WITHDRAWN

THE GHOST OF JAMIE McVAY

D1066938

R. G. ZIEMER

Black Rose Writing | Texas

© 2019 by R. G. Ziemer
All rights reserved. No part of this book may be reproduced, stored in a retrieval system or transmitted in any form or by any means without the prior written permission of the publishers, except by a reviewer who may quote brief passages in a review to be printed in a newspaper, magazine or journal.

The author grants the final approval for this literary material.

First printing

This is a work of fiction. Names, characters, businesses, places, events, and incidents are either the products of the author's imagination or used in a fictitious manner. Any resemblance to actual persons, living or dead, or actual events is purely coincidental.

ISBN: 978-1-68433-215-1
PUBLISHED BY BLACK ROSE WRITING
www.blackrosewriting.com

Printed in the United States of America
Suggested Retail Price (SRP) $18.95

The Ghost of Jamie McVay is printed in Plantagenet Cherokee

Praise for
THE GHOST OF JAMIE MCVAY

"Ray Ziemer's *The Ghost of Jamie McVay* has everything you could want from a novel: coming of age, family, secrets, danger, love, loss, life, death, after-life, and, most of all, redemption. Highly recommended."

–Donald J. Bingle, co-author of *The Love-Haight Case Files*

"This is a ghost story of revenge and redemption that pulls you in from the opening sentence…"

–Joanne Zienty, author of *The Things We Save*

"…unforgettable characters that will stay on your mind."

–Lou Holly, author of *South Side Hustle* and *Razorback*

"This psychological thriller incorporates young adult themes and avoids the campfire ghost story clichés that haunt lesser works."

–Thomas L. Croak Ph.D., English – *Robert Morris University*

"A well-written and thrilling ghost story with characters and settings you'll swear you know..."

–Wayne Turmel, author of *The Count of the Sahara* and *Acre's Orphans*

"Lighting the way to disaster… a spirit's remorse."

–Robert Walker, author of *Downstate*

"…one of those novels about teens that depicts them as they really are — not as they see themselves, and not as adults see them, but in their genuine nature, brave, troubled and curious."

–Greg Stolze, author of *Switchflipped* and *Mask of the Other*

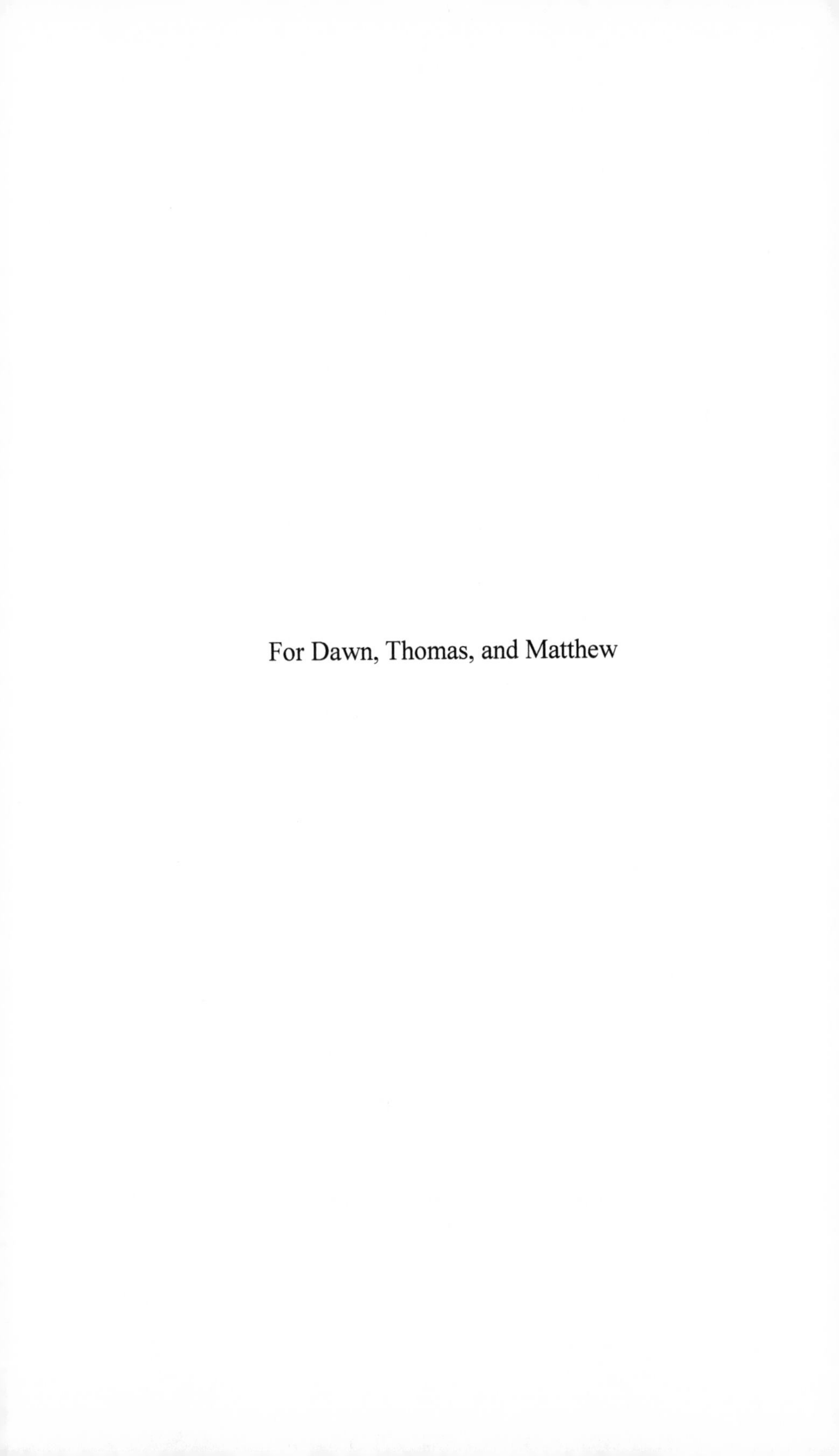

For Dawn, Thomas, and Matthew

ACKNOWLEDGMENTS

Thanks to Thomas and Matthew, who first met the Ghost of Jamie McVay on the Prairie Path. To Dawn who came to know him as she listened, proofread, and typed the original manuscript on her IBM Selectric. To my sisters – Barbara, who has ever been my muse; and Susan, who with my niece Allison breathed new life into the old story.

Thanks also to my best friend Tom Sheely for a lifetime of support and honest advice; and to Tom McCaffrey not only for his artistic talents but for years of joyful discovery and intelligent discussion.

Thanks to the members of the Naperville Writing Group for their encouragement and helpful criticism. To Mardelle Fortier and her group at College of DuPage, where lasting friendships were formed. And much appreciation also to the supportive folks at the Iowa Summer Writing Festival.

Thanks to the Fox Valley artists and writers who gave me the confidence and opportunity to share my writing: Paul and Kristin LaTour from Lit by the Bridge; the talented and prolific poet Frank Rutledge who led the Batavia Writing Group and continues to sponsor Harmonious Howl in Geneva; and the wonderful Waterline Writers led by Anne Veague and Kevin Moriarity, and now by James Joseph and Catherine Borders.

Much appreciation to friends old and new who read the manuscript and helped to make it better.

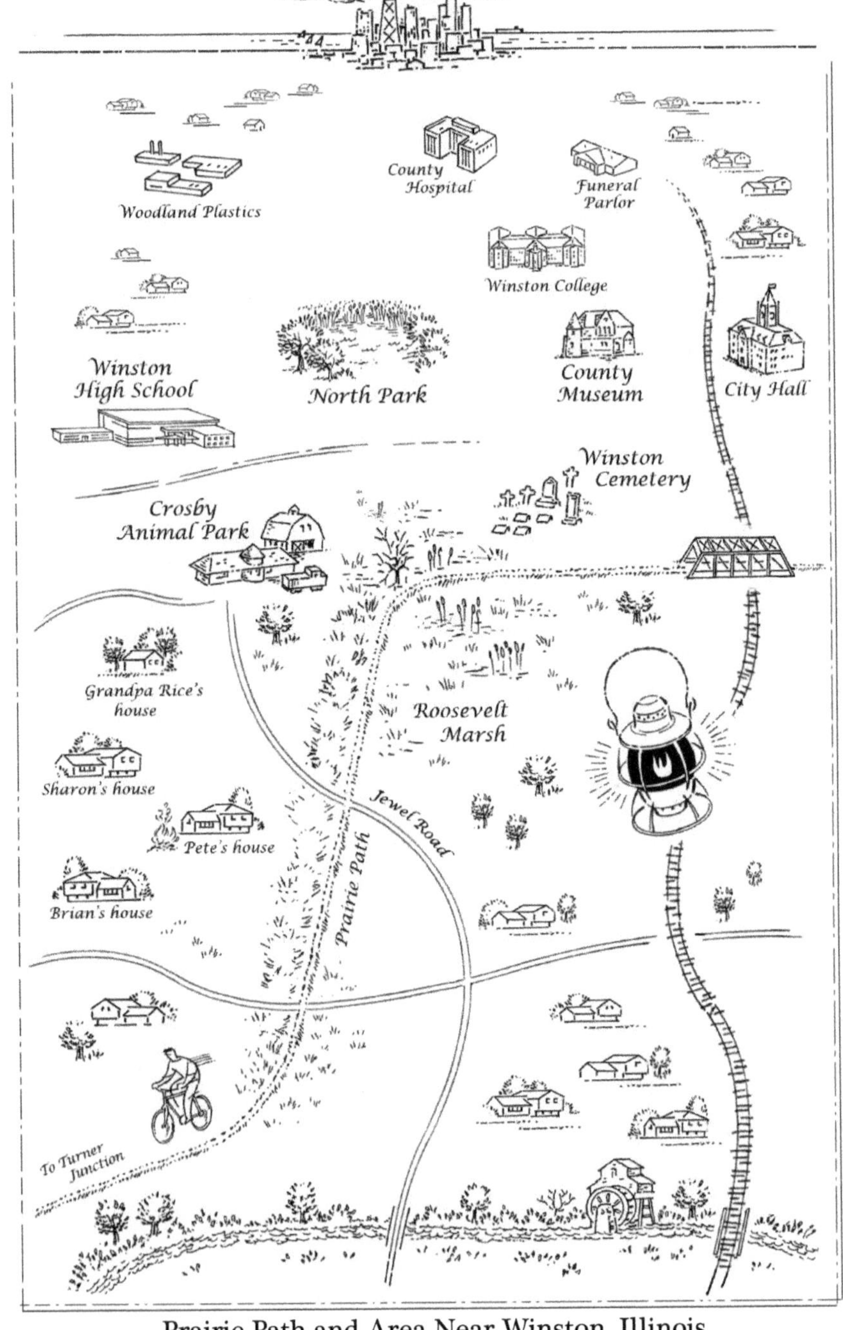

Prairie Path and Area Near Winston, Illinois

THE GHOST OF JAMIE McVAY

CHAPTER ONE

I bolted out of the house that summer night, running wild and I didn't care where. Just to put some distance between the old man and me, I tore off down our street, across empty lots and along the road, tears in my eyes, so mad I could hardly see. The narrow shoulder merged with a gravel path through the trees, so I let the fury drive me, and I raced by joggers and kids on bicycles and people with dogs, leaving them all behind. I don't know how long I ran. I kept on and on, trees and bushes and cattails just a blur around me, like I was plunging headlong into some dark hole in the landscape.

The trail climbed gradually after that, my legs burned, and I ran out of steam. Gasping, I pulled up and leaned over the rusty iron sides of an old bridge. In the fading light, steel rails glistened below me, curving out of view down a steep gorge, thirty or so feet deep. A smell of diesel oil hung over the gravel and railroad ties. The concrete bridge supports were cracked and overgrown, and painted here and there by the local punks: gang signs; a couple of choice obscenities; "Class of" some ancient year; in a fading heart, some names you couldn't read anymore. Not long ago somebody had sprayed there "LIFE SUCKS." I was inclined to agree.

I shouldn't have let the old man get to me. As usual, we'd been fighting over nothing. Just the two of us sitting at the table after supper, Mom gone to work, the Hamburger Helper finished off and me stewing about the whole situation. The old man popped open another beer and started up: Did I cut the grass like he told me to?

I just shook my head.

"Well?" he asked, but of course, he already knew.

"No."

"Why the heck not?"

"Because the mower wouldn't start, that's why not."

He gave me a gray-eyed warning look. "Did you choke it like I showed you?"

I just rolled my eyes.

"Did you check the gas?"

"I filled the tank."

"You didn't pull hard enough." He twisted his mouth, disgusted.

"I yanked on the rope till my arm was killing me. That mower is a piece of crap."

"You gotta adjust the choke like I showed you," he said, wagging his finger at me like I was a little kid.

"I'd like to see you get it going! Then I'll cut the grass." I jumped up and clanked my plate into the sink. "Maybe you can take some time out of your busy schedule tomorrow to work on that." I knew that would zing home.

He stood, teetering, his face turning red. "You don't talk to me like that!" Again with the finger.

"I'm just saying – You're the expert, Dad. What is it again that you do?"

He was fuming now, his mouth working before he sputtered, "You-you're not so big I can't put you over my knee!" He's been saying that since I was ten or so, the last time he actually put me over his knee. I looked at him, and he was so pathetic with his paunch and his grey whiskers. The rest of the mean things I had to say stuck in my throat. My head felt like I was going to explode – and that's when I turned and slammed out the back door running.

My blood was still pumping hard, my head throbbing, and my cramped guts kept me doubled up on the wooden planks of the bridge. Through the spaces between the boards was just nothing, just more of the emptiness I felt every day.

It was all gone – Gramps, our old house, the city and everything I'd ever known – gone. Here we were in this strange place – Mom working her tail off, me with no friends, Dad with no work and hitting the bottle like it was all he lived for. Everything was lost, and nobody cared. Nobody'd even care if *I* was gone. I could imagine myself sprawled out down there on the tracks, unconscious. In the gloom. Maybe a train coming. Would the old man even come looking for me? *What about when Mom gets home, 'Where's Brian?' And what does he say? Let them find me here, or find me too late. Let 'em sort that mess out after the train comes through, then there'll be some weeping and wailing when I'm dead and gone.*

I stifled a sob and straightened up. Walking unsteadily to the end of the bridge, I peered down the steep embankment at more graffiti on the concrete there. Curiosity drew me closer to the edge, and I stretched one leg out to step onto a piece of rusty steel sticking out of the dirt. Something – a flicker of light – made me look up and I turned quick, expecting somebody to be standing there or riding by – but no one was there. In the same instant, the loose foothold gave way under my weight, and I slipped, dancing half in the air, and grasped some small branch with one hand to catch my balance. The steel bracket tumbled down the slope and clanged dully onto the ballast stones.

I scrabbled back up, feeling my heart in my chest. Way down the trail I thought I saw a dim light, reddish and hazy in the dark. I stood up and started walking wooden-legged back toward home. Back to the same old routine. By now the old man would be passed out on the couch. But Mom would be home soon and she'd be worried about me.

The trail curved above a sea of cattails that rippled in the evening breeze. Right below the path spread an open patch of shallow water, brass colored like the sky. I paused to look at the way the sun was setting behind the dark fringe of willows on the far shore. Mosquitos whined, and I swatted one on my forehead. It was weird – no traffic, no houses, no people – like another time far away from my troubles and all the commotion.

Still – there was sadness here, a distant memory, but somehow tangible. And it got stronger as I stood there, swelling up like a lump in my throat, and a swirl of other feelings washed over me – pictures and sounds out of nowhere, too many thoughts cramming into my head all at the same time: Contorted faces, crackling flames, blasting heat, shrill screams – all twisting in and out of my mind, images in a mental kaleidoscope. I collapsed on a bench alongside the path and bent over, looking at my torn gym shoes, blood rushing in my ears. When I looked up, my head spun and the landscape kind of shivered. I realized the ground was vibrating, barely noticeable at first, but building up, like something big was coming up on me. I peered down the path both ways into the dark, but there was nothing to be seen.

A low hum came on, like the drone of an airplane way in the distance. Then I became aware of the smells, the rotten stink of black muck, and the weedy midsummer sting in my nostrils. But this had something else to it, hot grease, or machinery burning or something I couldn't quite figure. It got so thick I could taste it – and this heavy, oily smell like around telephone poles. That vibrating hum ramped up, and I was sitting there trying to figure all this out when it hit.

WHAM! This blast of air came out of nowhere and practically flattened me, cold and hot at the same time, wet and dry all at once, speeding a hundred miles an hour when it slammed me, and I thought I was dead with the devil come to get me. I gripped the edge of the bench while it all washed over me. White explosions of light flashed in my eyes, and the sound was all around, metallic thunder and lightning punctuated with an urgent jangling bell and rhythmic clicks and clacks clickety-clack, clickety-clack.

That was it of course. I remembered standing at a railway station when an express train blasted through. This was just like that – like I'd been standing a little too close to the edge of the platform when a big old train rumbled by, and its rush through the air whacked me enough to muss my hair. The sound diminished, dragged away in its wake, the bell clanging muted into the distance.

My ears followed the clatter way up the slope and around the bend in the trail, and my eyes tried to trace where the path disappeared in the gathering darkness and thickening mist. But of course there was nothing – there never had been. It was just me sitting there with chills and goosebumps and my hair standing on end.

I was losing my mind, I knew it. I shook my head, like trying to get water out of my ears, and rubbed my eyes. Everything was still. Was I hallucinating or –? No, it was just a weird feeling had come over me, that was all. And a squall had blown up, a sudden gust of wind. Maybe I'd dozed off for a second and this goofy daydream slipped in because of seeing those railroad tracks earlier. I still had the shivers and felt clammy all over, so I jumped up and jogged a few steps in place, shaking my head again to get those bells out of my ears.

It was dusky-dark now, and a genuine fog building up. I couldn't see more than twenty-five feet in any direction. But glowing way down the path, magnified in the chill of the cloud, was that red light, wavering, swaying back and forth. At least I wasn't the only weirdo out still running around in the dark. I walked toward it, expecting to catch sight of somebody on a bicycle with that red light, somebody carrying it in my direction. It never got any closer, though, twinkling and disappearing as the trail left the marsh behind and ducked back into its dark tunnel of trees. I turned and looked back up the path where swirling fog washed away the scene. Just as I was about to jog off again, I spotted that red gleam out in the middle of the nothing. Whoever it was must have left the path and struck out across the marsh, swinging his little dim red light like a signal to somebody unseen over on the other side.

CHAPTER TWO

We moved here outside Winston at the beginning of summer. Until then I'd never known any place but the city – the old neighborhood on the South Side of Chicago – and that was fine with me. Like people do, I took it for granted – my family, my life and home, my school and friends.... Then Gramps got sick, and that was the beginning of the end – the beginning of our hard times. Gramps just got worse and worse, in and out of the hospital. Well, anyway, he died, and that was that. From now on it was just me, Mom and Dad.

The cancer that ate Gramps up also ate up all the money, with hospital and doctor bills. Gramps's brick bungalow where we lived was all that was left. Then my aunt and uncles and the lawyers started pushing to sell the house so they could settle things and get their share. At first, Mom and Dad talked like we would possibly buy them out. But that wasn't going to happen.

Losing Gramps busted up my dad hard. He moped about like he'd let the old man down or something, and now he couldn't make it up. It nibbled away at him, and he spent more and more time lining up empties in the kitchen. It wasn't too long before one of the bosses at the plant got a whiff of him and he lost his job. Without his income, there was no more talk about buying the house.

Dad got a lot worse fast. Thinking back, I guess he always had been a sad and weepy drunk. He'd let Mom boss him around, and generally try to stay out of her way. But now with me, anyway, he was ornery all the time. We were always getting into it – him yelling and swearing, hurt feelings, one or both of us always doing or saying something we'd regret later. Gramps always used to say, a man should never have regrets, but Dad moped and drank like he had plenty to be sorry about.

Once it went up for sale, the sturdy old brick house went fast. Aunt Mary in Florida and Uncle Bill in Wisconsin just let the realtors and the lawyers handle it all. Uncle Bob, who lived in the city, gave us the bad news – that we had to get out and get out quick. Dad responded to that by knocking off a six-pack. Mom started making phone calls.

I'll never forget when she came home one afternoon and dumped the news on us like a bucket of ice water.

"I got a job as a waitress," she said, raised her eyebrows, and held her breath.

Dad stared up at her from the La-Z-Boy. "You're kidding."

"No way," I said. I knew how much she wanted to help and all, but really? I looked sideways quick at Dad's reaction. His mouth hung open.

"Yeah," she said, and smiled, blushing. "Andrea at the grocery store has a sister out in Winston, and they have this restaurant. They were looking for a waitress, so Andrea set it up for me to meet her brother-in-law. He says I can start next week."

Dad was still going over all this in his head. "How in hell are you going to get there?"

Mom sat on the couch across from him. "We have to move by the end of the month anyway. This Nick says he knows some houses out there for rent, so we can find a place in that neighborhood."

"Mom! What? Move?" I saw my past life pulling away from me in all directions. "What about school? What about my friends?"

She shook her head. "Brian, I looked for a job close to home. We've got to go where the work is."

Dad groaned, "Aww, some greasy spoon place, you couldn't find that around here? And what about factory jobs? What's out there for me?"

"Jim, there are lots of small shops and factories out there. You'll find something right away, I'll bet." Mom stood up and started to bustle around the kitchen picking up dirty dishes.

"Mom – what about *my life?"* It all seemed out of control.

But Mom stopped and looked me in the eye. "You'll make friends. You'll like it in the suburbs."

Before the end of the week, we had found this place to rent, a run-down ranch house – which any self-respecting rancher would have torn down long ago. It needed a lot of work. A month later we were still painting walls and washing windows, and unpacking our clothes out of cardboard boxes.

In a way it was nice to have a sort of modern house—it had a family room with a fireplace, an attached garage, and a big kitchen with sliding glass doors so you could walk out onto the patio. The problem was – whether I sat and looked out at the patchy weed lot of a lawn, or taped up posters on my bedroom walls – I didn't have anybody to share it with. At the end of the day, Mom was gone to work, and Dad was popping a beer in front of the TV. The summer was hot, so I ended up vegging out there, too, watching re-runs and soaking up the air conditioning.

At the time I didn't have a smartphone or wi-fi. Still, Winston isn't all that far from Chicago, a couple hours at most, by car. I called some of my buddies from the old neighborhood on the landline, but none of them had any way to get out here, if they were even interested.

I know how Mom's mind works. I know she figured to keep me too busy with chores to sit and feel sorry for myself, too tired to worry about the move. She was right, I guess. I had to clean the house – vacuum the floor, dust the furniture, and somebody had to mow that scraggy excuse for a lawn once a week. The landlord had left a rusty power mower in the shed, which Dad got running, but he pretty quick lost interest in using it. Which is why I was out there the day the trouble started with Pete the Pyro.

Our neighborhood is like a suburb of a suburb. It's what they call "unincorporated," which means we don't have sewers, sidewalks, street lights, libraries, or local ordinances against anything. Well, the sheriff's police ride through every once in a while, and there's a volunteer fire department.

Now I like to think about the things we *do* have. We do have our own water wells, and septic systems, old broken-down trees on big weedy lots littered with snowmobiles, tractors, and junk cars.

We've got freedom, too. People can do whatever they like in this neighborhood, no matter how it smells or sounds or looks or how much it scares the people next door. The old man by the creek's got some million ducks and geese. This Mike guy with his bushy mustache bangs away at all hours on the beater cars jammed end-to-end in his driveway across the street. And Pete the Pyro is the high priest of bonfires.

My first day in the new house, Pete Vincenzi tried to run me over in a stolen car. All right, I'll say a *borrowed* car, although I'm sure his parents didn't know he was hot-rodding the family Ford all over the neighborhood that day. He and a bunch of his stoner buddies were fishtailing all up and down the block, squealing around corners, spinning gravel, and just missing me on my way from the mailbox.

The Vincenzis live facing Richard Street and next to them is the vacant lot directly behind our house, which Pete has taken over, for bonfires and also for what we might loosely call "storage." For example, they have stored out there a rusty old van with a gaping hole in its side, a fenderless Camaro shrouded with a rotting green tarp, a crumpled fiberglass canoe, a mound of broken cinder block, and piles of old crates, skids, dead tree limbs, or any other kind of trash that Pete could scavenge for his next bonfire. This is the view from our kitchen window, or from our patio – if we'd be inclined to sit out there, or if we had any furniture to sit on.

For what it's worth, some spindly maple saplings and raspberry bushes back on the lot line screen us off from the Vincenzi house itself. When we first moved in, hearing the shouting over there, we just had to wonder what was going on. We'd see this poor miserable woman, Pete's mother, her face bruised and her dirt-colored hair all a tangle, scrawny as an ad for famine relief or something; she'd be striding up and down the street talking to herself, nodding and shaking her head, with her arms clasped to her belly. Mr.Vincenzi we didn't see much, except for his coming and going in the Ford at odd hours of the day or night; but we'd hear him cursing and swearing on their deck, throwing stuff around, and generally acting unpleasant. And speaking of unpleasant – there was Pete.

Dad and I were sitting in the family room just watching TV one hot night about a week after we'd moved in. The patio door was closed, the AC running. Dad was dozing, and I was barely awake, when all of a sudden – kaBAM! All the windows in the house shook, and we both jumped up to look out back, expecting to see the Vincenzi's' house blazing. But it was just an average-sized bonfire that Pete had got going in his favorite way – with a generous dose of gasoline and a cheer. Enormous flames, thirty or forty feet high, crackled and popped and lit up our whole yard. We just stared for a long time at the billowing, glowing red smoke and the sparks dancing wild into the black sky, while Pete the Pyro and his pals hooted and hunched about like druids, just shapes against the fire.

"Should I call the fire department or something?" I wondered.

Dad shook his head. "Don't make trouble. Prob'ly no law against it."

He craned his neck to watch some sparks drifting over our house, and gave me a meaningful look. "That kid could be dangerous."

***

The day after my fight with Dad and that strange experience on the Prairie Path, I had my first run-in with Pete the Pyro. It happened right in my own threadbare rag of a backyard, where I was yanking on the lawn mower to try and get the grass cut before it rained. It was a sticky, overcast afternoon. Thunder rumbled in the distance. For the last hour, this yellow Mustang with a loud exhaust and one gray primer fender had been circling the block, the engine revving up every time it approached our corner. Then I heard it screech to a stop in front of our house; car doors slammed, and a shrill voice called out. Around the garage stomped this gorgeous black-haired girl, all leggy in black shorts, with a bright white top showing off her tanned face and cleavage. She looked mad, scary, and beautiful in the skankiest way. I stood there like a big dummy and stared as she clomped across our yard, passing about ten yards away. I was still gaping when Pete Vincenzi came up and yanked her back by the arm.

"Get away from me!" she shrieked, and shook him off. Meanwhile, this other guy shows up at Pete's elbow, some buddy of his I'd seen before, a thickset freckle-faced character with a stubbly carpet of red hair and a dumb expression.

"Get back in that car!" Pete snarled and grabbed at her again. This time he caught a fistful of hair, jerking her head back hard. She screamed to pierce your eardrums, and spun like a cartoon Tasmanian Devil, swinging with both arms, trying to get a crack at Pete. He brushed off her open-handed swipes with little effort and stepped in close, bringing his fist in an arc, smack into her face.

She went down like a wounded goose and just lay there curled up on the ground, honking and whooping into her hands. That's when I had my stupidity attack. I'd been standing there like a jerk anyway, so now I made it official. "Hey!" I yelled, my voice cracking.

They all three looked at me as if they just now noticed I was there. Pete's face went blank. "Who the hell are you?"

"Brian Krueger," I fumbled out an answer. "I live here. "

Pete's lip curled. "Who gives a damn?" He turned to glare down at the girl, who was struggling to get up on all fours.

"You son of a bitch!" she cried, hurt and sullen now. Her knees were dirty and the white top smudged. She picked herself up rubbing her eye, the whole side of her face red. I walked over to them.

This was the first time I'd seen Pete the Pyro up close. A bit taller than me, but skinnier. Dark skin, cheeks pitted, a shadowy mustache under a long thin nose. Jeans with a tight black tee shirt, and out of the sleeves long brown arms that he let dangle now, flicking his wrists. He spat in my direction and stared with beady black eyes.

The girl glanced at him, then turned and looked at me, straightening up as if daring me to say something.

So I asked, "You okay?"

She swung back to Pete, touching her swollen cheek, and pouted, "Yeah, I'm okay."

Pete gave me a disdainful once-over, nodding his head and taking a couple purposeful steps in my direction. "Keep your frickin' nose out of it," he warned in his whiny voice. The other guy edged around until he was standing on the concrete patio to my right.

"Look," I said, spreading out my arms. "I see somebody hurtin' a girl in my backyard – what am I supposed to do?"

Pete shoved his long-nosed face right in front of mine so I could feel and smell his onion breath. "Stay the hell out of it!" he shouted into my eyes.

Chunky guy at my side leaned in, too, growling, "Yeah, that's right!"

I looked back over at the girl; her gaze flickered away. "Yeah, stay out of it," she sniffled.

That did it for me. I felt like a complete fool, so of course, I had to open my big mouth one more time. I took a deep breath. "Well, the next time you idiots have to punch each other around, do it somewhere else." Nervous but satisfied, I backed away.

The two guys started spouting curses at once – not real creative swearing, of course, but they made up for that in volume and intensity. Also, spit.

"Who you calling an idiot?" Pete was put breathing through his nose.

The heavy dude curled his fists and cocked his head, "Yeah, who you calling?"

"Assholes," I put forward, getting into the spirit.

Pete flung out a tiny fist that I could see coming at me, but somehow couldn't avoid. Just as I took that poke to the mouth, the other guy caught me in the gut, and the wind went out of me like I was a popped paper bag. The ground rose up to meet me. Pete stood over me, taunting, "Get up! Get up, sucker!"

I crouched, doubled over with one knee on the ground, wondering what to do next. Everything went into slow motion.

Thunder crashed, lightning flashed and just like that, big heavy drops of rain started splattering. At the same time, as if blown in with the weather, this short, blonde chunk of a teenaged girl in gym shorts and a blue sweatshirt swooped across the lawn. She swept along low to the ground with the sudden chilly wind and gathered up Pete and his pal in outspread arms, hustling them away like they were three-year-olds.

"Lay off now, Pete," she was saying. "Come on, go home and get out of the rain." She sheep-dogged them all the way back to the street and then let them go on their own momentum. Nobody so much as looked back in my direction as they sauntered through the raindrops and disappeared in the direction they'd been shoved. In a minute I heard the Mustang start up, rev its engine and peel out down the block.

The blonde peered at the other girl, who was still rubbing her red cheek and working her jaw. "Carla, what's the matter with you?"

Short blonde put a sympathetic hand on the other's back, and the two of them exchanged a few words up close. Tall brunette – Carla – busted out sobbing all of a sudden, then shuffled across the lawn through the increasing rain and slipped through the bushes to Pete's backyard.

The blonde girl looked up at the sky, smiled at me, and scurried over to stand under the eaves of our house for cover, grinning and blushing vivid pink. I had to smile when I saw that face. I couldn't help myself even with my sore mouth. "You just going to stand there and get soaked?" she said.

I felt giddy with relief now that the Pyro and his buddy were gone. I scurried over to the wall, grunting with the ache in my gut.

Blondie examined my puffy lip with a serious look and smiled again, saying good-naturedly, "You'll live." Gesturing with her thumb skyward, she added, "You must have somebody watching out for you – besides me, I mean."

CHAPTER THREE

I'd seen Sharon Rice around, coasting by on her bike and sometimes in the early morning jogging past the house, her blonde ponytail bouncing side to side. Sometimes she'd be dragging some of her brothers and her sister home to dinner. The rest of the brood were all of them just scaled-down versions of her, which is to say blonde, creamy-skinned, short, and plump. The little ones scampered all over the empty lots playing every sport known and some they invented. They roamed the streets on skateboards, home-made go-carts, big-wheel trikes, wagons, scooters and all sizes of bicycles. They filled the air – and the trees – with kites and Frisbees, baseballs and footballs, airplanes and rockets. Over on James Street, they had cobbled together the most amazing and dangerous-looking tree fort.

Sharon got around, too, although her energy was channeled into more civilized activities such as school, running, and talking. She knew everything and everybody and apparently intended to share it all with me. Catching the impatient look on my face, she stopped cataloging the Richard Street neighbors and put her hands on her hips.

"You could have saved yourself a fat lip," she pointed out, "if you'd known more about the Vincenzis." Undiscouraged, she went on. "Things have really livened up around here thanks to them. Big parties, big bonfires. Police raids. Fire engines."

"Yeah, they're a fun bunch," I agreed, kneading the sore spot in my middle. "What about the jerk who sucker-punched me?"

"Bill Melkovec. Lives over in the trailer park on County Farm Road.

His brother's in the Marines, and here's Bill joyriding his brother's car, probably without permission. Bill's stupid and mostly harmless – except when he's with Pete. Pete's the one to watch out for. He's a certified weirdo."

"Certified?"

"Well, at least when we were in junior high, there was a lit-tle fire incident, so the school headshrinkers worked on him."

"I'd like to work on him myself," I muttered, lightly patting my lip. "I hope the shrinks didn't get paid for finishing the job. You in the same class?"

"Same class of head case, or same class at school?" She grinned, showing small, even white teeth. "He's a year older – I'm a junior this year. You?"

"Same. At Winston, right?"

"But of course," she replied, in a fake English accent. "Winston North is the acme of learning in these precincts."

"Winston North!" I laughed, a little uncertain. "I suppose there is a Winston South, or an East or a West?"

"Hmm," she pretended to think about it. "I *do* believe they have all the compass points covered. If you must know, there's even a Winston Central – our arch rivals in every sport, mind you." In her normal voice she went on, "I guess it's not too original. Where the heck are *you* from, anyway?"

I told her a bit about the old neighborhood. "I was like you – I *used to* –know everybody on the block, knew all the side streets and back alleys, the pizza joints and taco stands. My old high school football team made it to the Semis last year – I was going out for the team this year…." I shook my head. No sense going into it.

Sharon looked me over through the awkward silence. "Sorry – it must be tough to have to move. I'd be a wreck, myself…."

She was cute, if a little pudgy, with the bluest eyes – the same color as her oversized Winston North sweatshirt. She was easy to talk to. (Well, so far she'd been doing most of the talking.) I mentioned I'd seen her run by the house, mornings.

"Oh, Lord!" she said, flushing pink and covering her eyes. "I thought

I was leaving early enough not to be spotted. I can't get up any earlier – not in the summer – I just can't."

"You don't have to get up in the dark on my account. I'm a runner myself – or used to be. I've been thinking about running again, get in shape for football."

Sharon's eyes lit up.

***

Next morning I looked out the window to see her on the front lawn stretching and waving to the neighbors who drove by on their way to work. I ducked into the bathroom and took stock: lower lip still puffy, but not that noticeable; no sign of a whisker, but no zits jumping out of the mirror, either. I dragged a comb through my hair, laced up my shoes and slugged down a glass of orange juice before stepping outside.

Sharon bounced up with a big smile and a perky "*Good* morning." I followed her onto the damp street.

It was already warm. We crossed the steamy creek and quickly covered the short blocks to Pleasant Hill Road. I recognized the name on the street sign and remembered my earlier wild, angry run. "I was here a couple weeks ago," I told her. "Where's the hill?"

"You're on it. Used to call the whole neighborhood Pleasant Hill," Sharon puffed as we veered off the paved road and onto the crushed limestone bed of the trail. A metal sign identified it as the Prairie Path. "Station used to be right there." She gestured with her thumb back toward the road. "Show you later where they moved it to."

"What kind of station?" Now in the dark tunnel of dripping foliage, it was cool and humid enough to show the vapor of our breath.

"Train," she answered. The path here led behind houses like mine and the rest of the neighborhood, kind of dilapidated. The bushy wooded area that bordered the path was muddy ground with piles of lawn clippings, old tires, garden sheds.

We came out of the woods into dazzling morning sunshine where the path crossed Jewel Road. A few cars coming from both directions forced us to mark time before crossing. Sharon, bouncing like a ball alongside me, pointed to the edge of the asphalt. "Still see the rails," she panted, and took off. Two flat shiny slabs of steel gleamed there, embedded in the paved surface of the road.

Railroad tracks? The path plunged into a ravine on the other side of the road; steep eroded banks rose twenty-five feet or so, cutting off any view of the surrounding neighborhood. As we traded the bright sunshine for blue shadow, the temperature abruptly dropped, and the sudden eerie chill raised goosebumps all over me. Now I saw it was a railway cutting through a hill, a slight downgrade almost unnoticeable to anyone but a runner. I recalled from before this gradual descent to the level of the marsh.

Wisps of fog hung in the low spots to either side, but the sun was steaming it away like a jungle movie set. Ahead of me, Sharon pointed to a sign I had missed last time: ROOSEVELT MARSH. It still smelled rank, although the previous day's rain had washed the place down a little. Sunlight sparkled gold in the water where ducks bobbed and gabbled among the reeds. Red-winged blackbirds chirped, locusts buzzed, a cicada rasped away, and our shoes crunched the gravel as we jogged through on the embankment. Not a particularly spooky place, I thought. And yet....

I couldn't help but compare this to my runs in the park back on the South Side, wide grassy paths around the lagoon and along tree-lined boulevards. This place was surprisingly wild. And you could run a long way in a straight line without stopping for traffic.

Running had always come pretty easy for me, but I was way out of shape now. My breath came harder, my legs felt like sticks, and my stomach ached where I'd been punched the day before. The sun streamed down hot, and now we were beginning to climb away from the wetland. I was working up a good sweat and a lot of admiration for Sharon, who never changed her pace but just chugged on as stubborn as the Little Engine That Could. I kicked into high gear to catch up with her.

We had come back to civilization. The marsh waters drained off into a shallow creek that zig-zagged away between a couple houses under a bridge, while our path began a wide curve back into the shade of tall maples, climbing higher. Pretty soon we could look down on the woods, over some of the shrubbery. Just the other side of a muddy ditch I saw files of cemetery tombstones standing like chessmen on a board of green and yellow. Then there were homes: huge old Victorian places, all cool in the shade. Tall catalpa trees were dripping with those Indian cigars, what Gramps called them.

The path leveled off, and packed gravel gave way to wooden planks. Sharon pulled up, leaned back on her heels, and bent at the waist, her arms dangling. I came up alongside her, huffing and puffing. "Fast," I panted. She couldn't hide the smile that triggered.

We were perched on the narrow trestle over the tracks I'd studied on my previous trip. Directly below were grease and grime, and life still sucked. Beyond the trees, the streets and sidewalks of Winston bustled with what passed for Life in Suburbia. When we'd both rested and gotten our voices back, Sharon returned to her tour guide act.

"This is where the C & F R crossed over the other railway and came into the yards. Look over there." She pointed through the iron struts of the bridge toward a cluster of white buildings. "See that place with that long curved wall? That used to be the roundhouse."

"So the Prairie Path used to be a railroad?" It was so obvious when you knew. "Must have been a long time ago."

"Yeah," she said, "I think it started way back when – early 1900's? When they first invented electric trains. It was an electric railway, with trolley wire strung overhead. Some places, they had a third rail."

"Like the 'L' trains in the city."

"Yeah. And it ran through Winston here and straight into Chicago alongside the Northwestern rails over there. The other direction, back through the marsh, the train went on through Turner Junction, and ended up beside the Fox River in Elgin. That's why it was the C & F R. Chicago and Fox River."

"How do you know all this stuff, anyway?"

"My grandfather used to work for them, a long time ago."

"So what happened? They just go broke?"

"Guess so. Couldn't compete with the cars and trucks hauling freight in the 50's I suppose. And there never was too much business out here, anyway. Grandpa said they picked up milk from the dairy farms, but most of them closed, too. The C & F R folded up, and the whattyacallit – the right-of-way was abandoned, all overgrown. The rails were scrapped, and people scrounged up the railroad ties. So the county cleared this path, and they keep it up now. Volunteers do things, too – they fixed up this bridge – so now *we* can take the path to Front Street for an ice cream cone. Come on."

Sharon went prattling on as we walked over to the business district. She must have known every piece of trivia about the town, including what time the ice cream shop opened. And she bought for both of us, too.

"Now, old Ezekial Winston settled this town. He had a cabin just two blocks down that street." Even a double chocolate fudge cone couldn't shut her up. We settled on a bench next to the railroad tracks across the street. "This antique shop used to be the old Amtrak station. The new station is just up there, see, toward the courthouse? There's a train there now."

No mistaking the tremendous clatter of the diesel-electric engine as it led the short commuter train in our direction. The locomotive belched black smoke and picked up speed, shaking the whole of downtown Winston. A rumble traveled through the ground, through me, and before I even wondered where else I'd ever felt that sensation, the hot pulsing engine was roaring by. A wall of hot air slammed into us, streamed over, and was gone. Just like that other train that was no train – on the railway that wasn't there anymore. Just like before, I shuddered, so even Sharon noticed.

"Give you the willies, huh?" she grinned, and raised her eyebrows to look me over. The hair on my crossed arms was standing straight out, and I rubbed my shivering shoulders. Sharon frowned. "Okay, let's just start walking back, so you can warm up. Some people just can't handle two scoops of ice cream. Better drink some water, too. You feel all right? You should see yourself. You're all pale, like you just saw a ghost or something."

I combed my fingers through my hair self-consciously. "Ghost?"

"That's it!" Sharon skipped up in front of me, walking backward and mocking me with a big smile. "You must have seen the ghost of Jamie McVay!"

"Very funny," I told her, trying to sound casual. "Another bit of Winston Folklore?"

"Yeah! Everybody knows about the ghost." Here she adopted a late night 'creature-feature' voice: "The ghost of Jamie McVay, who haunts the Winston by-ways – a headless apparition seeking to feed on the living...."

"How's he feed on anything if he doesn't have a head?"

She laughed with a toss of her ponytail and turned before she might have stumbled into a trash barrel. I double-stepped to catch up. She was quiet, though, as we climbed the path up to the railway bridge. "Well," I poked her with my elbow. "What's the matter? Run out of historical background?"

"I was just thinking – remembering. My grandpa used to tell that ghost story when I was little. He used to tell a lot of stories, but I can hardly remember them now." She sounded choked up. "He just had a stroke a couple months ago; he's using a walker now, and he doesn't even know people half the time. He can talk, but he doesn't always make sense. It just makes me...."

She couldn't finish. All of a sudden she broke into a run, so I fell in behind.

The day had turned into a real scorcher. Even in the damp shade of the path, the heat drained every bit of energy. We'd covered seven or eight miles, and I was pretty much done for. Just when I was wondering if I could match Sharon's pace all the way home, she pulled up flat-footed and downshifted to a weary walk. When we got to the little bridge over the creek, she plopped down under the willows with her feet dangling above the water. Before, she couldn't stop talking; now I wished she'd say something to break the uncomfortable quiet.

"So do you think you could tell me about the neighborhood?" I tried to imitate Sharon's "sophisticated" voice. "I'm thinking of relocating in the area – looking for a cozy little place with a big yard and lots of firewood – and your real estate firm was recommended to me by the Vincenzi family."

Sharon gave me a sour look. "I didn't think you were that enthused about our fair community."

"Well, so far, my dealings with the locals have been a little strained. All I've gotten out of it is a fat lip."

"And an ice cream cone."

"That's right. Thanks again." I thought about the old neighborhood and all the adventures. "It's just that – Winston isn't exactly the South Side."

"Ohhh-kay," she sighed. "Tell the country hick here all about life in the big city."

I kicked at the gravel, frustrated. "It's hard to explain. Things are just a lot more *real* in the city. Not so fake. And this neighborhood – it's all the same kinds of people, if you know what I mean."

"Excuse me, Mr. 'I'm-so-ghetto!'" she laughed, adding, with a sober look, "But you don't know what you're talking about. You'll see when school starts."

We both glanced up at a couple of red-faced men jogging by – gray-haired executive types with color-coordinated jogging shorts, shirts and socks, expensive running shoes. I'd been slogging along behind the trademarks on Sharon's heels all morning.

"Okay, you may be right," I said. "But you've got to admit, everything's about the labels around here, the status symbols. Everybody's so … going places." *And meanwhile my old man is flat on his ass at home, and we're going nowhere.*

She looked at me, her face hard as plaster, an indignant look in her eyes. "That's the way everybody is, everywhere, when they have the chance. My dad works hard for everything we've got. But it's all for the family, so why shouldn't we enjoy things?"

"Yeah, it's all about the things."

"No, it isn't. It's a hometown! *My* hometown. Just like you were talking about. Your old neighborhood was special because it was *yours*."

"Right," I said. "This is yours, and that was mine." Sharon stood up, looking irate. "Look," I went on. "It wasn't all perfect, but I was happy there. I didn't want to move out here, but we had to find another place after my Gramps died."

Tilting her head, Sharon raised her eyebrows and sighed. "Oh. Brian, I'm sorry."

I shrugged. "Yeah, well, that's why we're here anyway. No sense talking about it."

"What do you mean, no sense? Of course, you should talk about it. If it's bothering you, get it off your chest."

Sure, it bothered me, especially looking through the trees into that cemetery. Gramps used the same expression, *Get it off your chest.* He would have said, too, *Let's talk about it, Kiddo.* He used to look at me a certain way sometimes when I was feeling down, and he told me more than once, *You're sensitive, Kiddo. You feel things. You feel things other people don't, or can't.* But I didn't have him to talk to anymore.

Sharon reached out and touched me lightly on the shoulder, and it felt good. "Come on, let's walk." She returned to her breezy narration. "The Winston Cemetery here is way old – there are soldiers from the War of 1812 buried here and guys from the Civil War. There's some kind of a train monument, too."

The marsh shimmered in the heat, so we just took our time, strolling along. "You know, my Gramps, he did a lot of different jobs, worked in the steel mills most of his life. He used to tell railroad stories, 'cause he was a hobo when he was younger. *He* told stories about train wrecks."

Sharon paused at a section of wooden deck that served as a wildlife viewing platform. "Grandpa's story about the Ghost of Jamie McVay... that was about this big train disaster, too. It happened right here, in the marsh."

I looked around, and once again, my skin prickled. This was exactly where I had been standing that night... when I'd seen... whatever.

"I don't remember it all, but it had something to do with the Pleasant Hill Station, too." Sharon led me by the arm off the deck, and closer to the slope, that was edged with briars and wild roses. She pointed through some sumac trees to a cluster of rooftops just visible beyond the sea of cattails. "We'll have to go over there sometime. They moved the old station to that little park where they've got a children's zoo, a nature center, an old caboose and stuff."

From where we stood I could just make out a long, low roof with a fancy cupola sticking up, wavering in the heat. The marsh buzzed. I followed an emerald dragonfly's skimming, dipping flight across a stretch of green water. Once more, I thought, *Not a very spooky place in the daylight.* "So what else about the ghost?" I asked.

"The Ghost of Jamie McVay," Sharon recited. "Well, he's supposed to haunt the whole railroad, I guess —the Prairie Path now." She reverted to her "spooky" voice: "He would glide across the marsh, waving his lantern and chasing trains – and snatching at lost little city boys who wandered off the trail."

My smile might have been a little stiff. "Waving his lantern? Why? Whatever happened to Jamie McVay in the first place?"

"Like I told you." Sharon shrugged. "He must have been killed in the train wreck. I just remember Grandpa, how he'd say it: 'They never found his head!'"

A bell jangled behind us, and I spun around. A couple kids on bicycles shouted, clanged their bells again, and whirred away down the path.

CHAPTER FOUR

The run to Roosevelt Marsh got to be a regular thing, two or three times a week. Sometimes I went on my own, but more often Sharon showed up in the morning to get me moving. Like the first time, she wouldn't ring the bell or knock on the door, but waited out on the front yard, stretching and greeting the neighbors as they left for work. They'd give her a wave or a short beep of a car horn. The guy with the gigantic mustache might be standing across the street giving me hard looks, but Sharon would holler "Hey, Mike!" and he'd flash her a big old grin.

Mustache Mike, I called him, but not to his bristly face.

"Aww, he's a good guy," Sharon cooed. "He's a friend of the family, helps my Gram and Grandpa with stuff all the time. He's my godfather."

"He looks like a cowboy, and he'd like to hogtie and brand me."

Sharon laughed, "He doesn't *know* you. He's just suspicious."

The first time I got out early and jogged over to Sharon's place, I could barely find the house behind all their stuff. The driveway was a parking lot full of trucks and cars, tractors, backhoes, and other kinds of construction equipment. Mr. Rice was a masonry contractor, a guy who'd learned the bricklayer's trade and built his own business. On the lawn and around the garage they had a riding mower, a boat on a trailer, a camper, and a pair of snowmobiles. The spaces in between all these machines were taken up with toys or parts of toys. The little savages responsible for the carnage included three younger brothers and a sister. The twelve-year-old brother Allen would stand there looking at me, and then narrow his eyes and nod like we shared some dirty secret. The rest of the tribe would bounce alongside us hooting and teasing all the way to the end of the block.

Unfortunately, we had to run past the Vincenzi place, too. We usually didn't see Pete until we got back later in the morning. Then he might be out on the deck mocking us with scornful looks, or he'd straighten up from the engine compartment of the car in the drive and make some crack about Sharon, my "baby-sitter." Sometimes his girlfriend Carla would be there, too, lying on a lounge chair in a skimpy bathing suit, sneering at us and making comments.

My folks were saying things, too.

"So, did you run with your little girlfriend today?" Mom asked.

"If you mean Sharon, she's not my girlfriend," I told her.

Oh, Mom didn't mean any harm, and I suppose she didn't know it embarrassed me. Next day I'd hear something like, "Oh. Brian, there goes your little girlfriend. Aren't you going with her today?"

Mom slept in when she could, since she worked through dinner time, but once she got up, she bustled around the house to get housework done. She was the practical one, handling the family money, working her feet flat at the greasy spoon and trying to keep things together at home. I guess I should have done more to help, but there was Dad in the middle of it all, and it bugged me to have to clean up after *him*. But Mom was patient – she cut the Old Man a *lot* of slack.

Dad was often "not feeling too good" in the morning. He'd drag himself out of bed all bleary-eyed around ten o'clock, peel and salt a hard-boiled egg, and then sit in the family room in front of the television. It didn't matter what was on. After a while, he'd go to the refrigerator and pop open his first beer of the day.

Mom did most of the shopping and errands since she took the Chevy to work. But every once in a while, like if Dad needed to work on the car or something, he'd drop her off and then pick her up later.

One particular day, for instance, he was going to change the oil.

"Okay," Mom said, "I'll give you a list for groceries, too." Pulling me aside she added, "You better go with to make sure he gets everything."

"Yeah," Dad grumbled, "looks like we're gonna have to pick up a couple of six-packs anyway," which was code for twelve-packs. He dressed up for the occasion, putting on a shirt with a collar, socks and shoes for a change.

After dropping Mom off at the restaurant, we picked up the oil and filter at a discount place and then rambled through the grocery store. Driving back home, we passed the high school. Dad gestured with his thumb. "Isn't that your team out there?"

I glanced over at the white uniforms scattered across the field. We could hear shouting, and a coach's whistle. "I suppose so," I said.

He gave me a look – one thing is, he can see right through me. "You said you were going out for the team, right?"

I nodded. "Yeah, I'll have to get over there pretty soon, I guess. I don't know how I'll get to school or any place until the bus is running. Can't get anywhere around here without a car."

Dad ran his fingers through his gray-streaked hair. "Not like at home, huh, Kid? I mean, not like by the old house. Gotta drive everywhere, out here."

It struck me for the first time that Dad felt just as out of place here as I did since he'd been born and raised in the city.

"Yeah," he said, "we walked everywhere back in the old neighborhood. Walked to school, walked to church. Even your Gramps would walk, with his bad leg."

"Sure," I remembered. "We'd walk to the park – when I was little."

"Yeah," Dad nodded. "He was all excited when you were born. He always thought you were special." He straightened up and wiped his eyes as we pulled into the lot in front of the liquor store. He sat there for a minute after he turned the engine off. "He'd have loved to have seen you play football. Remember how he went to the track meet that time, to see you run?" In eighth grade, I had made it to the regional semis.

"Yeah, that was cool. Gramps used to talk about how you played basketball when you were a kid, too. He told me once he thought you played tougher than anybody in the league."

Dad sat quiet, but I could see he was trying to stifle a smile. After a while, he shrugged and said, "Yeah, he used to go to the park with me, too." The smile faded. "But it was different for me growing up. Your Gramps wanted more out of us than we could give."

***

I had these great fantasies about starting out in the new place: I'd become some kind of football hero, and guys would want to know me, girls would fight to go out with me, little kids would want to *be* me....

But the summer days came and went, and I didn't do anything about it. Sharon kept reminding me school was coming as if she was looking forward to it. Mom sat down with me at the computer, and we officially enrolled me in Winston North. After that was the physical exam, which cost more than we could afford, and which cost me half a day waiting in a doctor's office with a bunch of runny-nosed kids coughing and sneezing all over the place.

Finally, Mom drove me over to the school to write a check for the registration fees and all. We got me enrolled in Driver's Ed., too, but that fee would be due the second semester.

Leaving the school office, I reminded Mom I needed to see the football coach. We found our way through the cool halls toward the gym, where a teacher sent us back out into the heat to the field house. I stopped Mom at the door with a pleading look. "I better talk to him alone," I said.

"Okay," she said, "I'll wait out here."

I found Coach Nelson munching a sandwich over papers on a dusty desktop.

"You want a try-out now?" He kind of harrumphed and shook his head, looking up at me. Middle-aged but tan and fit, he looked clean and perfect with his white shorts and a polo shirt trimmed with the school's blue and gold.

I stammered something about not knowing when the cut-off was –

"Look," he interrupted me, "my boys have been out here bustin' their butts in the heat all summer, two-a-days, night practices. They had their conditioning, you understand?" He set the sandwich down and looked me over. "You bring exercise gear today?"

"No, I – uh, just came to register, I didn't –"

Coach snorted. "Well, see what I mean?"

"No, I thought I better –"

"Look, I'll give you a try-out, but I hope you're not going to waste our time here. We got a scrimmage this Friday, and our first game's in two weeks." His eyes bugged out the more he thought about it. "You better be serious. I got a couple of new kids out here, and they had the good sense to come out ready to kick behinds and get dirty."

"Well, if you tell me when to –"

He wagged his finger at me. "If you're serious, be here tomorrow at eight. We'll see if you got it in you. You got football shoes?"

I nodded, wondering if my old shoes would still fit me. Coach looked down his nose at me like I was a dirty handprint on his shirt. He reached over and gave me a printed form, walking past me to open the door. "Read this over and have a parent fill it out." He looked out to see Mom standing just a few feet away in the shade of the bleachers. He plucked the paper out of my fingers and strolled over to her with his stomach sucked in and the sickliest smile on his face. "Hi. Coach Nelson. The boy, here, trying out? You'll need to fill this out before the first practice."

"Thank you," Mom said carefully, sizing him up.

He was giving her the once-over, too. "Yeah, we're looking forward to quite a team this year. Quite a team, hmm?"

"Hmm." Mom skimmed over the paperwork.

"Of course he's already got his physical?"

"Yeah, I got that," I threw in.

"And he'll do the drug screening," Coach went on as if I wasn't there, "and then there's the activity fee, here," pointing at the paper.

Mom went pale for a second. Her eyes flickered over to me and back to the coach.

"We'll see you out here tomorrow, then," he dared me. "If you're serious."

Outside the gym, I picked up a flyer for the cross-country team, just on a whim. I was looking at it when we walked out front to the car. The parking lot was filled with bored kids hanging around their cars, depressed at the thought of school starting, but lured to the grounds out of morbid curiosity. Besides, when you know school opens in a week, what's the sense of starting anything else? Music blasted from car stereos, and I saw Pete Vincenzi sprawled over Melkovec's brother's Mustang with Carla and a bunch of her skinny girlfriends. I recognized another guy named Rick Wagner who hung out at Vincenzi's a lot.

"Brian! Over here!" Sharon Rice waved her arms. She was standing with a good-sized group of good-sized girls. Three of them managed to hide the outline of the Honda behind them. "Hi, Mrs. Krueger."

Mom waved but kept walking to our car, acting cool but giving me one of those knowing looks. "I'll wait," she said.

I went over and let Sharon introduce me to her friends. They were the Three Bears, Doreen being the Papa Bear, hulking and scary looking; tubby Margaret Bork, medium-sized Mama Bear; and Little Bear Sharon. We compared class schedules, and it turned out we'd all be seeing more of each other. "Great!" Sharon hopped her happy little bounce. "We both got Taylor for English. He's pretty cool."

"Hey Kroogler!" Pete Vincenzi yelled across the parking lot. "Hey, go for it, man! You got you some Big Mamas!"

"Big Mamas!" Melkovec repeated, and Wagner cackled.

I felt my face turning red, but Sharon and the girls managed to ignore him, I don't know how.

"Hey Koogler!" The Pyro played to the audience cracking up over there. "Let's share some of that action, man, don't be keepin' it all for yourself!"

"Doreen has her mom's car for the whole day," Sharon was saying. "We were thinking about a picnic. Want to go over to Crosby Park?"

"It's too much for one man, Koogler!"

"Too much, man!" Melkovec echoed.

I shook my head. "I gotta get back home, sorry. Lots to do...."

"We can drop you off at home after," Doreen offered.

"No, no, listen, my mom's waiting – I've got to go with her. Somewhere."

Sharon saw the lie right away. She walked a few steps with me, her head bowed. "Well, maybe we'll get a chance to run once more before school starts, huh?"

"Hey Klooger!" Pete called out. "Don't get trampled over there with all them beef cattle!"

Melkovec lifted his head up and mooed.

"Sure, sure – I'll call you."

"Ohhh-kay," she said, looking up at me with a squint. No bounce.

***

I ran by myself that evening, to the marsh and back, thinking. Coach Nelson was eating at me with his football challenge. I didn't much look forward to spending the next couple of months with him wondering if I "got it in me." But it was hard to give up on football. That was part of the daydream.

I was supposed to be making all kinds of friends. Making friends with terrific looking girls. Pete the Pyro wasn't supposed to be standing around cutting me down in front of the whole school. Carla and her skanky girlfriends weren't supposed to be making fun of me. The only friends I'd made so far were Sharon Rice and her hefty herd. And then I felt pretty bad about that mean thought, too, and for ditching Sharon and the rest.

Nothing was working out. Dad wasn't supposed to be bombed out of his mind and griping all the time, and Mom wasn't supposed to be scrounging for tips all night either.

Life sucks, I read against the old railroad bridge as I turned and headed back. I plodded up to one of the plank benches at the marsh and just leaned up against it, watching the sunset all orange in the hazy sky. A few other joggers padded by, puffing, in both directions, but after a while, it got quiet again. I could make out faint traffic sounds carrying over from Jewel Road, just a background hiss.

But then that sound rose again, just as it had that other time, getting louder; and then the vibration, the pungent smell, and pretty soon the hiss intensifying to a roar that climaxed with the rush of hot air blasting over me like a locomotive. As before, the invisible thing clattered away, its bell ringing desperately and its wake subsiding as it spread across the damp evening air.

Sweat beaded up on my skin, in spite of the chill. I'd been ready for it this time, after that first sensation; I'd known it was coming, but it still brought on a reflex shudder. And I thought I could predict what was coming next. Trembling I peered down the path. I knew just where it would be.

The red light glowed more brightly than it had the other time in the fog. Tonight the beam shone clear and sharp on the darkly shaded path, sparkling as it was carried off through the trees and down among the cattails. There it wagged and swung dancing from one clump of reeds to another until it abruptly winked out.

CHAPTER FIVE

I dragged myself out of bed early in the morning and slouched in the kitchen stirring a bowl of cereal. I hadn't said any more about football to Mom, and the permission form just lay there on the kitchen counter on top of a pile of weeks-old junk mail. The wall clock ticked away while I watched the minute hand creep closer to the end of my football dream. But inside my head I could hear stupid coach Nelson whining, "You want a try-out now?" At eight o'clock I heaved a deep sigh and ambled over to Sharon's house.

As if she'd been waiting for me, she flopped out the back door and ran past me, tossing "Hey," back over her shoulder. I just fell in behind, and neither of us said a word all down the path, until we reached the marsh and collapsed on the bench in the sunshine.

"Good run," I panted. "Faster pace today."

"Oh, you're the fast one," she breathed.

Another warm day, but the air had a frosty chill to it around Sharon, and I knew why.

"Sorry I couldn't go with you guys yesterday," I started. "Maybe we can all do something together some other time."

Sharon lifted the hem of her tank top and bent over to meet it, wiping the sweat from her pink face. She leaned back with her tanned legs stretched out and watched a sparrow hopping about in the tree limb over our heads. "Don't poop on me, bird," she warned. With a narrow-eyed glance at me, she added, "You neither."

I sighed. "I'm sorry. Your friends seem nice...."

"For a bunch of fat girls? Yeah, nice fat girls, every one of us!" she hissed, surprising me with the venom in her voice. My mouth went dry, and I couldn't think of a thing to say. For a while. For too long, until I looked hard and saw the hurt in her eyes.

"No, no, not –"

"Just forget it, Brian, okay? I get it. I understand completely. You're new, you want to make the right friends, I don't blame you." Now she turned and faced me. "I know my friends aren't popular. I'm not popular either. Not one of the cool kids. But you'll do okay. You'll make it at North just fine."

She really had my number. I stood up to get out from under that look. "I'm sorry. You *should* be mad at me. I was an asshole. I should be happy to know your friends, to be making all the friends I can." I swatted a mosquito for emphasis.

"Like I said," she muttered, "you'll make it just fine. You'll be hanging with the football jocks and going out with cheerleaders."

"Not likely. I blew off Coach Nelson today, so it doesn't look like football is in my future."

"Hah!" Sharon looked up at me, eyes widened. "I'm sure Coach is all broken up about that."

We both laughed, and I felt like the situation had relaxed a bit. I squatted in front of her, and looked her square in the eyes. "Anyway, I just want to say I'm sorry, and I want to be friends."

She nodded slightly, pursed her lips, and raised her hands with spread fingers between us. "Ohh-kay, Brian. Let's not talk about it anymore."

Startled by a passing runner's crunching footsteps, I stood and looked around. It was the same place I'd stopped the night before, the bench on the shoulder of the gravel path overlooking the rank green water. Now everything appeared so distinct in the summer sun, so real. A warm wind blew through the leaves, flies buzzed, birds chirped. Yesterday on this same spot I'd almost been run over by an invisible train. I'd watched a bobbing red light float through the air and disappear. Or I'd imagined it all.

Sharon was still sitting there at my elbow, giving me a curious look. I let out a nervous laugh and smiled self-consciously.

"What?" she asked.

"I'm wondering."

"About…?"

"I'm wondering if I'm going crazy or what?" I laughed again and shook my head.

"Crazy because…?" She wasn't laughing now. "Here's the deal, Brian: Let it out. Say what's on your mind and no more keeping things to yourself. Tell the truth – to me, to yourself."

"Right. Uh-huh." I took a deep breath. "I'm wondering what's real…."

"Ohh-kay." She waited a beat and shrugged. "I'm not getting it, Brian. What's real?"

"Your ghost is real," I said, wincing, knowing I'd just opened a big can of nightcrawlers.

She cocked her head. "My ghost?"

"The ghost of Jamie McVay." I waved my fingers, imitating her spooky story gesture.

She smiled, gesturing for me to go on.

So I did. I told her the whole thing, everything I'd felt and seen there in the marsh. She listened politely enough, raising her eyebrows to show interest and leaning intently toward me with mouth agape when I recalled the sensation of the speeding train. As I finished my tale, describing the mysterious red light, her eyes widened. Then a smile began to creep across her face in spite of her efforts to hide it.

I shrugged and crossed my arms. "Well. That's the way it was."

"Ohhh-kay." She raised her eyebrows. "Drugs do terrible things, Brian."

"I hope you know I'm dead serious. If it was a…a hallucination, it wasn't from anything I took. You know I – "

"I know, I know," she giggled. "I can see how serious you are."

"Damn it! You asked for the truth."

"Yeah, yeah." She waved her hands and paced up and down the path with a finger to her lips. "Let's look at this logically."

"I've looked at it from every angle."

She stopped and wagged a finger in my direction. "*Obviously*, this whole red light thing was just dug up by your brain, from the suggestion I planted there when I told you the story."

I shook my head. "No – I saw it *before* you told me about Jamie McVay. Before I even met you."

She waved that notion away. "Oh, you're just mixed up on that. Okay... what was the first thing you experienced?"

"The vibrations through the ground – like something heavy coming my way."

"All right. Now. There are all kinds of heavy things going by all the time. Just over there on Crosby Road, or back on Jewel – big trucks, construction machines – big and heavy enough to give you the bad vibes. What then?"

"The sound, which was definitely a train. Nothing else sounds like that."

"Okay, that might be true, but so what? There's plenty of trains here. There's nothing weird about that. *Listen*."

Perfectly on cue, there was a long blast of a train horn, and from way off I could hear the clatter. Sharon pointed west, out across the marsh, and there on the farthest margin was a Metra commuter train rattling away. I hadn't noticed the embankment there before.

"But it's not precisely the same sound," I argued, remembering. "I know what a diesel locomotive sounds like, and this was different."

"Hmm, now you're changing your story."

"I'm not...."

"Well, go on," she said with another wave of her hand. "What else was there?"

"A bell – there wasn't any long train whistle or diesel horn like that."

"But there's all kinds of bells – bicycle bells, church bells, doorbells... jingle bells –"

"Funny. No, it was a clangy *train* bell."

"You know what you heard? Somebody might have a bell on their back porch that they clang to call their kids at dinner time. People down the block used to do that."

"You've got an answer for everything. What about the smell?"

"Well… you must have smelled that stuff they soak the railroad ties with." She raised her pug nose up in the breeze to sniff, and began kicking through the weeds along the path.

This was so frustrating – but then I should have expected that.

"Over here," Sharon called in a minute. Sure enough, she'd found a couple of old, rotten ties lying on the side of the embankment. There was a tingle to the smell, I had to admit.

"Yeah … creosote, I think. Yeah, that's what they call it. But it's not just that. There's a different smell mixed in. Did you ever ride on the bumper cars at an amusement park?"

"Sure," she grinned. "Let's go. They've got bumper cars at Safari Land."

"What I'm saying is that it smells like the bumper cars."

She nodded encouragement. "Okay. Meanwhile…."

"There was the wind. Remember when the train went by just across from the ice cream place, and you said I looked sick? Well, that was because the wind was just like that train – it washed right over me – or *through* me."

"But Brian, come on – it was just the wind. You get these funny … *gusts* sometimes. There's nothing supernatural about it."

"And the light? I saw the light, too. Don't tell me there's nothing unusual about that."

"I have to tell you – there's a logical explanation for everything."

All I could do was shake my head. "I wish – I hope that's true. But all that stuff about Jamie McVay seemed to fit in somehow."

Sharon faced me with folded arms, a faint smile turning up the corners of her mouth. She snapped her fingers. "Well, if you really *did* see the ghost of Jamie McVay, we'd better go talk to somebody who knows the whole story."

"Who?"

"My grandpa. At least it's worth a try."

***

Grandma and Grandpa Rice lived at the far end of Richard Street in a little white cottage with rust-red shingles. Deep in the shade, huge cottonwoods rising up all around, it looked like some Disney cartoon fairy tale place. Grandma answered Sharon's knock at the back door, and she looked like a cartoon figure, too, with her bifocals, an apron, and white hair in a bun. The inside of the house was neat and clean. Lace doilies protected dark-finished tables from lamps with plastic-covered shades. There were religious pictures on the wall: Jesus knocking at a heavy wooden door, Jesus with a flock of sheep.

"I told Brian we could mooch some lemonade here," Sharon said by way of introduction.

"Well, that you can, that you can," the plump old woman said and chuckled. "Sit right down there in the kitchen where you can catch the breeze. How do you do?"

"I'm fine, thanks," I said. "Sure is hot already today."

"That's the truth, it truly is! Sharon, you're not out running in this heat, are you?"

"We're done for the day, Gram. Is Grandpa up?" Sharon peeked around a corner.

"Bathroom," Grandma said.

"How is he today?"

"Oh, pretty good," she sighed, setting out glasses, a bowl full of ice cubes, and a sweating pitcher of lemonade.

"The real reason we came," Sharon explained, "is because I wanted Brian to hear one of Grandpa's railroad stories."

Grandma frowned. "My gosh, I don't know if your grandpa's up to remembering any stories. We'll have to see about that."

"I thought it wouldn't hurt to come by and find out."

"Oh, of course not, Dear, of course not." Grandma brightened. Don't worry about it. We'll just have to see, that's all. What were you going to ask about?"

Sharon looked sheepish, covering her eyes. "The ghost of Jamie McVay."

Grandma peered over the tops of her glasses. "Well, you know I've never had any use for ghost stories or any of those old superstitions. Those railwaymen were all full of superstitions, just full of 'em. I never paid any attention to 'em myself."

"But Brian's new in the neighborhood, Grandma, and I thought he'd be interested in the story. I know something happened on the Prairie Path, but I don't remember the details."

Grandma looked me over again, more critically. "The Prairie Path?"

"I thought that's where the train wreck happened, over at Roosevelt Marsh."

"Ah-ha," she said, nodding, "that's what you're talking about, then – the Marsh Disaster is what we called it. Terrible, terrible wreck. All those children!"

"What happened?" Sharon leaned across the table. "I don't think Grandpa ever said anything about children."

"I should hope not! It would have given you nightmares." Grandma turned and busied herself at the sink.

"Come on, Gram. We're big kids. We can handle it."

"Think so, do you? Well, I'll have you know I had nightmares myself after the Disaster, and I was a grown woman. Must have been fifty years ago, now, because your Uncle Rudy was just a baby. Maybe that's why it affected me the way it did at the time. But I think everybody in town was just sick about it, just sick."

"Gram, come on."

The round woman turned and, clasping her elbows, leaned back against the counter. "There were three whole carloads of Sunday School children, and they'd been on a picnic – oh, I guess out at the Electric Park, the picnic grove on the Fox River. So it was evening, and they were almost home – I think they were from the Bible Church in town – when they stalled or something, there at the end of Roosevelt Marsh."

An eerie feeling came over me, sort of a chill from the inside out because I was picturing the scene in my mind, and somehow I knew exactly how it looked in the twilight with the sun set and fog wisping about.

Grandma Rice continued, her shoulders hunched. "A freight train came up fast on the stalled cars and rammed them from behind. It was just terrible – one car was pushed up inside the other, and so many of those children were horribly maimed. Then the cars caught fire, and children burned, too. I think there were a dozen killed altogether, and it's a miracle there weren't more."

Sharon let out a long breath. "I never knew the whole story," she said, shaking her head and looking at me with wide eyes. The hair was standing up on my arms. I'd just heard that doomed train go by the night before.

A door banged open around the corner, and Grandma scurried out of the room.

"Look here, Pa," Grandma said as she led the way back into the kitchen. "Sharon came over with one of her friends."

One step at a time, Grandpa Rice shuffled in, supporting himself with one of those tubular aluminum walkers. He was short, round, and bald with a fringe of sparse white hair to match a couple days' growth of white whiskers. Grandma held a kitchen chair for him to settle heavily onto, and he grinned amiably at us both.

"Who?" he said, frowning.

"It's Sharon, Pa," Grandma repeated, "and her friend Brian."

He smiled again warmly, but his blue-gray eyes were watery and somehow off-focus. Sharon's eyes teared up, too, as she went and knelt alongside him, her tiny hand on top of his fat, spotted one.

"Hi, Grandpa," she said, and he grinned once more, nodding, looking past her. "I was trying to remember the story you told me, about the ghost of Jamie McVay."

"Who?" He squinted, looking around.

"Jamie McVay."

"He doesn't remember," Grandma muttered. "Pa was on the section gang that worked in the marsh there, cleaning up the wreck after the Disaster. He worked for the C & F R until they shut down. I don't know... I think they all just tried to out-do each other with ghost stories."

"Do you remember Jamie McVay, Grandpa?" Sharon repeated patiently.

Grandpa stared at a calendar on the wall. Slowly he nodded. "Seen him," he declared, and looked about at us all, smiling wisely. "Seen the light. I did. Seen it with my own eyes."

A cold feeling flushed all through me. "What kind of light was it, Mr. Rice?" I asked.

"The red light," he said. "The signal light."

"Now, Pa," Grandma scolded, "you never saw any such thing, and you know it."

His eyes got real big, and he leaned toward me. "He almost got me, too."

"Here we go, now." Grandma rolled her eyes at us. "He knows I won't listen to this rubbish."

"When we were .... Me and... we were working on that bridge."

She crossed her arms and leveled an exasperated look at him. "He means the railway bridge in Winston."

"Yeah," he almost shouted, "we were up under there on the scaffold. We seen the light, all right!"

"He's told this story for years," Grandma interrupted. "There was part of the scaffolding had come apart, and it was hanging there over the tracks, right in the way of a Chicago & Northwestern train."

"Yeah! And we seen the light, wavin' at us. Jamie McVay comin' for us, but we got outa' there by the skin of our teeth!"

"Well, that's true, I guess. The whole scaffold was dragged down by the commuter train. They just barely got off in time."

"Yeah, he come for us, but we seen his light. Almost got us, but we seen his light." He thought for a while leaning over with his elbows on the table. "Jack – wasn't it Jack Vogl, Ma? He seen the head. But I just seen the light."

Grandma stepped over to him and put a gentling hand on his back. She turned and looked at me. "As if seeing a signal light is something unusual on a railroad. I swear! Those guys blamed everything on ghosts for years after, didn't they, Pa?"

"I seen the light," Grandpa blurted defensively.

"Now, Pa...."

"Light's lit, that's what."

"Pa...."

"Yeah, light's lit, you'll see. Leave the light on."

Grandma Rice nudged Sharon's elbow, shaking her head. "I'm sorry, Honey, I think it's about time for Grandpa to take his medicine and have a nap. Why don't you come back another time, though?"

"All right, Gram."

"Good-by, Mrs. Rice, Mr. Rice," I said, standing reluctantly. "Thanks for the lemonade."

The old man glanced up quick at Grandma, then leaned forward to fix me with haunted eyes. "You know they never found his head," he muttered.

Sharon sniffed, "Bye, Grandpa."

"Light's out now!" he called.

CHAPTER SIX

Our visit with Sharon's grandfather raised more questions than it answered. Walking home, I wasn't sure if I felt better or worse. On the positive side, somebody else had seen the same thing as I had at the marsh, so maybe I wasn't going crazy after all. But the bad thing was… *we were talking about a ghost.*

I was almost happy to walk into the house where our real-life situation was under discussion. Dad slumped on the couch with Mom standing behind him. She had just brought up the news that a local plant was hiring.

"I saw the sign yesterday," she said. "At one of those places on my way to work. Some kind of machine operator."

Dad grunted, and she leaned over to pat him on the shoulder. "Just about any kind of factory work, you could do it."

"Yeah, well, who knows?" he shrugged. "What *is* the place?"

"Woodland Plastics."

"Seems like a contradiction in terms," I said.

Dad laughed. "Okay, maybe I'll check 'em out."

Mom talked fast, now that she got a response. "You need to get over there quick, fill out an application! God knows how long it'll be available!" She looked at me. "Brian can go over there with you." I was shaking my head, but she was on a roll. "For moral support! Brian, you can go with, right? Sure you can."

So it was decided that we would drop Mom off at work and then go to this plastics place to check out the job opportunity. Dad shaved and changed while Mom, already wearing her waitress clothes, kept me in the game.

"Don't look so disgusted," she said, keeping her voice low. "He needs somebody to keep him company."

"Yeah, Mom – for moral support."

"Well, he hears it from me all the time. But you can reinforce the message a little bit, too. Let him know you believe in him?"

"Do I?"

Her eyes blazed for a second, but she took a deep breath and went on. "Yes, you do. You can keep him focused on the job, Brian. If you're there, he's more likely to go through with it. Otherwise … he might just lose confidence." She looked in the direction of the bedroom. "He doesn't have a lot of confidence."

Mom pointed the small factory out to us on the way to the restaurant. After we dropped her off, we swung the car around and headed back. Dad was more talkative than usual, nervous, I suppose.

"So, whatever happened with football?" he asked.

"Mm, not gonna happen this year, I guess."

"How come?"

"Just too late to get into it. They've been practicing, they already got teams picked – I'd probably just be warming the bench all year. Plus, the coach is a dick."

Dad chuckled, but warned me with a look. "Don't talk about your teachers like that. I thought their team was so great, they've got some champion coach or something."

"That's the head coach, for the varsity team. But I'd have to try out for Junior Varsity. And believe me, that coach, Nelson – you wouldn't like him."

He thought for a while. "Well, that's too bad. But you shouldn't let one bad coach keep you from your game. There's always going to be people you don't like, who you don't get along with. You can't let them stop you from doing things."

"I don't know, it's hard enough to break in on a new team without the coach having something against you."

"Well, there's other sports. You ought to join something – hell, join the Chess Club or something, it's a way to make friends, you starting a new school and all. How about baseball?"

"Maybe I'll check it out," I mumbled, "in the *spring*."

"Oh yeah, right."

We were driving down Gary Road where it goes along between North Park and the far side of Roosevelt Marsh. All of a sudden Dad jammed on the brakes, and we screeched to a stop, killing the engine. A kid in a blue tee shirt had appeared out of nowhere right in front of the car – he glanced our way and veered back to the side of the road, running along the shoulder ahead of us. A couple of seconds later, a whole string of kids came jogging out of the park in his wake.

"Damn!" Dad muttered, "where'd they come from?"

"Cross-country team, I'd guess."

Dad nodded and started the car up, easing past the runners. "Cross-country… well, there you go."

"There you go," I echoed. "So, you were big into baseball, too, I guess?"

"Softball," he nodded. "We played Chicago-style, 16-inch Clinchers."

"Right – so you told me when I asked for a glove for Christmas a while back."

"Who would use a glove to play softball?" he wondered, accusing me with a look.

"So… you played in a league, though, right – not in high school?"

"Yeah, I played shortstop on the company team. Wednesday nights out on the island at Marquette Park."

"Yeah, I remember – Me and some of the guys used to watch them play. With the slow pitch and all, they're so funny."

"We had some plays, all right – we had a double play, man ...."

"But I never watched *you* play," I said. "How come you quit?"

He didn't speak for a minute, but acted intent on his driving. "Ah, I was younger then," he finally said. "After you came along, who had time for games?" He shot me a self-conscious grin.

We pulled into the asphalt lot of Woodland Plastics, on a corner of the industrial park. A couple of cars pulled out, some men were going in, and it seemed like a lot of activity for a business like that. It was just another metal-sided building with an office out front, so you couldn't tell at all what they made there – wood that looked like plastic, or plastic that looked like wood? Dad examined himself in the rearview mirror, combed his hair, and breathed in and out deeply before he got out of the car.

"Go get 'em, Dad," I called as he walked into the building.

I reached over and turned the key he'd left in the ignition, and started fiddling with the radio, thinking. Funny – for all his stories about basketball, softball, fishing – *I* never once saw Dad in Marquette Park as long as *I* was going there. He never once went there with *me,* unless it was when I was little. Everybody agreed he was a good athlete, though. And I guess he'd been a good steady worker. Back then. Before *me*? Or before he hit the bottle so hard?"

The car door flew open and Dad threw himself into the driver's seat. He cranked the engine, and we careened out of the parking lot and onto the street.

"What happened?"

"Nothing happened," he snapped. "There must have been fifteen guys in there filling out applications. They'll have a hundred easy apply for that job." And that was that.

Late that night by the time Mom got home, Dad was bombed, so she knocked on my bedroom door. I put down the book I was reading. When I told her what happened, she just sagged on the bed.

"He was kind of brave about it, going in," I told her. "He was willing to give it a try."

Mom shook her head. "Yeah, I just had a hope that he was going to be positive."

"Well, things the way they are, it's not his fault – not this time."

We sat there quiet for a bit, Mom chewing the inside of her lip. When she spoke again, her voice cracked. "Your father has a hard time dealing with things. He didn't always, but...." She shrugged.

"But what changed? He was talking today about playing softball in the park, and you could tell he felt good thinking back on those days."

Mom smiled. "He loved going out there after work and messing around with the guys."

"So why did he stop? I think he might blame me – having a kid and all, like he couldn't go and goof off sometimes."

"No, no – Brian, no. It didn't have anything to do with you. He did change, though. Even before you were born, I think."

"Well, how, then?"

"I don't know… and he just talked about one time, and he was real funny about it…."

"Funny? Dad, funny?"

She scolded me with a look. "Funny strange. I don't know…."

"Well, what? Did something happen to him?"

"In his mind, something did. I think…."

"What?"

"I remember when it was, because I was pregnant with you. This little boy – about eight years old – drowned in the Marquette Park Lagoon. I remember there was a commotion when he was missing, and then real quick they found him in the water over near the island. It was right near the baseball diamonds."

"What did that have to do with Dad?"

"Nothing – I don't know, Brian. I just know it got him pretty upset. He went there to play ball a few times after that, but every time he'd come home … *spooked* somehow by the thing. Eventually, he just quit. I don't think he ever set foot in the park again after that."

"That's – that *is* so weird!"

Mom wiped her eyes and stood up. "Yeah, it was weird. He had bad feelings about the whole thing."

"So – he never went to the park with me, or came to watch me in the track meets or anything."

"It wasn't because he didn't care about you, Brian."

"Sometimes he acts like he doesn't care about anything."

"Don't say that. He cares, he really does. I think he cares too much. You know, he puts up a tough-guy front, but inside, he's – he's sensitive. *Yeah, sensitive."*

CHAPTER SEVEN

A few days later I found myself standing on the corner a block from home, waiting for the school bus with a dozen or so complete strangers. A couple of huge guys I hadn't seen before hefted equipment sacks full of football gear. Beefy arms bulged out of their tee-shirts. I figured them for seniors. They figured me for non-existent, never looking in my direction, which was fine with me. A pair of wise guys who must have been sophomores taunted some nervous little freshmen boys and girls. They all just looked me over, but I guess couldn't quite decide how I fit in; so they ended up just ignoring me and trying to act cool. I kept watching for Sharon.

Pretty soon here she came, hustling along flat-footed with a big old smile I could see a block away. She looked different – her hair wasn't tied up in the ponytail I'd gotten used to, and she wore a nice top and white shorts with dress-up shoes instead of the running sneakers. She was just a stone's throw from the bus stop when this beater of a Buick careened around the corner from Richard Street, spinning gravel and bearing down on her from behind. She ignored it at first, but the sound of the racing engine and squealing tires broke her nerve, and she scrambled from the road. Her feet slipped out from her in the wet grass on the edge of the ditch, and down she went on her behind.

Pete the Pyro and Company, meanwhile (because it had to be them behind the smudgy windows), raced on by with shouts and laughter. Even the coolest of the sophomores tip-toed over to the edge of the blacktop, and the senior football chumps grudgingly lurched over, staring after the car.

Sharon's smile was gone. "I'm going to get him for this!" she raged, coming up to me but announcing it to everybody. "Are my pants all wet? Are they muddy?" She turned in circles, trying to see for herself.

"Wet but not muddy," I told her.

She breathed hard through her nose, her face all flushed. "Guess I'll live, then," she muttered, glancing up at me. "But Vincenzi won't – not him or his buddies – not if I get my mitts on them!"

I was still admiring the effect of the wet shorts on her backside, marveling at the whole new first-day-of-school look: her hair, shaggy, but shiny and brightly dancing around her shoulders, and the blouse had a lacy top that brought the best out of her figure, which was....

"Hey!" she barked, and punched me in the arm. "What're *you* gawking at?"

"Ow! Take it easy! I'm just thinking...."

"What?"

"Well, you look... *nice.*"

She stepped back and crossed her arms, giving me an intense look. Then she busted out laughing and sidled up to say under her breath, "First time you've seen me without a sports bra on, I guess."

When the school bus rolled up, Sharon climbed the steps and went straight to the back where a couple of her girlfriends were yelling to her. I ended up sharing a seat with one of the skinny freshmen who eyed me uncertainly when I let him take the window. I turned to the inside trying to keep up with the girls' chatter. But it was all strange to me, all of them strangers except for Sharon. I didn't look forward to spending the whole day rubbing shoulders with strangers.

That's pretty much what it turned out to be. Oh, a few kids were friendly in a detached sort of way; Sharon's friends Margaret and Doreen were in my morning Geometry class. I sat at their table in the cafeteria for lunch, but felt embarrassed since I was the sole guy. The girls giggled a lot about nothing, yelled at each other, and screeched, attracting way too much attention. I looked for a table with some guys to sit with, but decided to stay put. Pete Vincenzi was holding court with an audience of his scroungy-looking pals.

After lunch, it turned out that one of them, that Rick Wagner whose Buick had almost dusted Sharon that morning, was in my English class, with Sharon and big Doreen.

"Hey, Sharon," Wagner greeted her, plunking himself down behind her. About my size, he wore a black AC/DC tee shirt and jeans. His dark hair was longish; too cool to tote a backpack, he dropped a couple of loose books and a pair of new gym shoes onto the floor under his desk. "I seen you were working on your broad jump this morning," he grinned.

"Ha ha," she gave him an icy smile. "And what were *you* working on? Not your driving skill. I'm surprised that piece of crap is even running."

"Well, the steering is a little loose, that's a problem. But you shouldn't walk down the middle of the street during rush hour, y'know?"

"Yeah, the streets aren't safe for anybody anymore – with you behind the wheel."

He snorted and inclined his head to look me over. "Who's your new club member?"

"My club?" Sharon grinned at me. "He's gonna have to pay his dues to be in my club."

"Maybe he should pay you protection – so much a week or Doreen camps out on his doorstep." Doreen looked around and discreetly flicked her middle finger in his direction. Wagner leaned back in his seat. "Hey, don't take it out on me if his heart belongs to someone else. Yeah, I hear this guy's really got it bad for Carla. "

The girls coughed up a laugh at that one, and I let out a groan.

"That's right my man," Wagner warned. "Pete's likely to take you apart if you mess around with her again."

I stifled a laugh – not that the memory of Vincenzi's twisted face was in any way humorous, or for that matter the image of the dark-hot Carla – but while Wagner made mean eyes at me, Sharon was slipping a gross-looking mushy banana into one his brand-new gym shoes. She stomped it down good and kicked it back under Wagner's desk. "Try to drive more carefully, Rick," she said earnestly.

Before anyone could say any more, Mr. Taylor came in to add to our growing pile of schoolwork. He was an okay guy, though, with a good sense of humor and the class went by quick.

I couldn't say the same thing about chemistry: I had kind of a sick feeling that I'd missed the first three weeks of class or something. Maybe this class was way beyond me; it was more of a foreign language than Spanish. There it was the opposite: most of the introductory stuff was everyday conversation in my old neighborhood, so I felt a little bit ahead of the game.

Last class of the day was Phys. Ed., which began with the embarrassing locker room ritual of taking your clothes off in front of a roomful of strangers. The Winston North-blue shorts were horrible baggy things that flared out from the hips, while the tee shirt was too tight. I looked like a ballerina with hairy legs in a wrinkled blue tutu. At least my new gym shoes were a good fit – I had tried them out myself at the mall, and they were a brand I didn't have to feel self-conscious about. Bad enough there had been an awkward conversation with Mom about the cost.

A storm of curses blew up from the next locker bay when Rick Wagner found out one of his gym shoes was flavored banana cream. I shouldn't have let him see my smile when he raged past – but I couldn't help it. Not only did he have to blot the mess out with paper towels, but Coach also assigned him twenty push-ups because he was late lining up for attendance. We filed outside, and I made a point to avoid him as we ran a few laps around the track, lined up for calisthenics, and broke up into squads for some touch football. Tossing the ball around outside cleared my mind, and it was exhilarating after a day in classrooms to just tear across the grass in the sunshine. By the time Coach called us in for showers, I had forgotten all about Wagner and his dark looks. I dressed and tucked my gym clothes in my backpack, and walked out of the locker room dangling my gym shoes tied together by the laces. I never noticed Wagner sidling up to me. In an instant he had snatched the shoes out of my hand, dancing away from me toward the exit doors at the end of the hall.

"Whoo! Krueger – these are some stinky shoes, man."

I made a quick charge in his direction, but he skipped backward laughing through the doors, a couple other guys slipping out with him. As the doors closed, my stomach roiled – I had to get those shoes back. Trembling, I pushed out the doors in pursuit. Wagner was standing a few yards out in the parking lot swinging my shoes like a pendulum.

"OK, Wagner, that's enough! Give 'em here!" I yelled, my voice cracking as I stalked toward him.

"That's enough?" he mocked me. "You want 'em? *Here!*" he shouted, and swung the shoes over my head where they were caught in a scramble by one of the other guys. Wagner's game of keep-away turned into one of hot potato, the other players reluctant to face me while holding onto the shoes. I decided I wasn't playing along.

As Wagner snagged the shoes out of the air again, I held out my hand, trying to keep it steady. "Done now? Let's have 'em," I said as calm as I could make it sound.

It looked as if Wagner had tired of the game, unsure himself where it was heading, when it shifted to another level. Who walked out the door into the middle of it all but Pete Vincenzi?

"Hey, what's goin' on, Kugler?" he sneered, and looked at Wagner for an explanation.

Rick nodded in my direction. "Krueger wants his gym shoes here," he laughed, flipping them underhand to Vincenzi.

As Pete reached out, I stepped up and grabbed at the shoes, but he blocked me with his body, gathering the pair in and continuing to walk out of the circle.

"Come on!" I almost cried with frustration.

Pete turned to Wagner, ignoring me. "Hey, I don't want the frickin' things." He paused as a school bus started up and pulled past, then casual as could be, swung the shoes in a lazy arc through the air. They tumbled end over end to land with a metallic *thunk* on the roof of the bus. Roaring as it went through its gears, the bus headed across the parking lot behind the school.

My heart sank as I watched it go. Somewhere in my guts, desperation turned to action, and I started to run. Upper-class students, going to their cars, looked up to see me darting past. The school bus had a good lead on me, but it was trundling along slowly through the lot. I had almost caught up when the driver made the turn into the driveway and hit the gas. The bus pulled away, and I shifted into another gear, too. The side drive went the full length of the building, but I kept up behind as the bus approached the horseshoe entrance of the school out front. It tilted around the corner, and my feet flew to meet it. I cut across the front lawn, angling to cut it off before it could leave the neighborhood. Gulping air, I dug in for my final sprint when, just like that, the school bus slowed and eased into place in front of the school, where of course it was positioned for students to board for the trip home. The driver, oblivious to the whole chase scene, looked up, gaping, as I clambered up the fender and onto the hood to snatch my shoes off the roof.

I glanced around warily, stuffing the shoes into my backpack. Although not many of the kids leaving school had even noticed, Rick Wagner had pulled his car out of the lot. He and Vincenzi hung out the windows applauding. Meanwhile, a tall, skinny teacher – younger guy in his twenties, maybe – had walked over from the front door. His sleeves were rolled up and his tie loose at the neck. He pushed his glasses up on his nose and asked with some concern, "Everything all okay?"

"Just fine, now," I told him.

He asked who I was and what year, and introduced himself as Mr. Konechny. "That was quite a sprint, there," he noted. "Play any sports?"

I grudgingly admitted that I did not.

"Hm-hm," he nodded. "Well, you look like a runner."

I looked at him. "Yeah, I run."

"Well," he said. "We could use runners, you know. I coach Cross-country. Ever run long distance?"

***

Anyway, that's how it came about that I joined the cross-country team. The J-V team had five meets in the fall. Morning runs were on our own – one circuit around my neighborhood would be a couple miles. There'd be some sprints and such on the track during practice after school. Then we would run two and a half miles, out the door and over to North Park, down the Prairie Path and back through Wick's Woods Forest Preserve.

The competition course would be 5 kilometers. The only thing that worried me was the $100 athletic fee, but Coach Konechny said it could be paid in installments.

Cross-country practice after school left me with less time for the piles of homework, though. After dinner – a casserole or something mom had left for us to put into the oven – I would sit in my bedroom at my little desk, which was just big enough for a notebook and the chemistry textbook. Dad would be leaning back in the La-Z-Boy chair in the family room, a can of beer in his hand, the TV just loud enough to be a distraction. This Friday night I had read the same paragraph over about three times, without it making a bit of sense, so I stomped down the hall. The TV blared some news show, but Dad was fumbling around in the kitchen. Idling over to the old bookcase, I let my eyes roam over the faded bindings. In amongst the several ceramic knickknacks, a couple dozen books had been haphazardly lined up when we moved into the house. Some of them were gifts my parents had accumulated over the years, most of them still unread in their dust jackets. A few "coffee table" picture books with nature photos were laid flat so they'd fit. One big volume stood out in bright glossy red and green dust jacket: *Railroading in the United States.* I'd bought that one myself, for Gramps's last birthday, but he never got a chance to read it. Now here it sat like an unopened letter, moved with the other books from Gramps's house to this place – this place that never felt his footsteps or heard his voice.

God what a storyteller that guy was! He'd been around – merchant marine, carnival roustabout, fruit picker – and he had a million stories about riding the rods, hobo-ing across the continent. The train stories, in particular, had always caught my attention, funny stories about the hobos he traveled with, and grisly tales about railroad accidents, too.

Plucking the book from the shelf, I paged through cheap reproductions of old engravings from early magazines – speeding steam locomotives, explosions, railway cars piled up on each other. Here was a story about an accident in Chatsworth, Illinois. A burning trestle collapsed under a passenger train, and eighty-two people were killed. The sleeper cars smashed together, telescoped and burned. That's what

Grandma Rice was describing when she told us about the Roosevelt Marsh Disaster – part of one car would slide right up inside another like parts of a telescope, crushing bodies, tearing off legs, arms and heads. Then those pinned inside often fell victim to flames that consumed the splintered wooden cars, especially in winter when the old carriages were heated by coal-burning stoves. Any crash would turn into an inferno.

On another page was an old newspaper-style drawing that gave me pause – there's a uniformed guy with a cap leaning over the tracks, swinging his kerosene signal lantern at arm's length in the face of an oncoming train. The locomotive looms big and black, its headlight beam freezing a desperate look on the signalman's face. And I felt like I'd been there. I could remember the pounding and the heavy trembling of the train as it passed through me in the marsh, that electric smell and somehow the signalman's dread panic in the pit of my own stomach.

The phone rang a few times before Dad answered it. "Your girlfriend!" he yelled.

I went into the kitchen to take the phone from Dad, brought it back in the family room, and turned off the TV.

"Hi," Sharon said. "Your Dad sounds kind of mad. Are you in trouble or something?"

"No, he's just grumpier than usual."

"Sorry. Listen, would you like to come with me Sunday to Crosby Park? You said you still wanted to go."

"Well, sure, I guess so, sure. I've got cross-country practice tomorrow, but Sunday's good. Who else is going?" I was thinking *is this like a date or what?*

"Umm, well there's good news and bad news."

"What's this now?"

"We'll go for lunch! It'll be a picnic!"

"Okay, I guess...."

"I'll supply the lunch!"

"What's the bad news?"

"Well, I'm babysitting while Mom and Dad go to a thing, and I got talked into taking the whole gang with."

"All of them? How many *is* that?"

"Who's counting? Anyway, it'd be a lot more fun if you were with."

"Yeah, you need somebody with a dog catcher's net to snag the kids when they try to run off. So what's the good news?"

"I already told you – I'm bringing lunch. Do you have a bike?"

"Yeah, sure, I'll have to check the tires...."

"Okay, it'll be great! Come over to our place around eleven?"

CHAPTER EIGHT

So Sunday we set out from the Rice's driveway like a caravan trekking off into the Sahara Desert. Sharon, looking cute in shorts and a tank top, led the way with a cooler bungeed to the back of her bike. Little Sammy wobbled on a tiny bike he'd just gotten the training wheels off of. Tommy pumped away doggedly on his twenty-inch. Ten-year-old Christine rode like a miniature of Sharon, blonde and a little pudgier, a little more pink-faced. Allen, the hardest and meanest brat of the batch, coasted circles around us, weaving in and out, his knees sticking up as he pedaled his stripped-down BMX-style bike.

Cars pulled over on the narrow street to let us pass as though we were the local Fourth of July event. We followed Sharon – me in the middle of this cycle gang on my dilapidated mountain bike – to the Prairie Path where we started threatening the lives of all the joggers and cyclists who were out here on this bright September morning. Before anybody could get much speed up on the path, though, we veered off onto Jewel Road.

"Stick together!" Sharon yelled. Instead of heading downhill toward Roosevelt Marsh, we rode down a sidewalk with a lot of ups and downs. Allen and Tommy kept swinging out onto the busy street in and out of people's driveways, and all of them kept up a steady racket of beeps and other horn imitations whenever another bike drew near. Fortunately, it wasn't far from the park.

Through a picnic grove of tall oaks, a gravel path led up to a brightly-painted one-story building with a fancy turret on top. "I told you about this before," Sharon said. "This is where they relocated the old Pleasant Hill train station to."

"Oh – from the Prairie Path?"

"Yeah, and they're just fixing it up now."

Alongside the platform stretched a set of steel rails for an old red caboose with fancy yellow lettering: "Crosby Park and Children's Zoo." A miniature farm spread out behind the station, with fenced yards for horses, cows, sheep, and goats; several smaller pens for pigs, chickens, ducks, and rabbits; a couple of good-sized barns and sheds offered shelter. Beyond those, a narrow gravel path wound past outdoor cages with raccoons, squirrels, foxes, pheasants, and whatever other local wildlife they could scare up.

The Rice kids started in, scaring up wildlife on their own, chasing chickens and ducks all over the place while caged doves and pigeons fluttered in a panic. Sammy hopped right into the pen with the rabbits. They fed twigs to the ponies and stampeded the sheep. Tommy let the baby goats out of their pen and got butted to the ground for thanks. They were wild animals themselves.

But they didn't seem to bother Sharon much. She just kept after them, reading their minds to head off some of their worst ideas before they could do any real damage. She'd see Tommy gazing across the park and yell, "Drop it!" The kid would just shrug and drop the rock he was just considering flinging at some unsuspecting squirrel. Seeing Christine take a running start toward a fence, she'd yell "Stay off!" and the little pudge would just change course and head over to the next challenge without missing a step.

All this commotion did attract more attention, of course. A couple park district staff, college kids working part-time, mostly looked the other way. But when Allen jumped a fence and headed for the horse barn, this old guy in bib overalls stepped out brandishing a pitchfork. It was scary enough to make Allen backtrack.

Sharon carried the cooler over to a shaded picnic bench near the caboose, so the maniacs could go ahead and clamber all over it while we watched. "Keep off the roof!" Sharon warned as Allen started up the ladder.

"Is there anything they can break in there?" I wondered.

"Nah, there's just a bunch of built-in bunks and a couple seats and desks. They like to climb into the top part there and look out. Then they jump down and run out again."

As she spoke, Christine came flying out the door and down the steps toward us, yammering about lemonade.

"Okay," Sharon said, "we might as well have lunch now."

Such a feast of peanut butter I had never seen, and hope never to see again. Besides the mountain of sandwiches, she had potato chips and pretzels and a bunch of apples.

"You packed this lunch?" I asked her.

"Nobody else. You got some problem with peanut butter?"

"Not by itself, but with lemonade, it's a little...."

"Yeah, well," she shrugged and crunched into an apple. "Never touch the stuff myself."

Meanwhile, the kids looked like peanut butter and jelly sandwiches that had risen from the grave. "I get to camp out here this year!" Christine boasted with her gummy mouth full.

"Oh, yeah, how come?"

"Her scout group," Sharon explained. "They do a real neat spook trail here for Halloween, and then the park lets different groups sleep overnight in the caboose."

"And this year it's our turn!" Christine ran back up the steps with the others.

The caboose was great for the kids to play in, but I was more interested in the old station. They had put a lot of work into restoring it, you could tell. The shake-shingled roof had several peaks and turrets. A built-in birdhouse fluttered with pigeons below one gable end, and in the middle was a big bay window. All the clapboard siding was painted a bright yellow, setting off the brown trim and posts that supported the roof over the station platform.

"What's in there?"

"Some kind of museum," Sharon said. She started cleaning up the mess on the picnic table. "It was closed for a long time while they worked on the inside." Sure enough, peering in through the bay window, I saw dusty furniture arranged in an old-fashioned parlor, and there looked to be pictures, hand-lettered signs, and stuff on shelves. A brittle old lady all powdered white looked up from reading as I opened the door and slipped inside. She nodded and smiled.

"Hello," I said and began to look around. The stationmaster's office was set up just as it might have been when the place was first built. Ropes kept visitors away from the big desk with its pigeonholes full of train schedules and whatnot. In what must have been the main waiting room stood display cases and cabinets full of donated items such as weathered woodworking tools, dolls in lacy dresses, fancy-design plates and teacups. It looked like an "Antiques Roadhouse" outtake, with rock collections, bug collections, arrowhead collections.

One wall held a display of old railroad tools: pry bars, picks, hammers, and a brakeman's rusty old signal lantern. Against another wall hung a sheaf of big, black plastic-covered mounting boards you could page through like a giant scrapbook or photo album. It was papered with brown newspaper clippings and fading photographs.

I browsed through a couple of the pages: There was a great old shot, fading to white, of some of the old trolley cars hooked together, zipping down the tracks of what might have been the Prairie Path – or I should say the old C & F R. Another picture showed a train with a pre-skyscraper Chicago skyline in the background. I turned the page and did a double-take at a blurry news photo of a pile of wrecked coaches. The caption read: *ROOSEVELT MARSH DISASTER!*

Something like ice water rushed through my veins as I read other clipped headlines: *13 KILLED AS FREIGHT RAMS STALLED INTERURBAN. 33 SUNDAY-SCHOOLERS INJURED. CHILDREN TRAPPED IN BURNING CARS.*

Sharon had come in behind me. "What'd you find?" she asked and then saw for herself. "Oh my God! Lookit – just like Gram said!" She pressed in beside me and began to read aloud from one of the clippings: "*Twelve children and one of their chaperones were killed early yesterday evening in the collision of an electric interurban freight train with an excursion train carrying over seventy youngsters. The three coaches of the Chicago and Fox River Valley train, returning from a Sunday School picnic on the Fox River, had apparently become disabled in the fog at the edge of a marsh just minutes from their destination, the Village of Winston. The freight, its motorman apparently unaware of the stalled train and seeing no signal, plunged into the cars, trapping many victims inside. The cries of mangled children rent the air as fire sped through the wooden coaches.*"

I turned away, watching the Rice kids clambering all over the caboose just outside the window. But the other scene was vivid in my mind.

Sharon was skimming and paraphrasing now. "Jeez… *estimated fifty miles an hour… couldn't see a thing in the fog…. Motorman of the excursion train leaped to safety seconds before impact… the embankment strewn with burning wreckage.* The engineer and brakeman of the freight were both injured, too. Look at this picture, though. It hardly hurt the engine at all."

She was pointing at another picture showing a funny, boxy little engine, in the middle of a blackened bonfire of the wreckage.

"You know," Sharon said softly, studying the photo, "one of these guys – the workmen standing by the cars – could be Grandpa." She shook her head. "Can't make anybody out though. There's nothing in here about – whoa! Brian! Look at this!" She pointed near the end of the page: "*Firemen lauded the rescue efforts of the excursion train's conductor, James McVay, who pulled many of the children from the wreck, saving them from certain doom. 'When we got here, all of them what could be saved were out of the wreck,' said one volunteer fireman.*"

"Jamie McVay – he was the conductor?"

"According to this," Sharon shrugged. "I always thought he was killed in the crash. The stuff about the floating head and all. Here it turns out he was a hero."

I thought back about the unbidden images that had flooded my brain in the marsh, the flames, the heat, the screams. If I'd been seeing into the mind of Jamie McVay, if those sensations were his feelings, too, they weren't the feelings of a hero. It didn't add up somehow. "Why would he haunt the scene of the crash?"

Sharon looked at me and rolled her eyes. "Who says he does? Nobody says he does except freaked-out teenagers and senile old men."

I drew her away to the door. "Hey, give me a break. *Or* at least give your grandpa some credit. Could be he really did see … the light." The pictures in my mind – Jamie McVay fighting smoke and flames to free the terrified children of the wreck – were jumbled up with things I had *felt* there in the marsh with my own senses. I had felt the phantom train. I'd seen the wavering light. I felt sure that Grandpa Rice had seen it, too. The light, and then … disaster.

Sharon bent to read more from the clipping: "*The motorman told reporters that the troller had come detached from the overhead wires causing the train to lose power.*" She looked back at me. "See, no power, no lights. Nobody saw any lights."

CHAPTER NINE

Out of all my classes, English was my favorite – maybe because it was the easiest – or was it easiest because it was my favorite? Anyway, Sharon was in the class, and that was cool – which made up for the fact that Rick Wagner was in there too. Mr. Taylor was this paunchy, short, round-faced guy who every day wore the same boring blue suit with a different goofy, old-fashioned tie. He also almost always wore a smile. You got the idea he didn't hate us too much.

"I have a great project coming up for the class," he said one day, grinning in response to all our moans and groans. "I knew you would be enthusiastic. Wait until you hear more about it! The project has to do with the Winston Sesquicentennial."

We muttered back and forth, and Wagner waved from the back of the room, "Mr. T, why do they call it a sexy centennial?"

"A ses-qui-cen-tennial," he pronounced carefully, "is the one hundred and fiftieth anniversary. Since you are plainly struggling with English, I wouldn't expect you to know the Latin – sesqui meaning half again, and centennial meaning the hundredth year celebration."

"Sexy! And a half!" Wagner called out.

Mr. Taylor went on, "In honor of this milestone in the town's history, we are going to begin a series of local history projects to further your understanding and appreciation of the area's rich cultural heritage. And also as an excuse to have you do a research paper," he chuckled. Oh, he was a riot, Mr. T.

He strode about the room all business-like, handing out the assignment details, calling out random individuals, as if he was prepping us for a commando raid on Turner High School. "The first step will be a simple report on some local history topic. It may be a historic building or person in town, or perhaps a significant event in the town's history."

Somebody poked me in the back to let me know that Sharon, a couple seats behind, was trying to get my attention. When I turned her face was lit up like it was her birthday or something. She was nodding and going, "All right! Great! All right!"

"And what, Miss Rice, has so captured your fancy about this assignment?"

"It's not just me, Mr. Taylor," she told him, unembarrassed. "Me and Brian have been – well, it's really *his* project – he's been doing some research on his own." She raised her eyebrows at me and nodded. "Tell him, Brian."

Taylor kept grinning, though he was starting to think this was a put-on. He was a good sport and went along with it. "Mr. Krueger, can this be true? You have gotten a jump on this assignment? You and Miss Rice have been … ah … *working* on something together?"

I felt my ears warming to red. The class loved it, coming out with a few hoots and good-natured exclamations. Wagner commented, "Oh, yeah, they're working it!"

"What, pray," asked Mr. Taylor, "has been the topic of your research?"

I cleared my dry throat. "The train wreck," I rasped. "The Roosevelt Marsh Disaster."

"What's that? I'm sorry?" He turned to Sharon. "What was the topic?"

"The ghost of Jamie McVay," she announced.

The class broke up again, with laughter from some, questions from others, and spooky movie noises from the rest. Taylor waved his hands to calm everybody down. "Well, that sounds intriguing. I'm thrilled that you have a topic that interests you, and I'll write you down for that on my list – both of you, since, yes, it's a two-person project. Now the rest of you need to find topics as well. If you can't think of one yourself, I have a whole list here."

More complaints erupted from the class. Mr. Taylor went on unfazed, "You may need to travel to the county museum or the public library for your research. You'll be spending several weeks on the project, so it would be a good idea to team up with someone … ah, with whom you are… ah … *compatible."* He raised his eyebrows at me and went on with the next part of the lesson.

I thought everybody'd had their fun with me for the day. But after school, walking to practice, a couple of the cross-country guys started giving me a hard time about Sharon.

"She's cool," I said, blushing. "We did some running together before school started."

They busted out laughing. "Get out, man," this guy Kenny said, "I saw little 'Thunder-thighs' run last year, and it was pretty scary. Broken windows, cracks in the pavement, stuff like that."

He fist-bumped skinny Ray. "You couldn't tell if it was her or a yellow beach ball bouncing down the street," Ray added. "She's so fat she's the same height lying down as standing up!"

"I don't suppose you comedians noticed," I said, seething, but trying not to show it, "but she's not so fat as all that. I don't know about last year, but she's dieting and all, and like I said, running."

"Well," Kenny considered. "She *is* cute, I'll give you that. But she doesn't look like she could run for help if she had to."

As if that wasn't enough to aggravate my liver, we had to walk past Vincenzi and friends where they lounged against Wagner's car in the parking lot. Obviously, Wagner had said something about our English class.

"Hey, check it out! It's the Ghostbuster!" Pete called when he saw me coming.

Freckle-faced Bill Melkovec looked up. "It's the ghost of Jesse James McVader!"

Wagner jabbed him in the ribs, cracking up, "Jamie McVay, Dumbass."

"Whatever," Melkovec grunted.

"Seriously, Krueger," Wagner said, stepping closer, "how can you suck up to a teacher like that?"

Pete gave me a sly look. "Maybe he's more interested in sucking up to the Rice bitch."

Seeing my shoulders stiffen, Pete kept on. "Yeah, Koogler, your fat little girlfriend thinks she's the Block Mom or something."

I flipped them all the finger and kept walking – steaming inside, but what could I do? Well, I could run. Running at practice helped get rid of the anger.

***

On the bus next day, I asked Sharon, "What'd you do to piss off Pete the Pyro?"

She shook her head with a sigh. "That family is so messed up! Last week Vincenzi's dad was at it again, and the mom ran out down the street past our house. My folks brought her in and called the cops. I wasn't supposed to say anything, but I'm surprised you didn't hear about it."

"I *did* see the squad car, and I was wondering. It's not the first time, though, is it?"

"Hardly. Anyway," Sharon went on, "Pete's dad was out there making excuses to the cops, the Mrs. was sobbing on our front stoop with Mom and me telling her 'it'll be all right,' while Pete was lurking there all sulky, staring daggers at us. I just went over to him to say something, you know, to make him feel better – and he went off all of a sudden, swearing at me and stomping around."

"Well," I told her, "he's still going on about it."

"Yeah, he's a real mess!"

"So whatever happened ... the other night?"

"Nothing, as usual. The Mrs. wouldn't press charges, the old man got a 'stern warning', and they all walked home happily ever after."

"Well, Pete's holding a grudge against you now."

***

Friday, when Coach gave us a short practice, Mom dropped Sharon and me off at the County Historical Museum in Winston. I had agreed to go do some research for the "project." We walked through the old mansion briskly, just glancing at the boring displays of old farm tools, political banners, and Civil War firearms. A couple of small rooms were done up as walk-in replicas of stores from the early 1900's. One whole parlor was devoted to trains, with a model layout of the old C & F R line from east of Winston to the Fox River, spiraling around and around from one station to the other.

"Nobody bothered to do the Roosevelt Marsh," I complained.

"Tell it to the Model Railroad Club," Sharon shoved me along. "They'll be closing up soon. Let's see what they've got up here." She prodded me to an upstairs room full of tacky, home-made displays with posters and dioramas in cardboard boxes lined up on tables.

"Looks like a bunch of old school projects," Sharon said. "Taylor would love this, wouldn't he?"

"Yeah, look – all this stuff was made by school kids and community groups for bicentennial projects."

They were pretty crude, not museum-quality dioramas or anything. Different sizes of figures were in all the wrong scale for the buildings and trees. In the Dixie-cup tepee Indian village, the area's original inhabitants were represented by store-bought plastic Indians. In another box was old Ezekiel Winston himself modeled of clay, almost twice the size of his "Lincoln Logs" cabin. Another little box used GI Joe as an early settler, building the first popsicle stick sawmill down on the river.

"So! This is the source of all your local folklore, is it?"

Sharon answered with wide-eyed innocence. "Hey, I haven't been here for years. I don't remember seeing any of this stuff before. It's a bunch of junk."

"*This* is pay-dirt, though," I claimed, pointing to the next cardboard box. A hand-lettered sign read *Roosevelt Marsh Disaster – Miss Anderson's 8th Grade, Winston Junior High School.*

Some kid must have had fun burning up the old toy trolley that was central to the scene. It was all smashed and blackened, bent where it had supposedly been rammed by the battered Lionel steam engine. Creepy little misshapen clay figures lay about the scene, looking way too much like the charred bodies in Grandpa's railroad book.

The caption had been neatly lettered on a yellowed index card. "*The worst railway accident in Winston's history happened*," Sharon read, "*when a passenger train broke down by Roosevelt Marsh, and a freight train ran into them.*"

"Check this out," I said, and my stomach tightened as I took it in. Off on the far left of the scene, supposedly in the distance, was a fair model of the Pleasant Hill Station. A small clay figure had been placed sitting with his knees hunched up on the platform, and a thin strip of paper labeled him *CONDUCTOR.* Some clever eighth grader had set beside Jamie McVay's form a miniature lantern, and on the other side, a tiny jug with a row of X's on it.

CHAPTER TEN

I barely saw Mom during the week, once I started running cross country. After school by the time I got home, she'd be gone to work. Dad would be pretty well soused, crashed on the couch, and not very talkative. One night, though, I noticed he had picked up the railroading book from where I'd left it and was staring off into the backyard. He looked so old and sad I couldn't ignore him.

"Thinking about Gramps?"

He glanced over at me and nodded. "Yeah, y'know, I miss him."

I nodded. "Yeah … not just – not just that he was Gramps and we loved him and all, but – he was fun to be around, to talk to…. All his stories…."

"Yeah, he had a million stories, that guy."

"Yeah – and some of those stories! Him riding the rails like a hobo…."

"Riding the *rods,* you mean. The rods are the steel brake rods under the train that they used to hang onto."

"Under the train? I didn't know that. Jeeze…."

"Yeah – pretty dangerous. That's one reason a lot of them didn't make it. Slip off the rods and you're right under the wheels."

"Hey, didn't Gramps know a guy that got run over by a train?"

Dad gave me a quick look, stood up and kind of shook himself before walking over to the window. "He *knew* the guy, all right – knew him before and for a long time after." Dad didn't say anything else, as if he was thinking, like I was, that what he'd just said didn't make sense.

"What do you mean?"

He glanced over his shoulder. "Ah, like I said. A million stories." He forced a grin.

"But this one," I said, "I *do* remember about one of the hobos getting run over." I stood next to Dad looking out at the dark backyard. "What was the story?"

"Well...." He shrugged and decided to go on. "That hobo – he was a wino buddy of your Gramps, name of Butch, from the neighborhood. Always with a bottle of wine in his hand, I guess. And they were hopping a freight in the switchyards on Claremont when he got killed. The way I remember it, Butch was trying to juggle that bottle when he lost his grip and fell under the wheels."

It was coming back to me now, too. "Okay, that was the guy – Butch – that Gramps used to say...."

Dad's eyes flicked me a sideways glance. "He used to say, whenever he went back to Claremont, he'd always –

"He'd always see that bottle in his mind's eye!" I said at the same time. "Butch's wine bottle!" I had to smile remembering Gramps. "What'd he mean by that, do you think?" Dad turned and finished off his beer without saying anything. "You think that was just Gramps saying 'Don't drink so much' or something bad could happen?"

Dad sighed, sounding like a low growl. "Yeah. That was it." He bumbled into the kitchen.

"Like a warning!" I called after him. "Like 'Watch your step!'"

"That's right," Dad said, menacing, "Watch your step!"

I stepped back to let him back into the family room. When I heard the pop of the beer can opening, I knew the conversation was over.

I slid the patio door open and stepped outside. Out by us, the sky is dark as a hole in the ground except for moon and stars. Off on the edges, light bleeds into the dark from nearby streets and strip malls, and there's a glow from the lights of Winston. But in spite of that, you could still see a lot of stars.

Gramps had shown me the stars, on a summer night, that time we all went up to Uncle Bill's in Wisconsin. Mom and Dad, my aunts and uncles, playing cards and yakking under the bright kitchen light, moths beating their dusty wings against the screens – Gramps took me by the hand and led me out into the dark, the screen door slamming behind us. He hoisted me up on his shoulder and trod across the wet grass, out from under the maple trees, onto the gravel road, and a little ways up the hill. Then he pointed out the constellations: Big Dipper, Cassiopeia, Scorpio… what were the others? I couldn't remember.

Looking up at the sky now, I was just confused. A whole sky full of stars, and I couldn't see any sense to it. But Gramps – all those years on the road, camping in the bush and sleeping in hobo jungles – he spent a lot of nights looking up at the stars, and he never let himself get confused about life.

I slipped through the trees on a path the neighborhood kids used as a shortcut to Pleasant Hill Road, and walked along the narrow shoulder for a while. A few street lights spread faint cones of light down at the cross streets. A couple of times car headlights beamed out from behind me to scare my shadow out ahead, until the speeding car roared by.

Where the Prairie Path crossed the road, a large triangular space was overgrown with weeds, shrubs, and small trees: The former site of the Pleasant Hill Station. You could scarcely make out a depression where the building had stood, and cinders from the old parking area mixed with the crushed limestone of the bike path that ran along one leg of the triangle. It was a weird feeling standing off from the road, hiding inside the tree-leaf shadows, with just the occasional car rushing past – like living on the margins of the real world, watching life go on, but not being part of it. Anybody looking would see through me as if I was a ghost.

I peered down the path. The faint light gray of the gravel faded out just a few feet down that dark alley. That far-off flash of silver might be a car passing on Jewel Road.

And the red light flickering there? No, that was nothing from the world I lived in. I'd seen that blood-red stain in the dark before, at the marsh, a lantern swinging from an unseen hand. I shivered, but the chill wouldn't shake off. Instead, it grew colder, and a feeling surged up like an electric charge of dread spiked with panic. The light almost emerged from the black trees, but close to the road it flickered and went out. At once the sensation left me, and I knew I was alone again. But Jamie McVay had stood there, near enough to touch me with that frightening lamp.

I didn't speak about this to Sharon or anyone else, of course. Sharon was obsessed with her new cell phone anyway. I had to look at all the apps and features that she was so excited about, and act like I was excited too.

I guess she picked up on that. "What's the matter?" she said and gave me a little shove. "Look at this – it's got a flashlight thingy, too. It's way bright!"

"Yeah, yeah, I guess you like bright and shiny things."

"Jealous?" Sharon made a sad face, mocking me, then cheered up. "Ah, you'll get one pretty soon, too, and then –"

"And then what? You'll be texting me all the time?"

"Maybe," she said and gave me a sly look. "Maybe I'll be sending you some interesting *pictures of myself! Hmmm? Hmmm?"* She giggled to let me take it as a joke.

Maybe. That stopped me for a minute, anyway. I couldn't decide if she was kidding or what. I shook the thought away. "Well, for now," I joked, "don't bother texting me – we still have one of those telephones on the wall that you have to turn the crank on."

"Poor Brian," she mocked again.

"Yeah, poor me! I still have to come up with the fee for cross country. And I'm signed up for Driver's Ed next term, and that's what, a couple hundred more?"

"You'll work it out," she said, and I wanted to strangle the optimism right out of her.

There was always running. I still hoped I could run out ahead and leave my worries and the weirdness behind. Saturday morning I ran a pretty good time in my first cross country meet at Winston South. Coach said some good stuff, and it felt amazing to have people cheering me on, even if they were just girls and guys from the freshman and varsity teams. It wasn't something I was used to.

I also wasn't expecting to see Mom show up at school after the meet.

She had scraped up some money, from tips or whatever, and the surprise was that she drove me over to the DMV for my learner's permit. I was pretty pumped up once I had that slim card in my wallet. Mom pulled off into the industrial park to give me a quick lesson and let me drive a little. There I was, back at Woodland Plastics, behind the wheel and feeling cool!

When we got back to our neighborhood, I had Mom drop me off in front of Sharon's. A rust-streaked red dump truck idled in the driveway. Mr. Rice stood talking with a tall guy in dusty jeans. They shook hands, and the man swung up into the cab, gunned the engine, and rattled away. Mr. Rice nodded to me. He wore a blue Cubs cap over his short-cropped blond hair. His big round arms and belly stretched out his tee shirt.

"Brian. Oh, Sharon's not home."

"Oh. Okay, well… Thanks, Mr. Rice."

A white-toothed grin appeared on his sunburned face all of a sudden, and he fell in alongside me.

"Hey, I've got a proposition for you," he said.

"What's that, Mr. Rice?"

"I need some unskilled labor. Look at this." He guided me to the edge of the driveway near the front of the garage and gestured at a jumbled pile of reddish-brown bricks. "This is a custom face brick, a *clinker* brick that we have to re-use in a remodeling job."

"Yeah?"

"Yeah, and I need somebody to chip the old mortar off the bricks, clean 'em off so we can re-use them on the room addition for a house."

I saw that most of the bricks had a thick dried frosting of gray mortar stuck to one or both sides.

"How about it – you interested?"

"Well…."

"I'll pay you – let's say, a hundred bucks to clean and stack the whole pile." He put his hands in his pockets and looked at me the way Sharon did when she knew what the answer had to be.

"Yeah, sure, I guess – I don't know when you need them – "

"Oh, you can come over and work on them whenever you get time. Long as you get 'em done by – let's say, October 15th."

"Okay, great! Maybe I could start tomorrow."

"Sounds good, Brian. Now, get yourself some decent work gloves. These things'll tear up your hands in no time. I'll give you a hammer to use, and a cold chisel. We got a deal?" He held out his hand, and we shook on it.

When I showed up the next day, Mr. Rice showed me how to use the mason's hammer to chip at an angle and break the crust of dried mortar off the bricks in big chunks. The first couple I tried resulted in broken bricks. Before I'd cleaned off a dozen bricks, I'd bashed my fingers a couple times. But I eventually got the hang of it, and it went faster. When I'd finished exactly twelve bricks, I had to line them up and pick them up with a big set of tongs that gripped the whole line at once, to be stacked on a pallet. Little by little, the jumbled pile shrank, and the pallet stack rose higher.

Sharon came out and talked to me for a while, helping to pass the time. The little brothers and sisters all had to pester me, too, until Mrs. Rice came out and assigned chores to all of them. She was a young-looking woman with short brown hair, a little thick around the waist – a good match for Mr. Rice's stocky frame. When they were all out there, doing their family thing, I had to smile – they were such a good family, a happy *normal* family. And then I'd think about what I'd find when I got back to my own house.

The situation there was getting desperate. Mom and Dad didn't always talk to me about money, but I knew Dad's unemployment checks were going to stop coming soon. We weren't going to make it on Mom's restaurant pay and tips. So she sat next to him at the computer to help him write a resume and look at job opportunities. He seemed interested, but he ran out of energy after a while and went back to the fridge for a beer.

One night later in the week, with Dad slouched in his chair at the kitchen table, I was watching TV when the phone rang. It was Mom. She had ridden to work at the restaurant with one of the other waitresses, but that girl was working an extra shift or something, so now Mom needed a ride home.

I ducked into the hall with the phone and told her in a low voice,

"Dad's not in very good shape to drive."

"You can drive," she answered after a hesitation. "He's just gotta be in the car with you, right?"

"Okay, if you say so – sounds good!" All of a sudden I was wide awake and excited to get behind the wheel for a nighttime drive. I told Dad what we were doing and grabbed the keys from their hook.

He tested an empty beer can with a shake. "We're supposed to jump and run out whenever she wants," he grumbled and, looking up at me, added, "That two-bit job's not worth the trouble." But he stood up, unsteady, and followed me through the door to the garage.

"It's all we've got at the moment," I said.

Dad muttered and growled behind me.

I had to back the car out before he could get in. The other side of the two-car garage was still full of containers and extra furniture from the old house. I let the car creep backward until it was beyond the last stack of cardboard boxes.

"Move over," Dad said, rapping his knuckles on my window. "I'm driving."

My stomach lurched. "I don't think that's a good idea."

"Open up!" He bent down and stabbed me with a look. "I'll drive!"

"Mom said I could drive, why don't you let me –"

"Open the door, Brian!"

What could I do? I pushed the door button.

He jerked the door open. "Move over, dammit!" He fell into the seat almost on top of me as I slid away from the steering wheel. He backed out of the driveway, shifted and accelerated down our street, turning wide at the next corner. I couldn't even look at him.

It was about ten o'clock, and our headlights were the only ones shining their cockeyed beam ahead on the dark road and the trees above. We eased over onto Pleasant Hill Road, and Dad sped up again, muttering, "God damn job…." He wouldn't look at me either.

"She's trying to help," I said. I didn't want to fight, but... "She's doing *something!*" I slumped in the seat, just staring out at the dark. Our lights flashed briefly onto the yellow diamond sign that marked the crossing of the Prairie Path.

"Christ!" Dad cried out. The car swerved, suddenly throwing me to the left. We skidded, wheels screeching, and Dad whipped against his door while I lurched toward him and back, with the world turning by in slow motion outside the window. Bicycles, kids with blank faces and wide staring eyes spun past, while too near in the headlights loomed a leafy wall of green. With a great snapping and tearing of limbs, we crashed into the trees.

CHAPTER ELEVEN

You really do see stars. An electric display of red and green lights flashed up behind my eyeballs when my head slammed the door. Dad had been slumped in his seat, his seat belt unbuckled, and when we angled in to hit the trees, the airbag bounced his head partly through the open window. His forehead bent the window rim and split open like a ripe watermelon. I gawked, dazed and confused by the frosty white of shattered windshield and the powder-coated airbag draped in my lap.

Dad moaned and put his hands to his head where dark blood oozed from between his fingers. I couldn't see his face, but I saw the blood. "Oh God, oh God, oh God," he moaned.

"It's okay, Dad, okay, don't move, just sit back." I didn't believe anything was okay, though. In fact, I was sure he was going to die on me any second. *Helpless*, I though, *I'm helpless*. I looked for something to wipe up the blood with, to apply pressure. Mom had a sweater in the back seat, and there was an oily rag on the floor. Funny, how you think at times like that. I reached for the sweater, but my hands were guided by the thought of Mom – the rag went up against Dad's forehead. I pressed hard on the gash, talking to him all the time. "It's okay, Dad, you just got a cut, that's all." This went on for what seemed a long time. I was surprised when I looked up and saw a couple of faces peering in at us. I remembered the kids I'd seen just before we crashed. "Get help!" I yelled.

"An ambulance is coming," somebody said. Other people were moving around the car now. I could hear their voices.

"He almost hit us, man!"

"— car spun right around!"

"— must have seen them at the last second."

"Are they okay?"

A face peered in through my window. "Are you all right?" the woman asked.

"Mm-my Dad –" I stuttered. Wasn't it obvious? I was holding a bloody rag to my father's forehead!

I don't know how long it was – a couple minutes, a half hour – before the flashing red and blue lights of a squad car lit the scene. Now time sped up. A cop came to the window and took over from me, his gloved hand putting pressure on a compress to stanch the old man's bleeding. Dad had stopped moaning and now just stared. The bleat of an ambulance announced the paramedics' arrival, and firefighters swarmed the car. Men strode back and forth, barking orders and yelling at me. Or so it seemed – I knew they were talking, but it all sounded like nonsense to my ears. I recoiled at the sudden appearance of this yellow steel monster at eye level – mechanical jaws that reached into the open window – and stared in horror to see them pry the doors off in a scream of metal.

Next thing, I was stepping up into the back of the emergency unit, looking over my shoulder as they kept their attention on Dad. I saw how the car had skidded into a shallow ditch and slammed into the trees – one big tree in particular that ended the little hatchback's days. I felt a pang of sentiment for the first car I ever drove.

Before I knew it, I was flying through the emergency room's blur of bright lights. Wheeled into a curtained stall, I sat for a while holding my pounding head. Gradually I understood by the groans and grumbling across the room that Dad was having his busted head sewn shut. A couple of cops stood just outside the stall.

An ER doctor finally pulled my curtain aside, peered and prodded and prattled on. His questions whirled around me, and I stammered to answer. He got up from his stool, writing as he spoke – "I think you may have a concussion – we'll get something for that headache." And then he was gone, leaving me alone in a sudden lull.

I perked up when I heard Mom's strained voice and peeked around to see her hanging over Dad on his bed. He was complaining about his neck. I sat back and let them have their moment. When she came over to me, I could hardly look her in the face. She kissed me on the cheek, sighing with eyes closed, "Oh, Brian, Honey!" then stepped back and looked me over. Spotting the doctor at the nurse's station, she strode over to him. After a few minutes, she came back with a sad smile. She clasped my hands, but hers were trembling.

"You poor thing!"

"I'm sorry, Mom. I should never have let him…" but I couldn't finish, choking on an unexpected sob.

She squeezed my shoulders tight and kissed my forehead gently. "Don't blame yourself, silly! I should have known better."

I shrugged her off. "How's he doing?"

"I think he's going to be fine. But they're going to keep him overnight. They drew some blood, and they're doing some tests." She knuckled tears aside from the corners of her eyes.

We walked across to Dad's bed. He was lying rigid with a foam collar around his neck. Both eyes were swollen almost shut, turning black and blue beneath a bloody bandage.

"How you doing, Dad?"

"Ten stitches," he answered. "How about you?" He looked up, but wouldn't meet my eyes. I couldn't think of a thing to say.

A male nurse in blue scrubs appeared with a gurney and a couple of attendants in brown.

"We're ready to take him upstairs now," he said, so we said our good-byes.

Mom kept an arm loosely around my waist as we staggered to the lobby, where Felipe – the cook who had brought Mom from work – was waiting to drive us home. Those county policemen were standing close by.

I sat down while Mom spoke to them. I recognized them from the scene of the accident, and they'd been lurking around the ER, talking to the doctors and the paramedics.

"Pretty lucky, huh?" One of the cops – a stern-looking guy with a shaved head and a bodybuilder's physique – stood looking at me with cold blue eyes. "Your father, no seat belt.... And those kids, I mean – they could have been hit by the car and somebody killed."

"Yeah," I told him. "Well, I never even saw any kids, at least not until right before we crashed. Dad swerved to avoid them."

"Oh, I know," he said. He was chewing gum, acting all casual, "It's pretty dark down there. And you guys must have been going... how fast would you say?" I just gave him a blank look. "Thirty?" he kept on, "Forty? Faster than that? Just curious."

"Yeah?"

"Well, it's being investigated," he emphasized, looking across the room at his partner. "So you didn't see the kids on their bikes."

"Nope."

"Well, it's just a lucky thing nobody was hurt worse. Your father says he just saw a light at the last second – a *red* light, he says – then he turned the wheel and slammed on the brakes. Does that sound about right?"

"I told you. I didn't see anything. I was looking out the window on my side."

He eyeballed me like I was a bug. "Funny, about the light. I looked at those bikes, there were three of them, and none of them had any lights on them. Two of them had red reflectors, but on the *backs* of the bikes, of course. Not on the front where your father would have seen them." He shrugged his knotty shoulders. "Riding around in the middle of the night, no lights on their bikes. Still, your father says he saw a red light over to his left, from the bike path...but you...."

"Never saw anything." I kept a straight face, but he saw how I tensed up. My head was killing me.

"Okay," the cop said, spreading his hands and clenching his jaw. "Kind of funny, though. Say ... *you* haven't had any alcohol tonight, have you?"

"No!"

He nodded. "And how much would you say your dad had to drink?"

I just looked at him.

He sort of chuckled. "Ok," he said. "Sorry you had to get banged up

– but it could have been a lot worse."

It got worse anyway. The doctor had told Mom "No physical exertion" for me until I was examined again and approved for sports according to the "concussion protocol." My cross-country career was over before it started.

The Chevy was totaled. It had been towed to a local shop, and next morning we got a call from the mechanic saying he'd put together an estimate for the insurance company, but it was a complete wreck.

"Mom," I asked, "the insurance will cover replacing the car, won't it?"

She coughed out a bitter laugh. "Hah! We don't have any coverage except the liability. They wouldn't pay much anyway to replace an old car like that." Her voice cracked though. She had liked that little car. The issue now was, how would she get to work – how could we get around?

The answer to that came a little later when Uncle Bob and Aunt Margie showed up. "Abby," my uncle said, "you can drive the Jeep as long as you need it – until you find something else."

Aunt Margie talked over Mom's protests. "No, don't worry about it. We can get by with just one car. Bob's got the pickup, and I take the 'L' to work anyway."

Uncle Bob pointed his finger at me. "Nice shiner, Kid." I'd gotten up with a black eye to match my mood, and my head was aching. "Got anything to put on that?"

"They gave me an ice pack. It's still in the freezer."

He shook his head. "Abby, you got any frozen peas?"

Mom jumped up. "Yeah, I think so. Good idea."

Uncle Bob nodded approval when she opened the carton and handed me the frosty bag. "I hear you're driving now, too."

I touched the peas to my face and let the cool seep in. "Just with a learner's permit."

"Well, you can drive the Jeep, too, then. Just keep it on the road." He warned me with a shake of his finger.

"I – I will – I won't – I'll be careful...."

"Oh, shoot," he said, "I was just kidding, I meant, like, don't take it off-road, four-wheeling, you know?"

We felt a little better for having the transportation problem under control. Mom called the hospital. They said we could pick Dad up any time.

Uncle Bob and Aunt Marge drove us to the hospital, and we were all in a good mood until we got up to Dad's room. Humbled by the thick foam collar about his neck and the heavy bandage on his forehead, Dad gave Uncle Bob a sour look and didn't contribute to the upbeat vibe. He was starting to dry out a little, and his hurts were hurting him more. I don't know what they'd given him for pain, but it wasn't enough. He would have preferred to get home and get a taste of his usual "medicine."

I studied the two brothers, so alike on the outside but so different inside their heads. I could see Gramps in both of them – the sturdy build, the strong chin – but the younger man had the lively eyes and knowing smile. I wondered all of a sudden – what else might Gramps have passed down? A sensitivity, maybe? Or a curse?

We followed along as an orderly pushed Dad in a wheelchair to the front entrance, while Uncle Bob got the car. In the lobby, just outside the sliding doors, thumbs hooked in the straps of his tactical vest, stood the muscular cop from the night before. With just a quick glance at me and Mom, he bent over to say to Dad, "Mr. Krueger. You're under arrest for driving under the influence."

"What?" Dad said. "No!"

"Sir," the other cop said, "you had a blood alcohol content of .10. That's two points over the legal limit."

They took him in a squad car – subdued and pathetic as he stiffly ducked into the back seat. We followed to the sheriff's headquarters where they fingerprinted him, took mug shots, tossed him in a holding cell – the whole works. And we were as helpless as he was. Sick at heart and helpless.

I waited in the car with Aunt Margie. Mom wasn't inside very long. Uncle Bob called and left a message for a lawyer he knew. "We'll get some help, get this straightened out, don't worry," he said. He told reassuring stories of other cases he had known, chattering away all the way back to drop him and Aunt Margie off at their house in the city. Mom and I sat in silence.

It was late in the day by the time we got home with Uncle Bob's Jeep.

We'd just got in the door when the phone rang. It was just Sharon.

"We're waiting for another call," I told her. "I can't talk." She was all about using the damn cell phone now. My head was still pounding, and I just wanted some peace and quiet. I was lying back on the couch when she appeared at the patio door.

She oohed over my black eye and listened sympathetically to the whole story. I mentioned the business about the red light from the Prairie Path, too. At that, she sat back and looked away.

"Damn it, Sharon, it wasn't me – it was Dad who saw the light this time."

"Your dad – distracted by the ghost of Jamie McVay, he piles up the car." She looked down and studied her fingernails. "Uh, and did you say he'd had a few?"

Okay. From her point of view, I was describing a drunk who saw things that weren't actually there. "Yeah, he was pretty loaded."

"And he didn't say he saw the ghost, did he?"

"No," I said closing my eyes. "Just drop it."

We were both quiet.

"Sucks about cross-country," she tossed out. "It's a good team this year."

"Well, they'll have to manage without me somehow."

"Yeah," she said, "I don't know *what* they'll do, now," and poked me in the ribs.

"AAH!" I yelled with the pain. "Jeeze, Sharon!"

"Ooh I'm sorry I'm sorry!" she sat back gesturing with her hands up between us. Again, an awkward silence crept in. "Well… you can still run with me any old time."

"Great. Thanks. When the doctor says I can, I'll run with the team again." I told her. "But the season'll be over by then. I was just getting going, getting to know the guys…."

"Well, look, Brian, it's not the end of your social life, you know. Those CC nerds you sit with will still let you sit at their lunch table. You've still got friends."

"Yeah," I said, and I was thinking, You and the Fat Chicks.

Like she was reading my mind, Sharon said, "You've got one good friend here, you know. I was worried about you when I couldn't get a hold of you this morning." She sighed. "And Pete the Pyro's looking for somebody to buy that beat-up dirt bike of his. You could make friends with him and solve your transportation problem at the same time."

"Very funny," I said. "You've got two cars and the pickup truck parked in front of your house. You can joke about it."

"Hey," she said, her eyebrows raised. "I don't have any cars, personally."

"You know what I mean. And besides, you even said your folks will give you your Mom's Jetta when she gets a new car next year."

"Well don't worry about me," Sharon said. "The important point is, you guys will buy another car soon."

"How in the hell are we gonna buy a new car? You don't get it, do you! We don't know how we're going to pay these hospital and doctor bills! You think everybody lives like you do? With all the cars, and snowmobiles, and jet skis, and cell phones, and a big house full of televisions?"

"My dad works hard to get it all, too!"

I turned away. "Nice, real nice. Bull's eye. You know where to hit a guy."

"I didn't mean anything bad about your father," she said calmly, "and you know it. Or you *should* know it. I wouldn't do anything to hurt you, Brian – not on purpose."

Some cold, stony thing inside kept me from turning to look at her, and a lump in my throat kept me from saying anything else just then. I heard the patio door sliding as Sharon left.

CHAPTER TWELVE

I thought we'd have Dad home pretty quick, but as it happened, he had to dry out in the county jail over the weekend. Mom talked to the lawyer, who explained that we wouldn't be able to get him out until a judge set bail in bond court on Monday. She did get to see Dad briefly. I hope it made him feel better; it didn't do much for Mom. She came home with her nose red and her eyes puffy from crying. There wasn't much I could do to help.

By Sunday morning my headache was a little better, but my vision was still blurry. I was also feeling somewhat fuzzy from the pills they'd prescribed at the hospital. Still, I wanted to *do* something. The best thing would have been to run, but I knew my head couldn't handle that, and Mom would never have allowed it, anyway. I sat for a while feeling sorry and mad – sorry for Mom and angry at Dad. Then I started feeling sorry for myself, over the family woes and money problems. That brought me back to being mad at Sharon all over again, for not understanding. Remembering our argument, I thought of the pile of bricks waiting for me on the Rice's driveway. There was *something* I could do, at any rate.

Grabbing my gloves, I filled a water bottle from the tap and walked my bike out of the garage. As I approached Sharon's house, I saw Rick Wagner's Buick pulled over in front. Sharon leaned in through the passenger side window. I've got to say that my heart sped up when I saw her, dressed for the beach with a filmy top over a two-piece swimsuit. She straightened when she saw me ride up and eyed me warily. "Hi."

Wagner acknowledged me with a toss of his head. "Hey, Krueger, I hear your old man crashed the car. He okay?"

"Not really," I told him, "he's banged up pretty good. But nothing too serious."

"Okay, okay." He peered out at me, zeroing in on the black eye. "Holy shit, man, looks like you got banged up, too! Tough luck!"

"It could have been worse," Sharon reminded us.

"No shit, I heard you almost took out a couple of dudes crossing the street."

"Three guys on bikes," I said. "Riding around in the dark? Don't ask me what they were doin' on the Prairie Path in the middle of the night."

Wagner's mouth drew into a smile, his eyes darted over to Sharon, and he chuckled. "Okay, I won't ask ya – heh." He rolled his eyes and shot Sharon another knowing look, partly for my benefit, and added sarcastically, "I wouldn't know *what* they were up to."

Mr. Rice had a trailer hitched to the pick-up truck, where he was checking the straps that kept the jet skis secured. He jumped down and walked over, scrutinizing my face. "So, you tried a frozen food ice pack?"

"Yeah, frozen peas work pretty good."

"There you go," he laughed. "But your dad's gonna be okay?"

"Yeah, I think so."

He clamped a thick hand on my shoulder, saying, "Okay, then, that's good to know." Sammy and Tommy climbed up and started bouncing on the trailer. The younger little pudge called out, "We're going to the lake!"

"Is that so?" I marveled. "With the jet skis and all? You sure you're not going to Crosby Park?" He stopped to think about that, saw the joke and couldn't contain a giggle.

"Where could we ride the jet skis at Crosby Park?"

"I don't know, maybe… in the duck pond!" That idea caught his imagination, I could tell. Allen, meanwhile, had walked by shaking his head. "Dumb," he muttered.

Mr. Rice strode over to the garage and rummaged through the tools on a workbench. He held up the brick tongs. "If you came over to work, here's the tongs, and the hammer's here, too. We're just about ready to go up to Wisconsin."

On that cue, Wagner started up the Buick. "Have a good one, Shar," he called as he drove off. "See you in school."

Sharon's mom appeared from the open garage door, carrying a couple plastic tote boxes. She smiled a greeting. "Brian, we heard about the accident. Is your father out of the hospital?" Sharon hurried to take one of the containers, placing it in the bed of the pickup truck.

"Yeah, thanks for asking," I said. "Need any help?"

"Nah," Sharon said, "this is about it. We're just going up to Lake Geneva for the day. Grandma and Grandpa are going to stay at Aunt Marcy's cottage all week."

The Rices' mini-van was drawn up next to the pick-up. Christine scampered out of the house with a backpack, yelled, "Hi, Brian!" and clambered in through the rear doors.

Drawing closer, I recognized Sharon's grandparents in the middle seats.

"Hello, Mrs. Rice, Mr. Rice," I said.

"Oh, hello, there," Grandma warbled. Grandpa looked alarmed, drawing back at my face in the van's window. "Pa, it's Sharon's friend...."

"Brian," I reminded them. "I stopped at your house a while back to ask about Jamie McVay. You told us about the Marsh Disaster."

Grandpa squinted at me and nodded his head. "Didja see him? Jamie McVay? Didja see the light?" Grandma sighed and rolled her eyes.

I thought about what the cop had said, what Dad had told him about the light on the Prairie Path. I leaned closer to the half-open window. "Yeah," I said, nodding. "I actually did."

His eyes widened. "You better watch out," he rasped. "He almost got me!"

"I know, Mr. Rice," I agreed. "He almost got me, too."

I watched the Rice entourage drive away and occupied myself with cleaning and stacking bricks for the next couple of hours. It was mindless work, but satisfying in the way the mortar would chip away cleanly from the brick, if you hit it just right. If you missed the angle, you'd knock most of the mortar off but leave a thin gray scab that had to be scraped off with a cold chisel. So part of your mind had to concentrate on the task at hand, but the rest of your thoughts could wander any which way they wanted.

My thoughts dwelled a bit on Sharon in her swimsuit, but eventually, my mind wandered back to the Prairie Path and Roosevelt Marsh, where the ghost of Jamie McVay roamed in the murk. He also apparently visited the site of the old Pleasant Hill Station, and his lantern light was enough to draw my dad's attention, causing him to wreck the car and almost take out a couple of kids on bicycles. And what the hell *were* they doing out there on the path in the middle of the night, anyway? Just hiding out to drink or smoke weed? Is that what Wagner was getting at? Every smarmy word and exaggerated gesture he had for Sharon dripped with suggestion. But I had a feeling he knew more. Whatever it was, it was enough to draw Jamie McVay out of the marsh.

Other questions needed answers, too. Dad said he saw the light. That made sense, if we shared the unique family vision. But others claimed to have seen the light as well, like old Grandpa Rice and different people over the years. So could Jamie McVay sometimes interact in other ways with the material world, whenever he wanted?

I was stacking the last of the clean bricks on the pallet when the sun dipped into the trees. It was satisfying to finish the job, knowing that I'd earned some cash to contribute to the cause. And I had worked up an appetite. The restaurant wasn't open on Sunday evenings, so Mom was off. Ordinarily, she would make something special for supper, like one of Dad's favorites, meatloaf with mashed potatoes. But this wouldn't be a typical Sunday night, would it? Dad was in the county jail, and Mom slumped at the kitchen table talking on the phone – to her sister, or maybe Grandma in Florida. She waved at me and pointed to the stove, where a hamburger patty sat cold in a greasy pan. That about said it all.

While I was nibbling at the dry burger, Mom hung up the phone and distractedly patted me on the head, muttering, "How's my guy doing, huh? How's my guy?" But she was just making noise to fill the empty space in the kitchen, not really asking for an answer.

I swallowed the last bit of food and stood up to open the garage door. "I'm going out for a little bit."

"Oh, don't be out late," Mom said softly and gave me a sad smile.

In the garage, I took a flashlight from the tool cabinet and duct-taped it to the handlebars of my bike. Walking it down the driveway, I hopped on and coasted out onto the darkening street. It didn't take long to pedal back along Pleasant Hill Road to the bike path crossing. I stopped to see the bent and skinned saplings and the raw scar left by the car's bumper on the big maple tree. Pausing just a minute, I turned down the path. My dim flashlight didn't penetrate very far into the black tunnel of trees, but did exaggerate everything on the ground – every dimple in the gravel became a huge pothole, every twig a tree branch stretching across the path. At Jewel Road I waited in the shadows for a couple cars to pass before emerging into the light to cross the street. Then I plunged back into the cold channel cut in the earth that signaled the downward grade to Roosevelt Marsh. Faint light silvered the path from a half-moon hanging over the broad basin, and the sky still simmered a tangerine glow in the west. At the observation deck, I turned the bike so the light shined out, highlighting the cattails that fringed the black water.

For ten or fifteen minutes I stood watching color fade from the sky. I thought I glimpsed Jamie McVay's red signal light among the reeds, and the hair rose on the back of my neck. A cold sensation crept up my spine. My flashlight dimmed and went dead. At the same time, I saw a light approaching down the Prairie Path: The yellow beam of a flashlight flickering along the path, accompanied by crunching footsteps on the gravel and a murmur of voices. In an instant of panic, I pushed my bike down the bank below the timbers of the observation deck and crouched in the shadows.

"It's all good, man, you'll see we're good." I recognized the whiny voice of Pete the Pyro.

"Yeah, we'll see, *cabron*," someone else said. I made out a small guy in a white tee shirt.

"Stop here, this is the spot." The gravelly voice had to be Melkovec's.

A fourth spoke up, another voice I didn't know, very close above my head. "This the spot, huh? Can't see shit out here." I heard the pattering of drops on the ground, liquid splashing on the leafy shrub beside me. I found myself shaking, with the sudden realization that I might have gotten myself into a dangerous situation. Willing myself to hold still, I listened for the pissing to stop. Then a zipper closed and the speaker grumbled, "Let's *do* it, man. Let's see the money."

I heard fumbling and rustling, and craning my neck, moving carefully, I was aware of the four figures leaning over the benches built into the observation deck. Pete Vincenzi shined a flashlight onto a pile of plastic baggies, sandwich bags which looked to be full of marijuana. "Count it up, man," he said. The white tee-shirt character stood beside him, looking down. Melkovec stepped up and flourished a wad of bills, holding it under the light. As the stranger reached out to take the money, Pete's flashlight winked out.

"Come on, damn it –" he muttered, whacking the flashlight against his pants.

"Stupid light, man, let me see – never mind, I got this." The guy pulled out a cell phone and fingered it a few seconds. A flood of white light expanded from his hand, blinding me for an instant where I hid from their sight.

"All right, that's good," Melkovec said, but while the glare flashed randomly at each of the figures, its light flared and died.

"*Hijo de puta*!" the phone's owner swore, poking the instrument and waving it around.

Pete paced back and forth, looking nervously up and down the path. "Come on, come on," he moaned.

Melkovec stepped up, fumbling with his phone. "What the hell! It can't be dead?"

The pisser was agitated. "Ain't no stinkin' cell service in this stinkin' swamp, man? What the hell!"

"No," Melkovec argued, "there's a frickin' cell tower right over there!"

"Here, here," Pete said, nervous and jerky. He brought out a cigarette lighter and flicked it over the pile of dope. Flicked it and clicked it to no purpose. "Oh, maaan…" he whined.

"This is bullshit, *cabron*!" White tee shirt was gathering up the baggies and stuffing them into a backpack. "Come on, we get out of here and go back to the street lights, stupid shit – "

The voices mingled in confusion and faded as their footsteps skittered away down the path. Ducking out from under the platform, I climbed the bank and peered back toward Jewel Road. The figures were silhouetted against the light from a street lamp – until that, too, winked out.

CHAPTER THIRTEEN

All the next week, I felt like a disembodied spirit myself, like Jamie McVay, out of step with the real world while regular people went about their business. The cross-country team was running strong, our first meet coming up, but I was out of action until a doctor cleared me. Coach delivered an uninspiring speech about still being an "integral part of the team." I could be helping the manager, for instance, which I supposed meant picking up towels in the locker room. I had to listen to this as the rest of the J-V team jogged by me like I was one of the goal posts.

Well, nobody cared that much about CC, anyway, the whole school obsessed with their big football team, which seemed headed to the playoffs. Everything revolved around football: If you weren't playing it, you were talking about it, or cheering for it, or marching in the band at the game, or going to the game on Friday night with a bunch of your friends – if you had any. And now with the whole school gearing up for Homecoming, Sharon and her friends stampeded to join the herd of social animals, hanging out with the cheerleaders and football players, and even working on the class float.

She and I were barely being civil to each other, which made for some awkward moments: she sat with her crew on the bus in the morning, nodding a cool greeting to me. In English we kept to ourselves. In the hall between periods, and even at the lunch table bunches of other people always clustered around. Rick Wagner, in particular, was nosing in at Sharon's locker and following her to class all the time. She didn't seem to mind, laughing and joking and only occasionally glancing in my direction. When I did catch her eye, though, I thought I saw a speck of hurt there. Even though I was the one with all the troubles! She had no reason to be upset with me. But I decided to pull her aside at lunchtime.

As usual, there wasn't any room at her cafeteria table, Sharon and her friends packed in like piglets at a trough, eating and squealing away in a barnyard frenzy. I stood there with my tray like an idiot for a minute before turning away to my usual lunch spot. I headed toward Kenny and Ray from cross-country, way at the other end of the room. I had to pass smirking Pete Vincenzi at his table, with all his buddies watching me.

"What's for lunch, Brian?" Rick Wagner stepped in front of me. He'd sneaked up behind me, to the amusement of his pals.

"Usual crap," I said, eyeing him warily. "Mystery meat, and some kind of rice, an apple, or –"

"Mmm, rice?" Quick as a snake he snatched the spoon off my plate, and scooped up a load of rice.

"Hey!" I backed away, trying not to let the plate slide off the tray.

Wagner grinned and jammed the spoonful into his mouth.

"You shithead!"

"Brian, Brian, Man, it's cool!" he said, chewing. "We're *sharin' rice* now, ain't we?" He swallowed and backed away a step as I shoved the tray at him. "Get it?" he laughed, "Sharon Rice?"

The tray and plateful sailed to the floor with a clatter. Wagner danced away back to Pete and the others, who were spastic with laughter, pounding the table and cheering. With all the commotion, and kids sidestepping the mess on the floor, I escaped before Dean Streck rushed up to the scene.

Those days I just got on the bus after school and acted like I was in a hurry to get home; of course, once I got there, I wished I was someplace else. Uncle Bob had put up the bond to get Dad home, so the old man now sat there in the recliner, sitting up straight watching television. He couldn't do much else wearing the foam collar, with this plastic-Velcroed brace contraption girdling his chunky midsection. A stunted forest of empty beer cans generally crowded the lamp table, and the television would blare out stupid game and reality shows for hours.

Mom was gone to work by this time. I would sit in the kitchen, feeling sorry for myself and trying to study, and then he'd yell from the family room, "Hey, Brian, bring me a cold one!"

By the end of the week, this routine had me fuming – *if it wasn't for the "cold ones,"* I thought, *you wouldn't be stuck in that chair in the first place.*

"Hey, Brian!"

He had the nerve.

"Brian, bring me a beer, would ya?"

He had the nerve to ask me to wait on him now, now that he'd screwed up so bad – his life, Mom's and mine! I heard the chair creak as he struggled to get up. Then he was standing there, all red in the face, in the doorway. "Did you hear me?"

My throat felt tight and numb, and I managed to nod my head yes.

"Well?"

I said nothing. Just looked at him.

"You – you little shit!" he swore, staring, then raised an arm to shake his fist. "When I tell you to do something, I expect you to do it, you hear?" He was spluttering, bubbles of spit on his lips. He was a wreck, a fat old drunken mess, and I wasn't afraid of him at all. As mean as he might want to get, he wasn't scary, he was pathetic. "Who do you think you are, anyway?"

I stood up and looked him in the eye. "I'm the guy who's supposed to be staying home to take care of you. And the one thing I'm not going to do is *serve* you any more beer. That's how I'm gonna take care of you. If you want to get it yourself, fine. I can't stop you. But I'm not going to help you."

His eyes narrowed in his mean drunk look, and he nodded slowly, as if to say, *Okay, that's the way it's gonna be.* He got his own beer.

I picked up my Spanish book and stomped out to the patio. It was still light out, but the sky was dimming to gray, and I leaned back in one patio chair with my legs stretched out onto another. Trying not to think. I could hear Pete Vincenzi in front of his house, fiddling with his old dirt bike. He cranked it up and raced the engine, from a low rumble to a painful shriek, blue burnt-oil smoke billowing across the neighborhood. Then Wagner's old piece of shit squealed around the corner and straight into the vacant lot. Rick opened the trunk and started to unload a pile of wood. Pete came over, and the two of them worked at building another bonfire.

The murmur of their voices faded and it got quiet, with just the hum of traffic noise creeping in from the main road, the fading drone of an airplane somewhere in the distance. I nodded over my book, eyelids drooping.

Then BLAMMO! I jumped up off the chair. A ball of fire rolled up over the lot, tongues of orange flame licking the sky. Black smoke hung in the air. Weeds on the shoulder of the road crackled with gas-reeking flame. But the pile of wood was unlit, intact; the Pyro and Wagner were nowhere in sight. As I peered through the trees, there was another blast of yellow flame along the road. Near the Vincenzi house, a movement gave them away. The two of them were prone under the redwood deck with an air rifle, shooting across the lot at their targets – bottles of liquid sitting in the grass fifteen feet or so apart. No sooner did I spot one than up it went with a flash.

"What the hell's going on out there?" Dad called, peeking his head out the sliding door.

"Our clever neighbor," I told him. "Pete the Pyro's learning to make bigger and better booms." I slipped back into the house.

Dad stood back, collapsing into his chair. "Figured as much."

"Somehow he's managed to avoid blowing himself up. I've been counting on him blowing himself up, y'know?"

"Everybody loves fireworks," he muttered, and cleared his throat. He looked paler than usual. Dad turned his head just a little, grimacing. "Like a boiler blowing, down at the yards."

"The railroad yards?"

He nodded. "Your Gramps… he told me about it. I guess he was hanging around, planning to hop a freight, when it happened. Loudest thing you – he ever heard. An old steam locomotive blew up, and it was still sitting on the track smoking, but the whole boiler was gone. There was nothing but steam tubes flipped about like spaghetti." Dad's voice softened. "The hogger was gone, too." He looked at his hands.

"The hogger?"

"The engineer." Dad looked away. "Pa took me there once. Years later, I mean. He pointed out the spot."

"Wow. What did you see?"

Dad clamped his jaw and gave his head a shake. "He shouldn't 've ever made me go there. Why *would* he want to do that?"

Like an old, old, man he lurched into the kitchen. I heard him at the refrigerator door, and then the hiss of an opening beer can.

What did Gramps want him to see?

***

Dad's railroad story reminded me of the English project for Taylor. It would have to be done, with or without Sharon Rice. I sat myself down a couple times to see what I could get on paper, but it never seemed to amount to much. I couldn't find anything about the train wreck on the internet. I needed to get back to the museum at Crosby Park and those old newspaper clippings. I wondered if Little Miss Socialite had taken time out of her after-school activities to work on the paper. I thought of calling her about a hundred times, but always shook off the thought before it could take hold.

Saturday was my chance to get out of the house. With a bunch of paper folded up in my back pocket and a pen tucked inside my socks, I rode my bike down the Prairie Path and Jewel Road to Crosby Park.

It was a beautiful cool September afternoon with a turquoise sky full of fluffy white clouds. Except for my cross-country team-mates going for gold across town at our first meet, every kid in the county must have been at Crosby Park. With the racket of kid noises and animal noises outside, I waded into the calm and cottony quiet inside the stuffy museum.

I remembered pretty well most of the story about the train wreck, but I knew Taylor wanted quotes and hard facts, so I reread all the posted articles with an eye for specific details. They mentioned "J. McVay of Turner Junction" a couple times, and quoted eyewitnesses and rescue workers. Another clipping listed the names of the dead and injured.

I was real industrious. It wasn't easy standing in front of the big display panels copying things onto my little folded squares of paper, but I kept at it until I couldn't hold my hands up anymore. Then I slipped out the door, bought a can of Pepsi from the machine, and sat down on the one-time railroad station platform. The crowd had thinned while I'd been inside; in fact, the park looked to be closing for the day. The old lady from the historical society came out and jingled her keys in the door. Then she stopped and bent over me.

"Were you done in there, young man?"

I nodded up at her powdered face. "Thanks for asking, yeah, I'm through."

"You were certainly very hard at work." She smiled.

"Notes for a school project," I explained.

"Oh, I see," she said, pursing her lips. "About the railroad accident?"

"Yes, ma'am." She looked curiously at my barely-legible notes. She was old enough to have been around back then, I thought. On an impulse I said, "Pardon me for asking – I hope you don't mind – but do you know anything about it, personally I mean?"

"Oh, no, I wasn't living here at the time, although I heard all about it afterward. No, I'm afraid I couldn't help you...." She looked past me, thinking, and shook her finger in the direction of the barn. "You know, Mr. Freund is the one to talk to." Seeing my questioning look, she explained, "Mr. Freund is the caretaker here. He's the one you should talk to. I just saw him entering the barn."

I stood up and finished my drink. "Well, thanks a lot, ma'am, I appreciate it. I *will* have to talk to him sometime."

Before I could do or say anything else she had stepped off the platform and was fluttering towards the barn, cupping her hands to her mouth and yelling, "Mr. Freund! Oh, Mr. Freund!" The pot-bellied old guy with a green cap magically appeared framed inside the barn doors. He leaned on a pitchfork and scowled in our direction. The old lady stopped. She didn't seem particularly anxious to get any closer to him. She turned, flushed and panting a little, and made a shooing motion at me. "That's him," she said. "You just go right over there and talk to him, now."

CHAPTER FOURTEEN

The museum lady waved to Mr. Freund and arched her drawn-on eyebrows at me. Over at the barn, the old man turned and, leaning his pitchfork against the top rail of the fence, stamped the crud off his black rubber boots. My white-haired helper took a step back and gestured again, faltering, "Well, go ahead."

I sighed and, feeling Freund's eyes on me, walked along the path to where he stood spread-legged. "Hi."

He pursed his lips, crossed his arms over the bib of his overalls, and eyed me up and down. He'd sweated through a flannel shirt buttoned to the neck, grimy sleeves rolled once just above his wrists. From the shirt collar up, a scruffy neckbeard faded back along his jawline.

I gave him a quick grin and offered my hand. "I'm Brian – I go to Winston North. The lady thought you might be able to help me with my school project." I tossed my head in the direction of the woman, and glimpsed her picking her way down the broad leafy path to the parking lot.

Freund ignored my outstretched hand and nodded, squinting. "Winston, huh?"

"Uh, yeah, I'm working on this project for my English class – "

"Damn Winston kids're always comin' out here," he growled, working his tongue around inside his cheeks. "Messin' with the animals." He spat.

"Oh, wow, uh … that's too bad. I'm sorry to hear that." I looked down, shifting my feet.

Freund straightened his John Deere cap, then turned and stalked back into the barn. I followed him into the dark, cool interior as he went back to shoveling manure, pitching hay, and filling troughs. I just stood there sort of helpless. At one point he struggled, dragging a feed bag from an empty stall, so I grabbed it from him. "Here, let me give you a hand."

He rolled his eyes but let me drag the sack over to an empty bin. "So," I said, looking up, "the – uh, volunteer lady seemed to think you were an expert on Winston history."

He grunted. "Lived here all my life."

"Yeah," I nodded, "I thought so. Well, I was wondering if you knew anything about the Roosevelt Marsh Train Disaster."

His eyes narrowed. "I guess I do."

"Great, great. Um, well, it must have been a pretty big story, so…."

He cocked his head.

"Well, I mean, I read what they said in the papers and all, in the newspapers they've got in the museum. I just wondered what you remember about it."

He turned and walked out without a word. I followed him out to the rail fence of the barnyard where a couple of nappy sheep were nosing about. He stood there a while, glancing over when I approached.

"Happened right over there," he said, with a nod toward the marsh and the Prairie Path. His raspy voice grew soft. "The train just went dead and rolled to a stop."

A group of park stragglers came up the path, two women with little ones in strollers and a couple of toddlers. Freund waved them off. "Park's closed, folks. Critters got to eat and sleep."

I walked behind as he made the rounds, past the raccoon cages, the pacing red fox, the pheasants. Plodding along, he herded parents and kids in the direction of the gate. I realized he'd be kicking me out pretty soon, too.

"So what I was wondering about," I said, "was about Jamie McVay, the conductor?"

Freund pulled off the cap to scratch his pink scalp. "Him," he said.

"Yeah, what about him?"

"Well, they say he saved a bunch of kids from the wreck."

Freund nodded and worked his mouth. "He did that, I guess."

Talking to the man was like talking to a…a sheep! "But was he hurt or anything? The first time I heard the story, I thought he died in the crash."

"Hmm. Maybe he should have. But, no, he died later."

"What do you mean, 'He should have'?"

Freund shrugged. "Well, it was him who caused the crash himself, after all, wasn't it?" He pulled the wide gate shut and ensured it had latched, then headed back up the path to the buildings.

I scuttled to keep up with him. "What? How did he cause the crash?"

Freund puffed out his cheeks, and talked as we walked. "When the train stalled out, McVay was supposed to signal any other trains to stop. He walked back down to the Pleasant Hill Station…." Freund looked up at the fancy moldings of the old station building. "This very place," he said with a wry twist to his mouth. He checked the doors. Turning to look about the park, he adjusted the bill of his cap and narrowed his eyes. "Jamie McVay was a drunk," he stated. "Fell asleep – passed out – right here on the platform, and let his signal light go out. He was supposed to signal the freight… but he didn't." Freund rubbed his scruffy neck whiskers and stumped back to the barn. I watched him nudge the sheep inside and close one side of the double doors before I hurried back over. He was changing clothes in a stall under a bare light bulb. I stopped near the entrance.

"So," I wondered, "McVay wasn't the hero they made him out to be?"

Freund leaned out. He was wearing regular baggy jeans. The overalls and green cap had been hung on a peg. "Hero?" he sighed. "Oh, sure he was." I looked back as Freund unbuttoned the long-sleeved shirt and peeled it off. In the dim light, his thick arms hanging out of the sweat-soaked undershirt glistened with livid scar tissue. Wispy gray hairs sprouted from the taut, wrinkled and seared flesh that had been hidden by the high collar. Old burns, but still terrible to look at. "He pulled *me* out of the car where I was pinned," Freund said, "snuffed out my burning clothes, picked me up and laid me down like a baby. He was like a crazy man. Had us all lined up on the side of the track, and him goin' back and forth from one to the next, screaming, 'Jesus, Mary, and Joseph,' and holdin' his head like it was about to come off." Freund stepped back into his little alcove to hang up the flannel shirt.

In disbelief I drew out and unfolded the papers from my back pocket, scanning my penciled notes. Of course, there was his name in the list of injured children: William Freund, age eight.

He came out, buttoning up a clean plaid shirt, and stopped for a second. "I remember I seen him lyin' there in the row with the dead, where they was lined up. Passed out or exhausted, but you woulda taken him for dead, all black with soot and soakin' with blood." Freund huffed, jangling his keys, and I followed him out. The sun was setting out over the marsh, coppery light blazing through the trees along the one-time railway path. "Old Jamie McVay, yeah, I guess he was a hero, he did good – saved my bacon, you'd say." He chuckled without humor at the thought. "But still – it was him who was responsible for all those lost lives, in the first place. All the pain and all the suffering."

He turned and swung the barn door shut. "Well," he said. He inclined his head toward the entrance gate. "I'll be locking up."

Just like that, the interview was over. But there was so much more to know!

"Um … One more thing...."

He hesitated, his hand on the latch.

"Mr. Freund? People – *some* people say they've seen the ghost of Jamie McVay – that he haunts the Prairie Path...."

Freund looked out over the marsh.

"What do you think about that?" I asked.

Turning back to me, he raked both hands through the thin threads of his hair. His shoulders drooped, and he let his arms dangle at his side. "I've seen things," he said. "It could be him. And why not? Why should *he* get to rest?"

I stared. What could I say? What could I tell this scarred old working man about who deserves what?

Freund looked back toward the barn, where his charges rustled in their beds of straw.

I said my thanks and good-bye, mounted my bike and pedaled down Jewel Road. Headlights glared on the road until I turned into the deep shadows of the Prairie Path. Looking back, I thought, *Right down there, I've seen it through the memories of Jamie McVay: the blazing cars, thick smoke burning in his throat, the moans and cries.* The raggedy ribbon of sky glowed almost purple, reflected in the marsh through the screen of branches. The path inside the tunnel of trees was gray on black, but – like a taunt, a red pinpoint of light appeared, glowing for a second before vanishing at a twist in the trail.

I pedaled toward it. As times before, the light reappeared way down the path, wavering and flickering behind the trees. A faint rumble came up, and a smell of gasoline tinged the damp, cool air. When I came out of the shadows at the timber deck, the light was gone. The sunset glow faded, color dying as I stood there astride the bike. Below the horizon, all was black, except for a few pools of water reflecting the sky now like dull steel. Then a glimmer of red, a flash of light silhouetted a clump of cattails. That low rumbling sound rose and fell, and rose again.

Over to the east the lights blinked out at Crosby Park. A few minutes later a pair of headlights went on in the parking lot. I pictured Freund driving off in the old pick-up truck I'd seen there earlier, as the lights joined others streaming past on Jewel Road.

I imagined McVay that night of the Disaster. My skin prickling and clammy, I pictured him hunched up on the station platform at Pleasant Hill like the figure in the museum diorama, sleeping and snoring away – that insensible sleep of the drunk I knew well enough. He'd have wakened, though, panic-stricken, as the freight train rumbled past. I see him turning in circles, wondering what to do. He looks down at his old signal lantern sitting there burned out, cold and dark. He fumbles with a match to relight it. He races down the track screaming at the noisy old freight, but it's left him far behind. Maybe the brakeman peers out from the cupola of the caboose, but he sees no signal light from Jamie McVay. Running full-tilt, stumbling over railroad ties, McVay reaches Jewel Road – this crossing here behind me – and thinks he might still have a chance. If he angles through the marsh, he might still head off the freight as it makes its wide curve over the wetlands. He might still get a warning to the motorman and the passengers on his stalled train. He plunges down the embankment, but the marsh is shrouded with fog, both trains invisible in the murky darkness. He stumbles, flounders in the mire, shouts, waves the signal lantern, and helplessly watches the oscillating headlight beam of the freight train emerge from the trees and come sweeping around the bend. Like magic, the frail little trolley cars full of children appear suddenly in that white light. He hears the screeching wheels, the tearing, shrieking crash; he sees the coaches crumple, telescope, and burst into flame. Worlds end, lives snuffed out, as Jamie McVay staggers and stands helpless. The image held like a yellowed old photograph in my mind.

A sudden flash of white light blinded me and roaring behind it something big and black loomed, as an unholy chorus of screams tore the night. I tumbled off my bike into the bushes, sliding down the stony embankment, scrabbling in confusion, clutching at twigs, branches slipping through my fingers.

A second light, and then a third appeared above me. Whoops and shouts came from the dark figures dancing beyond the glare.

"Gotcha!"

"Hooo! Jump, you sucker!"

"Haha! Krueger, you are so lame! Oh, man!" Rick Wagner collapsed laughing over a big-wheeled all-terrain vehicle that rumbled at idle, its headlight beaming through the trees.

Pete Vincenzi, straddling his mud-caked dirt bike, pumped his fists in the air, hooting, "You dumb shit!" He high-fived Melkovec, on his own dirt bike, rearing back with a belly laugh.

"You bastards!" I swore, clambering up the slope. They'd got me, all right.

The Pyro lit a cigarette, coughing, "Oh, maaan," bent over his handlebars struggling for breath.

"Real funny, assholes!" I muttered, reaching the path. Melkovec revved his engine and his bike leapt ahead just as I gained my feet. I dodged out of the way, provoking more ridicule. My knees wobbled as I groped for a tree and stood up straight.

Pete leaned back, exhaling smoke, and crossed his arms with a malicious grin. "Yeah, *real* funny, Kugler. And you're the joke." He raced the wheezy engine and spun his rear wheel, gravel flying. The bike lurched forward, and the others followed. I watched the four-wheeler speed away, its one loose tail light wagging back and forth, back and forth, as it flickered red and disappeared.

CHAPTER FIFTEEN

Whap! Mr. Taylor slapped the literature book down flat on his desk. Startled kids jumped, their ears perked up like Labrador retrievers. "And before the bell rings," he announced, "let me remind you that your research projects will be due soon. We've talked about the importance of using firsthand research, so if you still haven't found someone to interview, please talk to me." A couple of hands went up, and Taylor went over to help.

Sharon was looking up at the ceiling. Turning I leaned into the aisle.

"Sharon!" At her answering look, I spread my empty hands with the question on my face. "What are we doing?"

"Oh, I think … English!" she laughed.

"All right – the paper! Are you working on the paper?"

"Yea-ah," she said, making two syllables of it. "I've got some pretty good stuff."

"Well – can we talk about this or what? Are we still –?"

Mr. Taylor's voice broke over all the chatter in the room. "People! One more thing. Don't forget that we meet in the auditorium tomorrow for a special sesquicentennial presentation from the County History Museum." The bell overlapped his last phrase, and students snatched up their packs to surge through the door. I stood up helpless as Sharon squeezed into the hall.

"Any problems, Mr. Krueger?"

I turned with a fake smile pasted on and gave him a thumbs-up. "No problems, Mr. T."

He nodded, eyebrows raised, and looked past me back where Sharon had disappeared. "All right, then."

I tried again to approach Sharon at her locker after school. I had to catch her before she rode home with Doreen and company. She spotted me heading her way and got incredibly interested in selecting textbooks and stuffing them into her backpack.

"So," I said, getting to the point, "when are we gonna put this report all together?"

She heaved a deep breath and kept studying the neatly-stacked contents of her locker. "I don't know," she said. "If you're sure you want to – "

"What *else* would I do? We're supposed to be *collaborating* on this, aren't we?"

"Yeah, well, partnerships are overrated, sometimes." She turned and looked at me with her cool blue eyes.

"Well, look – we should finish what we started. Together."

"Like I said. If you really want to – if you don't mind working with somebody so *privileged* – then give me a call." She looked past me, where Doreen was coming our way. Behind her, Pete the Pyro was pantomiming the big girl's characteristic waddle, with Melkovec and Wagner clowning along behind him. Doreen moved in like a loaded barge, crowding me back, while Wagner slipped alongside Sharon with an oily smile.

"What's *hap*hin', girls?"

Sharon got busy with her books again, and Doreen spun around to give Pete the evil eye.

The Pyro mouthed an obscenity at her and kept walking, bumping me with a shoulder on his way.

"Big Bad Brian," Melkovec laughed.

Wagner chuckled, "Yeah, better watch this guy, Sharon. Krueger'll try to get you out on the Prairie Path to hunt for ghosts with him. He's out there haunting the *hell* out of the neighborhood these nights! Aren't you, Krueger?"

"Well," Sharon turned with a good-natured smile, "I don't go out ghost-busting with just *anybody,* you know." With a slam of her locker, she tramped out with Doreen to the parking lot, Wagner covering their retreat.

Oh, Little Miss "If you really want to!" She put me in my place. I stewed all night, humbled and angry, but no way inclined to call Sharon Rice.

***

Next day we settled into the school auditorium watching the hundred-and-fifty year history of the Village of Winston pass before our eyes in – could it only have been fifteen minutes gone by?

A deep voice droned on as one sepia-toned photo dissolved into another on the big screen above the stage. In the plush seats, heads nodded, some dozing, some ducking to whisper across the rows, others secretly checking their phones. A dulcimer jangled annoying background music as the narrator continued.

"*Ezekial Winston and the first pioneers had settled on the river because it provided power for the saw mill and later the grist mill that became the center of the community. But it would be the railroads that put Winston on the map.*"

A puffing old steam engine appeared in the photo. I recognized the tops of the buildings on Front Street behind the train. Meanwhile, a wave of yawns rippled through my row. Behind me, Rick Wagner whispered something and Sharon stifled a laugh.

I let the narration wash over me and sort of zoned out on the slide show: more whiskery Winstons, grumpy guys in suits, 50's cars on Front Street….

"*… and with expressways and improvements to the local road system, fewer Winstonians utilized the electric interurban trains. When the old C &F R ceased operations, local railroading became a footnote to history, its relics consigned to local museums.*"

Tell me about it, I thought, as the camera panned over walls covered with old photos. The images dissolved into an assortment of museum displays. I recognized the old brakeman's lantern from the Pleasant Hill

Station at Crosby Park. There was the model train layout from the County Museum. That faded into a display of old timetables and train tickets, and presiding over that was the headless form of a conductor in a blue coat with gold trim and a familiar-looking patch and – *what the – ?*

I leaned ahead in my seat, recognizing the symbol of the old C & F R. As if following my gaze the camera zoomed in on the uniformed manikin, the gold braid, the brass buttons, and the nameplate alongside the coat's lapel: *McVay.*

Holy shit! I looked around, as if anybody else might take note of the detail, but of course, it would only mean anything to Sharon –

"Sharon!" I spun and waved to get her attention. "See that?"

Her blonde head tilted up, but the screen had changed. She looked and shrugged. Frowning, she settled back in her seat.

When the video was over, Mr. Taylor introduced Mr. Niederman, a gloomy-looking old guy in a tweedy sports coat, who had once taught history at Winston North. He answered some questions, prattling on about early fur trappers and Civil War heroes. There were other English classes besides our own in the auditorium, so the Q & A session went on until the bell rang. As most everyone filed up to the exits, I pushed my way down to the stage.

"Mr. Taylor!" He was talking to the historian at the speaker's podium. "I was wondering…." They looked at me expectantly. "Where'd that stuff come from? Some of those railroad things in the movie, like the train uniform?"

"Hmm," Mr. Niedermeyer thought. "You must be talking about the display from Turner Junction."

"The new museum on Main Street?" Taylor asked. "I haven't been there. It looks as though they have a fair number of railroad items."

"Yes, well, Turner Junction *was* the railway junction for the region." Mr. Niederman produced a business card. "E-mail me at this address, and I'll send you more information, the hours and phone number. They may only be open on weekends."

Glancing around real quick, I saw Sharon, hesitating a second at the door. I waved to her and caught her eye. She gave an exaggerated sigh and left her friends to stroll down the aisle. "What's up?" she said.

"They've got some Jamie McVay stuff at that museum in Turner."

"Yeah?"

"We should be able to find information for our project, right Mr. Taylor?"

"I'd be very surprised if you didn't," he said with a smile.

"As I was saying," Mr. Niederman went on, "the Turner Museum specializes in railroad memorabilia."

"Well, we'll check with you to see when it's open, and then Sharon and I will get over there. Right?" I asked, staring her in the face.

"Ohhh-kay, yeah," Sharon said. "Right-o." She didn't like the way I put her on the spot. But the important thing was, I got her to commit.

***

Mr. Taylor arranged for us to visit the Turner Museum on Friday night. Mom dropped me off before heading to her shift at the restaurant. Sharon's mother would bring me home later. At first, I was looking for this "new" museum Mr. Taylor had mentioned, but we pulled up tentatively in front of a weathered brick storefront on the main drag of old Turner Junction. Limestone cornices of the upper story crumbled above a carved *1889*. The front windows had been painted black, but a neatly-lettered wooden sign identified the home of the Turner Historical Society. I pushed the heavy front door open and entered under a jingling bell. Mr. Taylor stood near the entrance with Mr. Niederman, whose sport coat sleeves were powdered with dust.

"Brian, Mr. Niederman is staying late to keep the museum open for us today." Taylor's light blue shirt sleeves were rolled up.

"Thanks, Mr. Niederman, I appreciate it."

He nodded with enthusiasm. "Happy to be of assistance! Your teachers are smart to get you kids involved in the local history."

I looked around. The place was a mess. A fake kitchen was set up, with an old enamel wood-burning stove and hutches full of odd utensils and dusty dishes, everything strewn all over with no sense of order. "They're still getting organized," Niederman explained with a weak smile. "All volunteers, you see."

I looked past a jumble of old carpenter's tools in the front window to see Sharon crossing the street from her mother's car. She pushed on the door as I pulled it open, spilling her into the room.

"Miss Rice," Taylor chuckled, "nice of you to drop in."

Sharon flushed and laughed in spite of herself. "Ohhh-kay, here I am."

"Well," he went on, "Mr. Niederman knows that you're researching the Roosevelt Marsh Disaster."

"And the conductor of the wrecked train was a Turner Junction man," Niederman nodded. "Most of the rail memorabilia is upstairs." He gestured to a door where a narrow wooden staircase turned out of sight. Sharon poked her head around the corner. Looking back at me, she shrugged and climbed gingerly up the creaky stairs. "It's a bit disorganized," Niederman called after her.

Following Sharon up, I stepped out into a big room with bare brick walls and a worn plank floor. Motes of dust hung in the air like flakes of gold as a beam of the low sun flashed in from a rear window. Boxes and old trunks were stacked about the room. A few big glass display cases crammed full of junk stood against one wall. The focal point, though – the object of our visit, actually – was the headless model with the blue conductor's coat I'd seen in the video: the gold-trimmed sleeves, the shoulder patch of the C & F R, and the narrow brass *McVay* nameplate above the breast pocket. I gestured toward it with my outstretched hand. "So, I wasn't going crazy."

Sharon shook her head. "That is unbelievable!"

Groaning wood from the stairway announced the appearance one at a time of Mr. Taylor with the puffing Niederman. "I see you found what you were looking for."

"Yeah," I said. "Where did you even get this from?"

"Well," Mr. Niederman wheezed, "a lot of this memorabilia's donated by local folks."

"Can you tell us who donated this coat?"

"Well . . ." he hesitated, looking uncomfortably at Taylor.

"I'm sure there'd be no issue in disclosing that," Taylor put in. "It's part of the public record, after all."

"I suppose so," Niederman mused. "I can look it up in the records. It's all on the computer now." He studied the coat and name tag. "*McVay*," he chuckled.

"What's funny?" Mr. Taylor asked.

"Well, we wanted to have one of our re-enactors wear this for the Ghost Walk, but look, it's so small. It wouldn't fit any of our people. McVay was a small man."

"You know who he was?" Sharon asked.

"Well, sure, he's one of the characters in the Halloween Ghost Walk."

"What's that?"

"A very popular event for Halloween," Niederman explained. "I'll be one of the guides leading visitors from here to meet the famous ghosts of Turner Junction – some young volunteers dressed up, you understand." He peered over his glasses with a smile. "We walk to the river to see the Ghost of Gray's Mill, and from there we go to the Cat Lady's House – "

"Cat Lady?" Taylor laughed.

"Yes, the Cat Lady of Catalpa Street. Poisoned her boarders, cut them up and fed them to her cats, they say."

"And Jamie McVay?" I asked.

Niederman nodded. "Then from the Cat Lady's House it's just a half block down to the railroad tracks – there's an old signal shack, where the headless ghost of Jamie McVay will pop out and scare the daylights out of people." He tittered self-consciously.

"So," Sharon spoke up, "they tell the Jamie McVay stories in Turner Junction, too?"

"Oh, yes. He was a Turner man when he died, you know, though his family I think was originally from Winston. But we've got a number of accounts told by local people."

"Accounts of . . .?"

"Well, I guess you'd call them hauntings."

CHAPTER SIXTEEN

"Hauntings," Sharon repeated. "Ohhh-kay! Let's hear more."

Niderman blushed. "Well, the truth is, my Uncle Harold even told a story."

"No kidding," I said, "we'd definitely like to hear it."

Sharon dug into her purse and came up punching buttons on her phone. "Yeah, what's the story? You don't mind if I record it, do you?" The golden sunlight had flicked off suddenly, leaving us in a murky dusk.

Niederman backed up a little, and cleared his throat; he pursed his thin lips in a kind of smile and began. "Well, Uncle Harold told about meeting the ghost at the High Lake Spur. That spur line, with a siding along High Lake Road, served a number of dairy farms along the way. My grandfather's was one of them. They'd bring the milk cans to different stops on the High Lake Spur, and the C & F R train would run them in to the dairy in Cloverdale." He wrinkled his forehead, picturing the map in his mind, I guess, while Sharon stepped closer holding her phone up to his face.

"And what happened?"

"Well," he laughed, "Uncle Harold and one of the farm hands backed their truck up to the platform there as usual, and unloaded the milk cans. They were lying back, smoking, on an old flatcar parked on the siding, waiting for the early morning train to come down the spur. And Uncle Harold always said how Jamie McVay tried to sneak up on them."

"How?"

"Well, the ghost didn't really *sneak* up, because the men could hear the train coming. They sat up and were looking down the track, and they could hear the train, but couldn't see it. Then Uncle Harold turned and sure enough! Here it came, a couple of passenger coaches heading their way from the opposite direction! The train was free-wheeling down the siding where they sat, just rolling down the grade from High Lake, forty miles an hour or so. And as it came on, they saw that there was no motorman – it was a runaway, running dark! Not hooked to the electric line, you see, and no bells, no running lights – except at the front step they saw a light – like somebody was swinging a red signal lantern. But ..." Niederman paused for dramatic effect: "... there wasn't any hand holding the lantern. It was the ghost of Jamie McVay, lighting the way to disaster!"

Taylor made an appreciative noise, and Sharon let out an "ooh."

Niederman nodded solemnly. "Well, they jumped, and the runaway train crashed into the flat car about the same time as they hit the ground. It was a very close thing, according to Uncle Harold."

"Did they see the ghost after that?" Sharon asked.

Niederman crossed his arms. "They never did. He'd done his work, leading the train off the mainline, Uncle Harold always said. Except..."

"Except...?"

"The farmhand. He saw the head."

"He saw Jamie McVay's head?"

Niederman shrugged. "That's what Uncle Harold said."

"Great story," Mr. Taylor grinned, clapping his hands.

"And Jamie McVay *led* the runaway train onto your uncle?" Sharon pressed.

"That's the story. That's *one* story of the ghost haunting, coming after people along the line."

"But ... why would he do that?" I asked.

"Well ..." Niederman's smile faded. "The legend, you know, is that he haunts –"

"Yeah, but *why?*"

"Well, he's a *ghost,* isn't he?" He smirked and, then, exasperated, looked to Taylor for help. Taylor shrugged his shoulders.

"Even a ghost has a reason," I insisted.

Niederman sighed. "Well, maybe he's just *angry.* He lost his head, after all! Maybe he's just *mad* because of being killed in the wreck!"

"But he *wasn't."*

"He wasn't mad? I don't know, I sure would be," Niederman chuckled.

"He wasn't killed in the wreck!"

Niederman's eyes narrowed. "Well, that's the story."

"The story's wrong! He was there that night rescuing people. He was a hero!" I spun around the blue coat, muttering a little too loudly to Taylor, "I thought this was a *history* museum!"

Mr. Taylor bit his lower lip and cleared his throat.

"Now, that's uncalled for," Niederman said, hurt. He drew back and looked down his nose. "I gave you all a bit of *oral history* just now. That's history!" He stomped to the top of the stairs and pivoted, flushed. "I'll have you know that we have access to historical records right here in this museum. I can get to the bottom of this presently." He clomped down the stairs.

Mr. Taylor shook his head and rolled his eyes, making a nervous humming noise. Sharon walked over and looked at me askance with her mouth open. "Nice one, Brian," she muttered. "Got everybody all riled up."

Mr. Taylor worked his mouth back and forth a couple times and strolled over real casual-like. "What is your point here, Mr. Krueger?" he asked.

"The legend says Jamie McVay haunts the railroad. That *might* even be true. But it's not because he was killed in the Marsh Disaster. We know he actually *saved* kids from the wreck that night. Mr. Freund said he died later."

"Well, we should be able to find out the truth. Mr. Niederman says they have access to the data base with local newspaper archives." Mr. Taylor turned and descended the stairs as if expecting them to collapse with every step.

Sharon studied the table where McVay's uniform was displayed.

Train timetables and old tickets lay on the dusty surface. I moved up alongside her. "Sharon, look – "

She waved a hand to stop me. "I know, I know, we need to finish the paper. I'm here now, aren't I?"

"It's not just that."

She squared herself up to me with her arms crossed. "Well, what else is it?"

Her blue eyes had gone gray like everything else. As many times as I'd said to myself how I felt, the words wouldn't come now at all. I looked at Sharon's upturned face and felt hopelessly dumb. She heaved a deep sigh and turned away. Down the creaky stairs she went, leaving me all regretful in the darkening room. After a few minutes, the street lights came on out front, silhouetting Jamie McVay's headless coat against the diffused glare of the windows.

Downstairs everybody crowded into the little office. Niederman was typing and gaping at the monitor with Mr. Taylor peering over his shoulder. Sharon had squeezed in to look over the other shoulder. Mr. Taylor reached to pull out the page just spat out by the printer.

"Here you go, Brian. This is from the *Turner Junction Chronicle*: '*Conductor James McVay was officially censured yesterday by the Railway Safety Board, one week after the Roosevelt Marsh Disaster, for drunkenness on the job and dereliction of duty. The C & F R Railroad also suspended the Turner resident from all work without pay, pending the findings of the formal investigation and subsequent court inquiry by the American Interurban Railway Authority.*"

"This is your hero," Niederman muttered. His fingers clicked on the keyboard.

"Like I said," I pointed out, "he didn't die in the crash."

"No, here's something else though, a few days after that one – oh – Hmm."

Taylor, reading the screen, said, "Print that one out, will you?"

Niederman glanced up at me sullenly. Mr. Taylor plucked at the page as it popped up. He skimmed over it and handed it to Sharon, who read aloud: *"Another Tragedy on the Tracks! Marsh Disaster Conductor Dies in Tragic Accident! James McVay, indicted by the Railway Authority for his role in the Roosevelt Marsh Disaster, was struck and killed by a commuter train Friday night… no witnesses … speculation that alcohol may have been a factor… decapitated…"* She passed the printout to me with lowered eyes.

The room was quiet while I skimmed over the article: *McVay's death provides railroad officials with one more reason to work toward improvement of safety measures…blah blah … Possible suicide... Survivors and relatives of victims of the Marsh Disaster comment on McVay's death…'curse his soul' cries mother of the crash victim….*

Niederman's hands fluttered again, and the printer hummed. Mr. Taylor passed along an image from the last page. The black and white portrait showed a surprisingly youthful Jamie McVay in his uniform – possibly the same empty coat that gathered dust upstairs – wearing a cap emblazoned with the C & F R logo. Rendered in the black and gray dots of the old newspaper the face took shape: fair hair, broad forehead, light eyebrows, bright eyes crinkled playfully in spite of the jaw clenched to maintain a serious pose. Maybe a flush to the cheeks and nose?

Mr. Taylor broke the uncomfortable silence. "Not exactly the face of a ghostly fiend."

The face of a good-natured drunk, I thought, *a dangerous drunk.* But despair and a lonely death had turned him into a woeful monster.

We had some time to digest all of the old news while waiting for Mrs. Rice to come and pick us up. Mr. Niederman also grudgingly pulled up the record identifying the donor of Jamie McVay's uniform. "I remember her now, Mrs. Runyon – a *very* nice lady. Widow woman, her husband worked for the Chicago & Northwestern. She was getting rid of all those railroad collectibles."

We only had the woman's Turner address, but Sharon's stubby fingers played over her phone and quickly came up with a telephone number. Without hesitation, she thumbed in the call, but no one answered. "No message," she said, pouting. "Well, you can try again later." She wrote the number on one of our print-outs and walked over to the front window.

"So," I said, sidling up to her, "when do you think we should sit down and combine all our notes?"

She thought for a minute, gazing out at the traffic. "Tell you what – you take the newspaper stuff here, and copy it out in your own words. I'll figure out some kind of an outline for how we can use it." She turned and flashed me a quick, cautious smile. "Maybe we can get together this week." I walked away so she wouldn't see me grinning.

The Rices' mini-van pulled up in front. In addition to Sharon's mom, it seemed to be full of kids, all jabbering away and jumping up and down. They got even more exercised when Sharon announced that she'd drive. Tommy's outburst – "Oh, no, we're all gonna die!" – and Christine's good-natured suggestion – "Don't forget to buckle up!" – overlapped with Allen's helpful observation that "the front wheels are goin' backward!" All I could do was sit quiet with an uncomfortable grimace pasted on, helpless and humbled to have Sharon drive me home.

***

I spent Saturday morning helping Mom with some chores and fiddling with the goofy lawn mower. I ran it back and forth over the leaf-strewn yard a couple times and watched the Pyro pile up scrap wood for the weekend bonfire in the vacant lot.

After lunch I walked over to Sharon's. Her father was working on a concrete saw in the open garage, but he put it down when I walked up.

"How you doin', buddy? Y'know, Sharon's not home."

"Oh, okay. Thought I'd talk to her about school." I put my hands in my pockets, a little self-conscious.

"Yeah – hey! I owe you some money, don't I?" He strode into the house and was back in a minute with a wad of bills folded in half. "Here you go – thanks for the good work."

"You're welcome. Any time I can help, just…."

"Right, well, listen – I might be able to use somebody to tidy up the equipment yard, and the machine shed this winter."

"Just let me know when."

I was feeling pretty important when I brought that slim sheaf of cash home and laid it on the kitchen counter in front of my mom. "For the Driver's Ed fee," I told her.

She eyed the thin stack of bills with her mouth open. "You sneaky little bugger!" she laughed, pulling me over for a hug. "You shouldn't worry about that school fee. We've got it under control."

"I know, but – there's that, and the cross-country you had to pay for, too. So I hope it helps a little."

She picked up the money and hefted it in her hand like it was some huge bank haul or something. "I'll bet you could use this for something special."

I shrugged. "What have I got going?"

"Well – like Homecoming or something?" She smiled and raised her eyebrows. I must have looked completely clueless. Mom nudged me and cocked her head. "No? Aren't you taking little Sharon to Homecoming?"

"Mom. We're not – it's not like that."

"No? Does Sharon know that?"

"No – yeah, I mean – and even if it was, how could I take her? I can't afford to…" but Mom was pulling twenty-dollar bills from the stack and waving them at me one at a time. "Forget it."

"Oh, Brian," she sighed.

CHAPTER SEVENTEEN

Monday morning I was surprised to see Dad shuffling about the kitchen in his robe. Usually, he was still asleep when I left the house.

"Listen, Brian, I might not be here when you get back from school. Your Uncle Bob is picking me up to take me to the lawyer this afternoon."

We sat at the table a while, not talking.

"He thinks I might get my license back." Dad swirled the coffee around in his cup and took a gulp. "But it could be a year."

I had nothing to say to that.

"It could be worse." He stared at the cup. "There could be some jail time." His voice caught. He gave me a guarded look. "How's the head today? Feeling any better?"

I shrugged. "Mostly okay. I still get a headache now and then, but not all the time. The pills help."

He nodded, "Good, good," and chewed the inside of his lip. "'Cause they look at the injuries, you know? To decide how serious to charge you." He leaned back and sighed. "If you wouldn't have been hurt, it'd probably go easier."

"Sorry about that."

"No, no, I didn't mean – "

I got up to go.

"Brian, I'm sorry, all right?" he called after me.

***

I plodded from class to class all morning, trying not to think about what was going to happen to Dad. Every time I cleared that out of my brain, a certain pudgy little blonde edged in. What Mom had said about Homecoming sort of made it a real possibility. But nowadays I never saw Sharon in the hall without a pack of other people. I kept second-guessing myself, supposing she may have hinted something about Homecoming and I was just too dense to pick up on it. Would she even consider going with me? What would "going to Homecoming" even mean? Her Mom driving us to the dance in the mini-van? Dance? Who, me? I needed to talk to somebody, *anybody.* At lunchtime, I slipped through the food line with my tray and walked a self-conscious straight line to the table where Kenny sat shoveling macaroni into his mouth.

"Hey, man," I said.

"Man."

We sat there concentrating on eating. A couple of sophomore guys from Cross-country sat down, and you might have heard the munching, if the rest of the cafeteria hadn't been so noisy. One by one, as they finished eating, each of them brought out his phone and played games or listened to music.

"So, you guys going to Homecoming?"

Kenny gaped. "The game?"

"No, I mean the dance."

The two nerds across from us busted out laughing. Kenny's eyes flicked a beam of hate over at them, and narrowed suspiciously back at me. "No way."

"How come?"

He shrugged. "No date." He studied the macaroni on his shirt for a second, as if that explained everything, and maybe it did.

I looked across the room to where Sharon was having an animated conversation with her group. Kenny followed my gaze and scoffed.

"What?"

He shook his head. "If you're thinking about asking Sharon Rice out, you are *way* late to that track meet."

"What? What do you mean?"

"These girls make such a big deal about dances and all. It's almost like Prom. Most of them bought their Homecoming dresses before school started." He nodded at me knowingly.

"Even before anybody asked them out? That's – "

"Crazy, yeah, but that's the way they are. But in *her* case –" He cocked his head toward the girls – "I think you *know* who she's going with."

"No." I glared at him.

"No? Check it out."

I knew what he meant, but even as we watched, Rick Wagner sauntered over to the girls' table and made some clever remark that got a big response. I couldn't bear to watch.

I figured I'd have a chance to talk to Sharon in English class, so I got there as fast as I could and waited for her outside the door. When she and Doreen came up, she couldn't ignore me.

"Sharon, we've got to talk."

"Yeah, we do!" she said, giving Doreen a nod to let her in ahead of us.

"There's a lot to say, but first of all, when are we getting together to work on that paper?"

"Uh… I don't know. Want to call me tonight, and we'll see?"

"Okay," I said, leaning closer to whisper, "I want to talk to you about the ghost."

She sighed and rolled her eyes just as the bell rang, and we slipped into the room.

Mr. Taylor kept the class busy right up to the end, so there was no more time to talk. Then when we were dismissed, Rick Wagner cut me off before I could catch up with Sharon at the door. "Hey, Sharon," he called, giving me a backward glance. "Lemme talk to you about something?"

She groaned all dramatic, but slowed down and let him catch up, and the two of them moved down the hall – him bent in her direction and Sharon turning pink over something he said.

"Trouble in Paradise, Brian?" Mr. Taylor stood beside my desk with his arms folded. He nodded toward the doorway, his mouth twisted.

"Whatever," I sighed.

***

When I got home after school, Uncle Bob's pickup truck was in the driveway. He and Dad were talking over some beers in the kitchen.

"How'd it go with the lawyer?"

Dad wagged his head from side to side. "Ah, I don't know. It'll prob'ly be okay." He cleared his throat and took a swig.

Uncle Bob straightened up. "Yeah, it should go all right. This guy knows what he's doing. Just, a lot depends on the judge. Your dad's got a clean record, so – the judge oughta be reasonable."

Dad bubbled out a belch and slumped in his chair.

"I've got some homework," I said.

"Hey," Uncle Bob called after me, "when you're done, I'm buying at Chili's, okay?"

I took care of my schoolwork and then called Sharon. She wasn't home yet. Her mom didn't volunteer anything, but I guessed Sharon was working on the float again. All the way to the restaurant I brooded, all this stuff brimming up inside me. I still hadn't talked to her about Freund or Niederman's uncle or anybody else who had seen the ghost.

When we finally got a booth at Chili's, Dad ordered another beer. Uncle Bob's mouth tightened, but he didn't say anything, just got Cokes for him and me. The place was noisy, but he went on with what he'd been saying in the car.

"So the lawyer wants to make the point that your Dad only hit the tree because he swerved to avoid those kids."

"The light," Dad growled.

Uncle Bob tapped his fingers on the table. "The light?" he repeated. "Which was... what?"

"The red light – by the bike path."

"Okay, so that was one of the bicycles?"

"No," I put in, "it wasn't a bicycle light." I turned to focus on Dad, who slumped further down in the seat beside me.

Uncle Bob looked back and forth between the two of us.

"It was the ghost of Jamie McVay." I don't know what made me say it.

His brother raised his eyebrows, then nodded once. "Okay, then."

The waiter appeared with our drinks, not a moment too soon for

Dad, who drank through the foam on top of his glass. It took forever to order hamburgers all around, the three of us fumbling with oversized menus, the waiter talking too much. Meanwhile an awkward presence, the ghost, now that I'd named him, almost seemed to be sitting there, too. Nervous, I looked around the restaurant when the waiter left, but of course in that crowded place, nobody could hear us even if they wanted to.

Uncle Bob was thoughtful, folding and unfolding his hands as if he couldn't think of the proper before-dinner prayer. Finally, he leaned toward Dad. "Did you see him?" he asked.

Dad glanced up at him and shrugged. "I don't know. Maybe."

"Did *you* see him?" he asked me.

"Not then," I told him, "but I know that's who it was. I've seen him before."

Dad groaned, his eyes closed, his fingers gripping the beer glass tightly.

Uncle Bob took a deep breath and leaned back in the booth. "Okay, out with it, then. Tell us all about it."

In a matter of minutes, the whole story spilled out of me, from the first time I'd felt that speeding train on the Prairie Path to the waving lantern at Pleasant Hill Road. Uncle Bob listened with his head cocked and didn't interrupt. Dad stared straight ahead, his mouth open and his jaw dropping a little lower as I went on.

"So I'm pretty sure it was Jamie McVay's signal light that Dad saw that night." My heart thumped, and my palms were wet.

Uncle Bob kept his level look at me and nodded silently. My father groaned and bent over the table with his hands over his ears.

"And you didn't know about this? About Brian's..." Uncle Bob asked him.

Dad shook his head.

Uncle Bob leaned over toward me. "It's okay, Brian, I understand. Your dad understands."

I glanced over at Dad. *Did he understand?*

"Do you know *why* we understand?"

The question hung there for a few seconds before I answered. "I think so." I remembered Mom telling me, *he's sensitive.*

Dad banged his glass hard on the table and straightened up, his gaze meeting mine, then wavering away. He drained his glass and looked at me accusingly. "You should've told me."

I shrugged my shoulders. "It's hard to say it. Hard to tell."

He nodded. "Still ... you're too young. You're too young to have to see those things."

"I guess *not*," Uncle Bob said. "He's sixteen years old, right? Well, what did you think? How old were *you*?"

Dad looked at his empty glass.

"Well, you knew this day would come, didn't you? It had to happen sometime."

"HERE we go!" The server appeared out of nowhere, whipping plates onto the table with a flourish. "And can I get you another beverage?"

"Oh, yeah," Dad said.

It didn't seem possible to talk any more. We ate without another word. Each bite of my hamburger grew bigger in my mouth.

It wasn't until we left the restaurant and got into the pickup that the conversation continued.

"So, Uncle Bob," I asked, "are you saying you've seen ... things... yourself?"

He looked at me as he turned to back out of the parking space. "Yeah, me and your Dad have seen a lot of things in our time, right Jimmy?"

Dad slouched in the passenger seat. "'Things' is right," he grumbled.

"And both of you see things nobody else can see?"

"Well, of course Pops – your Gramps – had the gift. Pops said it's been in the family since forever," Uncle Bob went on, "but it follows the male line in our family. At least Sis never had it, and I don't expect our girls have ever seen anything. But Bill did, I know that."

"Uncle Bill in Wisconsin."

"Yeah, before he moved up north of the border. He told a few tales."

"Anybody else?"

"I don't know for sure – maybe another person could see what we see, if we were close to each other, touching, or close mentally or something. Your Aunt Mary claimed she saw a spirit when Pops took her someplace, and he was holding her hand. I've had people tell me strange things happened – poltergeist stuff – when I knew it was a spirit nearby. There may well be a lot of people who wouldn't admit it."

He chuckled. "Let's face it, people who talk about seeing ghosts … nobody takes them seriously anyway. That's the first thing you figure out – you can't actually tell anybody about it. Get me? You haven't said anything to anybody, have you?" He caught my eye in the rearview mirror. "Because, first – they'll just think you're pulling their leg, you know, just fooling around. But then if you keep at it, they will decide you're plain crazy. No one would believe such a thing. Keep up with it, and you'd find yourself doped up in a loony bin someplace!" He sighed. "We could tell some tales, huh, Jim?"

"Like what?" I asked.

"Well, over on Tallman, in the old neighborhood – there was that lady that stabbed her husband." Uncle Bob glanced back at me with a half-smile. "That was a good example. Nobody even knew about it except us. It had happened years before; people said that the house had caught fire and the man and wife and their baby died there. So the house was rebuilt and sold to another family – the Sajewskis, wasn't it?" He looked over at Dad.

"Salewskis," Dad corrected.

"Yeah, so sometimes at night you'd walk past that house, and you'd swear it was on fire – see the flames, smell the smoke, feel the heat, even – and you'd want to run and call the fire department.

"First time I saw that, I ran up on the porch, thinking people needed to get out of the house, and I looked in the window and saw the fire shining on this long knife, this fiery blade. I never really saw the woman, but somehow I knew it was a woman standing there in the flames, holding the knife raised up in her hand. And howling, just howling…." Uncle Bob paused, remembering those sensations. "Well, it was pretty… intense…."

Dad turned to look at him. "Pretty intense!" he mocked. "Yeah, it was pretty intense to find yourself inside that miserable woman's head. To know how her old man had been beating on her and beating their baby until one night he beat the child to death." Dad's voice grew louder.

"He'd kicked her, stomped her, left the baby dying in her bed, and late that night the woman plucked a butcher knife from the kitchen drawer and stabbed the bastard to death in his sleep. Then she set the house afire and sat down in the middle of it and died." Dad sniffed. "Pretty intense."

Uncle Bob nodded. "Yeah, you're right ... it was pretty bad."

"Pretty bad, yeah. So time after time I walked past that burning house and that wailing woman and her bloody knife on fire, and her guilt and rage. And you know what? She's howling still, isn't she, because she's stuck there in that hell and nothing can get her out of it." Dad grunted, turning stiffly to me in the back. "*That's* the kind of tale *we* can tell!"

The rest of the ride home was quiet. Pulling up in our driveway, Uncle Bob turned off the engine and came around to lead Dad stumbling to the front door. Inside, Dad collapsed into the La-Z-Boy without switching on the lamp.

"Got any coffee?" Uncle Bob asked me.

"Sure, I'll fix some up."

He sat on the couch facing Dad, the two brothers silent in the dark but somehow communicating. I started the coffee maker and sat down next to my uncle. He clamped an arm over my shoulder and rubbed my back. "Kid," he said. "Your dad wants to protect you – but he can't. He never let Pops or me say anything to your mom or you about it, and I respect that. But there's no denying it. You've got the gift –"

"The curse!" Dad growled.

"— and you're going to see and feel things sometimes. You're –"

"Sensitive," I said.

"Yeah, that's a good way to put it," he nodded. "'Sensitive' like a dog can hear higher sounds than we can, or as if your eye could see different wavelengths of light or something. And your mind can hear and feel and see what's in the mind of those –"

"– Things," Dad said.

"– *People* is what I was going to say. I think we can call them *people*. And your Dad's right – it's bad, it's sad – it's *horrible* to feel what they are going through – and to know there's nothing we can do for them.

It's real depressing, if you let it get to you."

I was thinking hard while I got up to pour coffee. Here was my uncle inclined to talk about the supernatural explanations I'd been needing all this while. Out of the sea of questions floating in my head, one big one rose to the top. "Is this it, then? For everybody, Uncle Bob? Is it hell for everybody, or what?"

"No, no, Brian, don't think that." He got up and followed me into the kitchen. "These people are few and far between. No, most of us go … 'to a better place' as they say. I'm sure of it!"

"Then what went wrong for these – like Jamie McVay, or the woman in the burning house, or the kid who drowned in Marquette Park lagoon?"

"Oh, yeah, that was a bad one, wasn't it? Your dad told you? Well, I'll tell you what I think – and he and I have talked about this." He paused, and we both heard the purr of Dad snoring in his chair. "Well, who knows? But I think these people get stuck – yeah, because of something brutal or violent that happened at the moment of their deaths – but also because their guilt, their shame, and their hopelessness was so powerful. Because of something left undone, maybe. That woman on Tallman Avenue? Her mind was all full of the child she failed to protect. The little kid in the park? Go by there, and you're hit with waves of fear and guilt because he'd run away after a fight with his mother, and gone to play near the water in defiance. Your railroad guy? From what you tell me, how he caused that train wreck? I'll bet he couldn't deal with the guilt. These are the kinds of people that get snagged after their deaths and can't move on."

"And we're the kind of people," I said, "that have to see and feel them suffer? And we can't do anything for them?"

Uncle Bob hung his head. "Let me tell you something else you should know about these people." He took a sip of coffee and looked up. "You've got to remember, they're damaged goods, Brian. They're not normal, healthy minds that you're hearing. They're souls that have been torn up by the bad things that happened to them. Pieces of them are missing, and they aren't rational – they're shreds of the people they used to be, locked into a loop they can never get out of. They're messed up –

and powerful."

A shiver went down my spine. "What can they do?"

He chewed his lip and considered me. "They can reach out of … wherever, whatever they are – and they can make things happen somehow. Don't underestimate your Jamie McVay, Brian. He *could* be dangerous."

CHAPTER EIGHTEEN

In school the next day I was determined to talk to Sharon, even if she was avoiding me. I made my move at the end of lunch when she got up to return her tray to the kitchen. But just as I started in her direction, the ruddy face of Nelson, the football coach, appeared in front of me.

"You Krueger?" He eyed me, trying to remember if we'd ever met. "Mr. Konechny wants you." He gestured with his thumb over his shoulder. Coach Konechny stood in the doorway monitoring foot traffic in and out of the locker rooms. He was looking my way and waved me over. Sharon meanwhile had turned and scurried back to the noisy group at her table. With a sigh, I let Coach Nelson herd me over toward the doors.

"Mr. Krueger, how's the noggin these days?" Coach asked.

"Feels pretty good, Coach. No more headaches, anyway."

"Great, great. Do you have a doctor's appointment? I'd like to get you back running."

"I don't, uh, really have a doctor like that."

"Hmm." He got a pained look. "Well, in the meantime, you could be out on the field helping out, you know. . . ."

I could see where this was going. "Yeah, I just need to get home most days to help my dad out – he got banged up in the accident, you know. . . ."

"Oh, right, right." Konechny cocked his head, thinking. "Well, if you have to drop out, I can understand..."

"Quitting the team?" Coach Nelson crowded in, looking down at me with a sneer. He sort of remembered me now. "This guy's a quitter! Doesn't he look like a quitter?"

Some shoving match broke out down the hall as kids coming out of the locker room ran into those leaving the cafeteria. Konechny looked to see what the commotion was, but he turned back to me briefly. "Well, why don't you come and see me at practice today? Maybe we can figure something out."

Coach Nelson pushed through the crowd, bellowing, "Vincenzi! Put him down now!" Coach Konechny strode after him.

***

I did get a chance to talk to Sharon just before English. "I left a message for that Mrs. Runyon from Turner," I said. "Don't you wonder what her connection is to Jamie McVay?"

Sharon thought for a second and snapped her fingers. "Maybe *she's* the demented cat lady!" We both laughed.

"I haven't gotten through to her yet, though," I told her. "You ought to try. You might have better luck."

"I'm *so* sorry, Brian. It's getting busy with the Homecoming float and all, and they asked me and Doreen to pick up some stuff we need."

"So, they've got you running errands for the cheerleaders?"

She stiffened. "Well," she said, with a quick roll of her eyes, "everybody pitches in however they can – like *you*, doing your part for the cross-country team, right?"

"Yeah, as a matter of fact, I'm going to practice today after school. I still can't run, but…."

"Ohh-kay, there you go! It's nice to be part of the team, isn't it?"

Rick Wagner, walking into the classroom, heard part of that. "Smells like team spirit," he threw out as he brushed by.

"You know," I said, my voice lower now, "the only reason they're being nice to you guys – to Doreen, I mean – is because she's got a car."

Sharon blinked and tilted her head up at me. "That's a mean thing to say."

"It's not mean, it's the truth!"

"Are you saying we're not – what? Not *worthy* of the group? Is that it?"

"I'm saying that's what *they* think."

Sharon clenched her jaw and breathed hard through her nose.

"They're just using you, is all," I told her. "*They* aren't worthy of *you*!"

Sharon plopped herself down at her desk as Mr. Taylor began the lesson.

After class, she charged out like a racehorse at the sound of the bell. And after school, feeling guilty, I figured I'd better talk to the coach.

I got out to the field and messed around doing some listless stretches and half-hearted calisthenics with the guys, until Coach brought everybody together for a team meeting. Thursday was our turn to host the Crosstown Meet, with the four Winston high schools competing in the city-wide rivalry.

"Today and tomorrow we'll practice that course," he told us. "It's a pretty straightforward two laps around North Park, which makes a nice three-mile run." He went through the list of competing racers, and made a few other announcements before sending the team out. They would jog from the athletic fields, off school grounds, and a half mile through the neighborhood to the park. I waited while Coach organized some things and zipped his duffle bag shut.

"So, Krueger," he called at last, "I thought maybe you could do sign-ins and tags and such."

"Well, I suppose I could."

He looked me over. "Look, I know it's not very exciting, but I have to know I can count on you to help out where we need you."

"Everybody pitches in, right?"

"Right. Of course, we'd rather have you running. But when will that be? Only the doctor can say."

"Yeah, like I said, I don't have a doctor just now. The last one I saw was at the Emergency Room."

"Well, why don't we see if the team doctor can examine you? Dr. Kolbe comes to all the football games, and he's always on call for CC meets. I'll give him a call, and you can talk to him Thursday. Deal?"

"Deal."

So I'd been drawn back into the cross-country world, by Sharon who shamed me into it, and by Coach Konechny who persuaded me with rah-rah talk. And also by stupid Coach Nelson, who challenged people by insulting them. I refused to let him call me a quitter.

Wednesday after English I was able to sidle up to Sharon, trying to get back to some kind of level ground with her. She kept looking straight ahead while I babbled on, pretending that I hadn't ticked her off the last time we talked.

"So, I'll be over at North Park after school, with the team."

That earned me a skeptical look.

"What, you don't believe me? I talked to Coach yesterday, and he's got me helping out, even if I don't run."

"You're giving so much for the team!" she mocked.

We trudged along. Finally, I said, "You kind of made me feel guilty – about not going to practice." She didn't respond to that, so I went on, "So I'll be out there after school the next couple days, in case you can't get hold of me."

Approaching down the hall were Melkovec and a couple other guys, and slinking around behind them was Pete Vincenzi. Sharon spotted him and stomped through the blockade to stand in his way.

"Vincenzi, you are in some big trouble!"

He cringed in mock terror. "Me? What'd *I* do?"

"Tommy and Allen told me what you did!"

I stepped up behind Sharon. "What happened? What did he do?"

"Chased my brothers out of their tree fort and set it on fire!"

"Jesus, Pete!"

He straightened up now and moved up to me. "Yeah? What's it to *you?*"

Sharon stepped between us and shoved him hard. "They said you were shooting at them with your damn bb gun! You're just lucky you didn't hit anybody, or my dad would have shoved that gun where you'd never use it again!"

"It wasn't me," Pete whined. "I wouldn't do something like that!"

"You're the *only* one goofy enough to do something like that! I'm just warning you – better leave my family alone!" Her face was bright red, her little fists clenched and trembling.

"Yes, ma'am, I'll look out for the Rice Family!" he laughed, scuttling away.

Rick Wagner had been hanging back. "Hey, Sharon, he wasn't trying to hurt anybody." Now he came up to where she stood, staring laser beams in Pete's direction. "I told him he better be careful. I was kind of looking out for the kids, you know?"

She shook her head and hustled off with Wagner at her side.

After school I helped get the course ready at North Park, staking out the chute and sorting through name tags. I have to admit it was nice to be back with the team, and I got caught up in the excitement of hosting the Crosstown meet. True, the football teams got all the attention, especially the week before Homecoming. But in our own world of cross-country runners, we felt important. And it *was* nice to belong to something, to have a job to do, to walk back to school after practice and ride the late bus with the guys.

***

Thursday was warm, with puffy white clouds dotting the summery sky, and trees all turning orange, red, and brown. I helped Coach get our runners lined up for their race. The girls' team ran first, so I had some time to watch their race before our guys lined up. Coach pointed out Dr. Kolbe when he drove up, and motioned for me to approach him.

"Dr. Kolbe?"

"Yes?" He looked fit and young except for the gray mixed into his short brown hair.

"Uh, Coach Konechny said I should talk to you about a physical." I explained the situation, and the doc started with the questions.

"Any dizziness?"

"Not anymore."

"Nausea or vomiting?"

"Nope."

"Balance okay?"

"Fine."

"Sensitivity to light? To noise?"

I decided not to mention red signal lights and roaring ghost trains. "I'm all good, Sir."

"Well," he said, "it's been three weeks, so if you're not showing any symptoms, I expect you'd be able to run now."

"Now?"

"Easy now – I'd say take it slow at first and see how it goes. Light jogging to start."

"Coach says he needs something in writing."

"Of course he does. You'll have to stop at my office for a visit. But we won't need to do a full physical." He handed me his card – his office was on Front St. in Winston. "Just stop in – let's say Saturday morning – and tell the nurse what you want. I'll have it ready."

Coach Konechny sent me out to the two-mile marker with a stopwatch to monitor times and rally the runners on to the home stretch. I jogged across the park on a direct line from the parking lot and starting line, stepping lightly for fear that my racing pulse would pound into a headache. Once I pulled up on the little knoll, though, and settled down, I felt just fine. It was so warm I peeled my sweatshirt off, down to my tee shirt, and enjoyed the afternoon sunshine on my face and bare arms. From my outpost of quiet, I looked toward Jewel Road, where a stream of cars and yellow buses was stacking up from the school drive. Across the river of rush-hour traffic, Crosby Animal Park and Roosevelt Marsh spread like some peaceful foreign country.

Hard to believe I could walk among the trees there and conjure up those images of fire and terror. Hard to believe a restless spirit lurked and I alone could see him. *In my mind,* I reminded myself.

From down the hill, shouts and cheers signaled the start of the race, but the crowd noise soon faded to a murmur. A couple dozen spectators had come over from school, boyfriends and girlfriends, brothers and sisters of runners. I was surprised to see the number of parents who showed up – mothers with little kids in strollers, and even some fathers in business suits. I let myself enjoy a fantasy for a minute, in which my Dad stood at the finish line clapping and cheering as I sprinted across leading the pack. But then, I wasn't running, and he wasn't standing.

The first runners appeared, flying by in a cluster. A string of individuals followed, and then several packs, as the guys sorted themselves according to their abilities. In almost no time at all, the line thinned to just a few stragglers. For all the anticipation and preparation, and even with separate races for varsity and J-V, boys and girls, the actual cross-country meet was over pretty soon. Even the awards ceremony afterward wrapped up fast. In this case, our gang came in second to our nemesis Winston South, with three runners in the top twenty. The proud J-V winners picked up their ribbons, and we all enjoyed our brief superiority over the varsity, who didn't do nearly as well.

Coaches and team members shambled back to school, and while the lucky few jumped into cars and rode off with their parents, I hung back. After the organized commotion of the meet, it was nice to have the park to myself. Tightening up the straps on my backpack I trotted back to the tramped-down grassy corner of the course at the edge of Jewel Road. Traffic was still heavy, the rush of tires on the pavement surging into the quiet of the park. Across the road and beyond Crosby Park, the backlit reeds and rushes of Lincoln Marsh glowed gold. The raised bank of the Prairie Path cut a fuzzy black line across it. I had run this far plenty times before, so I could easily jog on home from here.

Nevertheless, after dodging across the road, instead of continuing down Jewel to the path, I slowed to walk through the entrance gate of Crosby Park. A few families strolled around, some couples – older teens and college twosomes – and baby-sitters chasing young kids who were themselves chasing chickens and baby goats. The place rang with noise, surprisingly for just before closing time on a weekday. I walked over to the barn, figuring old Freund would likely be there feeding the animals. Edging around the bleating sheep and a braying donkey, I knocked on the wood trim next to the open barn door. I heard Freund inside, pouring sacks of feed into troughs.

"Hi ya," I called and stepped inside the cool, dark building.

Freund peered out from a stall. He grunted, gave me a nod, and went back to his task. His buttoned-up long-sleeved denim shirt was stained with sweat from hard work on this warm day.

"How you doing, Mr. Freund?" I asked. "Remember me, Brian? I was here talking to you about ... the, uh, Marsh Disaster?"

"Uh-huh." He didn't look up.

"Need any help?"

Freund straightened up and eyeballed me suspiciously. "Okay," he said. "Grab that sack of corn from inside there. Behind you," he gestured with his thumb.

Inside the little hay-strewn nook was a neat cot with blanket and pillow. A weathered highboy dresser stood against the wall with a coffee pot and a hot plate on top. Plastic feed bags were stacked at the door. I picked one up with two hands and lugged it over to him. "All the comforts of home, eh?" I said.

He blinked and hung his head. "Sometimes I sleep here overnight. The boss knows about it, though. Sometimes I've gotta be here all night. For the animals, I mean."

Outside a cow complained loudly, and Freund jerked his head toward the door. "Damn kids...." Tossing an empty sack to the floor, he stalked to the doorway and peered out into the fenced corral, muttering, "I'd like to get my hands on 'em."

There was a *pop,* and one of the sheep baaed and leaped. Freund stepped toward it, but a movement outside the fence caught his eye.

"Get the hell out of here!" he roared.

I followed his look and saw someone dart out among the scrubby bushes that bordered the animal pens. I recognized the rumble of Wagner's four-wheeler, and a second later saw it bounding over the tussocks of grass into the cattails of the marsh. Melkovec appeared on his whining dirt bike, and pulled up to look back in our direction. Freund, beyond speech with anger, let out an animal growl and tromped through the pen. Just the other side of the five-foot-high chain-link fence, calm as could be, stood grinning Pete the Pyro with his air rifle.

"Up yours, you old fart!" he yelled good-naturedly. He raised the gun and fired another pellet toward the bleating sheep before backing away into the tall weeds.

I heard him trying to start his bike, but the engine didn't want to catch. *This could be interesting*, I thought. Freund plodded through the mud and manure with murder in his eyes. He had reached the fence when Pete, suddenly frightened, burst out of the weeds, desperately pushing the dirt bike along the fenceline where the shrubs were cut back. Freund lunged over the top of the fence at him, and Pete recoiled, scrambling backward in the weeds to avoid his grasp.

"Get away from me, you old re-tard," he whined.

Freund put two hands on the top rail of the fence and started to clamber over, his feet in their big boots flopping uselessly against the woven chain link. He tried to get his big belly across the top, but couldn't quite get there, and he slipped down with a grunt. As he fell, the fence caught his shirt, ripping it open in front from the top button down. He landed on his behind and floundered for a moment to get back up in the muck.

The Pyro regained his nerve and stood up with a nasty laugh. Then he stopped and stared at the mess of purple creases that scarred the old man's chest. "Jesus," he said, "what the hell *are* you?" I walked out into the yard to help Freund. Pete's lip curled, and he called to me, "What the hell, Krueger? Is this your old man or something? Freddy Freakin' Krueger?"

He laughed at his own joke, and Melkovec, coasting up behind him, yelled, "It's a nightmare on Oak Street!"

"That is some sick messed-up shit, Freddy," Pete brayed.

Freund struggled to his feet, snarling, "You little son of a –!" He reached down with a sweep of his arm and, grunting, sent a handful of fresh cow dung sailing through the air. It splattered over the Pyro before he shut his mouth.

"Shit!" Pete spat. "Oh, that's it!" Spluttering he wiped his face with his shirt. "You're dead meat, old man! I mean it!" He hawked and spit again, and brandished the pellet gun.

From behind him, Melkovec's voice boomed, "C'mon man! Let's go!"

Pete hesitated. Without a word, Freund scooped up another wad of ammunition. "I mean it, sucker," Vincenzi warned. "You're gonna be sorry!" He straddled the bike and kicked it into its stuttering racket. Saluting with a defiant middle finger, he swerved off among the cattails.

CHAPTER NINETEEN

Saturday morning I put up my hoodie and rode down the Prairie Path into town. I was ready for the chill in the old railway cutting on the edge of the marsh. Sunlight sparkled on the dewy reeds, but the lingering patches of drifting fog sucked the light into their gray murk. I leaned ahead and pedaled through it.

As promised, Doc Kolbe was waiting for me at his office. A nurse had me fill out a form, and I waited just a few minutes before they called me in. The doc gave me a once-over with the stethoscope, peered into my eyes and ears and declared me fit. The nurse provided an envelope to bring home to my folks and just like that, I was out on the street and good to run again. I hustled to get over to school in time for the team bus.

The cross-country meet was out in the Fox Valley with some of the northern county schools. Coach was surprised to see me finish in the top twenty, but I was just happy to run. It felt so good to get my legs moving, to make speed! In the end, the J-V once more outshone the varsity runners, so there was a little good-natured teasing on the ride back.

Eventually, the talk turned to Homecoming. Kenny explained that the cross-country teams would get a brief intro at the pep rally Thursday night before the rah-rah shouting about the football squads.

"No need to dress up, Krueger. Unless," he added slyly, "you've got a date after all?"

Ray gave him a shove. "He's still hoping he's got a shot with Sharon Rice, man!"

"Oh, sorry I brought it up," Kenny grimaced. "Seriously, did you ever even talk to her?"

I shook my head. "She's too busy all the time, working on the damn float," I explained. "What the hell is it anyway?"

"That's always a secret, bro!" Ray said. "You have to go to the parade to find out."

"I can hardly wait. It better be like the Taj Mahal or something."

Kenny nodded. "They'll bring the floats out to the Freshman Bonfire Thursday night."

"If there *is* a Freshman Bonfire!" Ray laughed. "Did you *see* that sad-lookin' pile of wood?"

I hadn't noticed.

"Looks like something for roasting marshmallows, that's about it." Kenny said.

"Yeah, they've been calling around and cruising the whole neighborhood looking for scrap wood, but they're not finding much."

"I'll bet I know why," I told them.

***

Pete Vincenzi had gotten the jump on them. The Pyro's woodpile in the vacant lot stood about twelve feet high now, a jumble of boxes, pallets, and old furniture, topped with a tepee of yellow pine 2 x 4's that must have walked away from some construction site.

Mom and Dad were sitting on the patio when I got home, watching through the trees as Pete rolled a couple logs from the back of somebody's van. "Gonna be another big Saturday night in the suburbs," Dad sighed and gulped his beer.

"I guess he's not hurting anything, right?" Mom wondered. I held my tongue – no sense giving her something else to worry about. "Hey, Bri – who's this Mrs. Runyon that called?"

"Oh, that's the lady I'm supposed to interview for my project. Who donated the stuff to the Turner Museum."

Mom screened me with her Mother Radar.

"Mom, I'm not in trouble or anything. I left her a message asking her to call me back."

"Mm-hmm. Well, she said she'd be home tonight if you want to try her again. Say, how'd the meet go?"

I told them all about the day and gave them the envelope from the doctor. When we went back into the house, I waited for Mom to get supper into the oven before I phoned Mrs. Runyon back.

A smooth, calm voice answered. I explained who I was and that I had gotten her name from the Turner Museum. "Yes, how can I help you?"

"Well, my friend and I would like to ask you some questions about the Marsh Disaster ... and Jamie McVay."

There was a long pause.

I went on, "Um, according to that Mr. Whatshisname, you donated the conductor's uniform and some other railroad ... stuff. So...."

"Yes, I see...."

"Well, for our paper, I guess, we just wanted to get some more... *facts,* you know.... Instead of, like, *ghost stories."*

"Excuse me?"

"Well, you know – ghost stories about Jamie McVay. It seems everybody's got stories from people who say they've seen the ghost."

I could hear Mrs. Runyon draw in her breath over the phone. "Oh?"

Something made me babble on to this quiet voice. "*Yes,"* I said. "Like by the marsh. Different places along the railroad path."

She didn't respond at once, not directly. I strained to hear faint mutterings: "Yes... I see... by the marsh... well...." Then, more clearly, "Yes, I imagine I should talk with you about all this, then. Is tomorrow all right? For tea?"

Tea? I thought. *Very weird.* Mrs. Runyon had just hung up when I was punching in Sharon's number. I knew her rushed and breathy recording by heart: "Hiya, leave me a message, and I'll call ya back."

"Sharon*!* I got us a meeting with that Mrs. Runyon from Turner. Tomorrow! Give me a call – please!*"* I paced about the house for a while, wondering where she was and when she might get back to me. After dinner I stomped out of the house and headed to the Rices'.

The sun had set, leaving a tangerine-colored sky and darkened streets. The glow from lighted windows made the homes look warm and inviting, even the Pyro's place – which I imagined to be a virtual house of horrors behind its split-level facade. Pete spotted me from his observation post on their back deck, and I heard him clattering down the step to cut me off as I passed in front. He pretended to be going to the car in the driveway and acted surprised to see me.

"Hey, Kroooger!"

I slowed but didn't stop.

"Hey, man! I'm talkin' to *you!*"

"Yeah, Pete, what do you want?" I said, turning to him and walking backward.

He pointed a long finger at me. "Just you better keep your mouth shut about that shit at the zoo over there."

I stopped walking. "Me? Seems like *you're* the one should have kept his mouth shut!"

"That old freak's gonna be sorry. And you too! Just remember."

"You've got some real problems," I said, and turned to go.

"If you're goin' to see your *girlfriend,"* he called, "she ain't home."

"No? And how would *you* know?" I wondered, aggravated with myself for carrying on the conversation.

He grinned and leaned back against the car, folding his arms across his chest. "Oh, I know some shit, Krooger. I know."

"Yeah, right," I said, walking back to him. "And does that include knowing where she is, then?"

His eyes turned hard. "Maybe."

I stopped and crossed my arms in imitation of his pose, and we stood facing each other nodding like a pair of bobble-head dolls. I had to give in and break the spell. "*Well?"*

Pete's mouth twisted into what he supposed was a smile. "Well, I know I saw Wagner's car in their driveway this afternoon – and it could've been Sharon that got into that car." He saw he was getting to me, so he drew it out. "It *could* have been the two of them driving away…."

"Yeah, yeah, Pete, cut the crap. You know where they went?"

He shrugged his shoulders. "I don't ask where Wagner takes his girls. That *his* business, y'know?"

"Screw you, Pete!" I spun and stomped on down the block.

All the Rices' vehicles were lined up in the driveway, and the house was lit up like a Christmas tree. As I hesitated on the street, a shadow moved under one of the tall branching maples out front. I peered into the darkness.

A shape detached itself from the tree trunk and took the chunky form of Sharon's brother Allen. He idly plunked the rubber band of an industrial-grade aluminum-handled slingshot. "What do *you* want?" he demanded.

"Is Sharon home?" I looked up at the house, wondering if I could make it to the door before the kid dropped me with a stone.

"Nah, she's gone." He held the slingshot at arm's length, aiming it here and there – at me, at the garage door, the mini-van … back at me.

"Any idea where she went, or when she'll be back?"

"Yeah, well, she *says* she's working on the class float." He squinted, aiming with one eye. "But who knows? That Rick guy picked her up."

"Rick Wagner."

"Yeah, one of Vincenzi's *minions."* Allen let a pebble fly with a twang, and I heard it thunk into a tree trunk fifty feet away. "He's lucky I didn't catch him one upside the head. If him and the Vincenzi Gang show up again, I'll be ready for 'em."

"Jeez, Allen, be careful with that thing. You could hurt somebody!"

He nodded solemnly. "That's right, Krueger. And you better watch it too. My sister says you're clueless. You better not be jerkin' her around."

"What? She said I'm *what*?"

Allen formed his fingers into a vee and pointed the *My eyes are watching you* sign in my direction before gliding back into the shadows.

***

"Hiya, leave me a message, and I'll call ya back!"

If I heard that recording one more time Sunday morning, I thought

I'd lose my mind. I had called the home phone, too, and left a message there. At last I jogged over to Richard Street, just in time to see the Rice minivan disappear around the corner. I knew if the family were going to church, they might not be back for a while, because sometimes afterward, they'd take Grandma and Grandpa to brunch. *Why the hell won't she answer my message?*

I tried again throughout the day, but never got an answer. Finally, it was time to visit Mrs. Runyon in Turner Junction.

I rode my bike down the street and over to the path, enjoying the cool breeze and warm sunshine, in spite of my aggravation. The Prairie Path west of Winston rose over more marshlands, cattails waving and blue sky reflected in the open water. It bridged the meandering river where an old man and a kid stood fishing. Reminded me of Gramps, of course, and how he and Dad used to take me to Pell Lake near the old cottage. *Those were my good ole' days*, I thought.

The path entered a narrow tunnel of trees before I emerged into an old neighborhood of big Victorian houses, where the trolley tracks once ran down the main street. That route took me past the Turner Museum, a resale shop, and a couple of vacant storefronts. The Mexican restaurant on the corner seemed to be doing business. I noticed a poster in the window as I rode by: *Halloween! Old Turner Junction Spook Trail!*

Mrs. Runyon lived in a sort of gingerbread house on an avenue shaded by yellow-leafed maples.

A small woman came to the door, her tied-back hair the color of the sky on a rainy day. She was slim but sturdy-looking, with smooth pale skin touched with pink. She spoke in the low, easy voice I'd heard on the phone.

"I'm sorry if you had trouble reaching me this week. I keep quite busy with my church work…" and her voice trailed off, like the rest of the sentence was only to herself. She seated me in the parlor and actually served tea, pouring into delicate cups from a china teapot. I felt as if I'd stepped into an old sepia photograph, with the old-fashioned fabric of the furniture, the knick-knacks on lace doilies. "Please have a cookie," she said, offering a plate full of tasty-looking sugar wafers. I took two, hoping that was the polite number, and munched them self-consciously while Mrs. Runyon sat in an armchair facing me and smoothed her black skirt. Her calm blue eyes brightened when she smiled. "I understood you to say you had a partner in your project."

I nodded. "My friend Sharon – but I never managed to get in touch with her. I'm sorry she couldn't come. She's really the brains behind this paper. She grew up here and knows the area. She's the one who told me the story of the – of Jamie McVay."

Mrs. Runyon cleared her throat delicately. "Hm ... well. I see. I hope I can help you. After we spoke on the phone, I looked at some old photograph albums and a few keepsakes to help me remember the old days. Would you be interested in seeing them?"

"Yes, ma'am! Very interested!" I laid my napkin onto the tablecloth and pulled my notebook and a pen out of my backpack.

"Why don't we sit together on the sofa," she said and picked up a large album from the end table. Once we'd gotten settled, she opened the stiff old book with her blue-veined hands. "Here are some photographs of my late husband. Here he is with a crew at the Chicago and Northwestern yard." The brittle black-and-white photos showed a tall man in a rumpled suit. "Mr. Runyon was a mechanical inspector." She paged through the book, commenting on the pictures and pointing out details. I scribbled a few notes as she talked.

Turning the last page, she closed the book with a sigh and after a slight hesitation reached for another. The very first picture was a portrait of Jamie McVay. I recognized him right away and looked up at Mrs. Runyon expectantly. The widow folded her white hands in her lap and blinked her eyes – those same mild, light eyes, crinkled in the corners, of the man in the photograph. "My father," she said.

Of course! I shouldn't have been surprised.

Mrs. Runyon turned the page. The next photo showed McVay hunched and grumpy-looking on the steps of a rickety porch. He was dressed in work clothes and looked tired, as though taking a break from some yard work. A bottle of beer dangled from his hand.

"That's the house in Winston where we lived when I was a child. I believe it's still there on Acadia Lane."

Another snapshot had McVay posing arm in arm with two of his buddies, clowning around or singing. There was another of McVay the sober conductor, posturing in possibly the same uniform we'd seen in the museum. One picture, in particular, struck me, though. There was McVay with a big grin, playfully holding his toddler daughter up to the camera. Alongside him knelt his wife. You could see where Mrs. Runyon got her smooth, good looks. Her mother was laughing, looking at them both with pride but a touch of embarrassment. I'd seen that look on my own mom's face plenty of times.

"Are you the little girl?"

"Yes. How he'd rough-house with me! I was the son he never had...." She looked away. "I have the fondest memories of my father. Papa would pick me up and toss me through the air like a toy. Ride me all over the neighborhood on his shoulders. Then when it was time to jump down, off I'd leap with a somersault – he held my hands, of course – and I'd land facing him for a kiss." She gazed at the picture for quite a while before turning the page. A teardrop traced its way down her powdered cheek. She dabbed at it with a tissue and continued. "I was an only child until my mother remarried, that is. After my father's death. Since you are interested in him, I gather you already know somewhat of those circumstances."

I hesitated. "Well, I've read some of the old newspaper stories, and talked to some people...." Ms. Runyon signaled with raised eyebrows for me to go on. I described what Sharon and I had found out for our reports. Sharon would have known a tactful way to pry for more information. "One thing we don't know, I guess, is how ... the paper only reported that he was killed in an accident...."

Mrs. Runyon stood up and clasped her arms across her chest. "Yes, a terrible accident...." She moved to the window and peered out through the curtains absently. "You've come to take a special interest in my father's story, Brian?"

"Well, I guess you could say so." I was compelled to open up to this woman. "It's more than just an English assignment, I suppose. Anyone would be curious. About what happened to him after the Roosevelt Marsh Disaster. I mean, from what I read, he was a hero that night, even if he was partly responsible. Did he have to take the whole rap, just for falling asleep on the job?"

"That, yes – he paid the price for that." She closed her eyes again and cocked her head, as if listening to a far-off tune. "He was suspended from work, after the Marsh Disaster, so he had plenty of time to think about what he'd done. He was racked with guilt, Mother said. It tore him inside and out, destroyed his mind – and cost him his soul. He found some oblivion in drink, as was his habit, but even that was insufficient. His drunken stupors were filled with horrible nightmares, I'm sure."

She turned back to me tiredly. "Of course there's no mystery at all about his death," she said. "One night, after we'd gone to bed, my father left the house. He walked to the station and without a word to anyone boarded the westbound milk train out of the Winston roundhouse. He walked through the first car without a word to the motorman and stood on the platform between that carriage and the freight car. I picture him there as the train passed through the burned area of the marsh, the crash site. The track, the wires, and the roadbed had just been given temporary repairs, so the train crawled up the grade to Pleasant Hill. When they stopped at the station … he wasn't there anymore.

"I suppose many people suspected suicide, but there was no way to prove it. That was fortunate, as Mother's small railroad insurance benefit was uncontested. Mother was a devout Catholic, so I know she had difficulty accepting it for spiritual reasons. Of course, I didn't know for certain myself, not until years later, when I found the suicide note my mother had hidden among her things."

She closed her eyes and seemed to be reading from her memory. "He knew there was nothing he could do to bring back those he'd killed by his drunken negligence. And so felt there was no possible atonement for his soul in this world. He prayed to be granted peace and forgiveness in the next world instead." She sighed. "What a sad secret the poor woman kept all those years.

"The tragedy," said Mrs. Runyon her voice catching, "is that he was so wrong. He did just the wrong thing, didn't he? He did the one thing that would destroy any chance he might have had for atonement. He left his soul without a chance. If he'd made his peace with God, he would have found forgiveness for his sins at once. And then he would have lived to find some way to make up for what he'd done. But death closed the door on him. And the Lord condemned him to the torment he endures even now."

"Even now," I echoed and scratched helplessly in my notebook.

What could I write?

Mrs. Runyon sat back down next to me, wringing her hands and looking across the room. "Last night, when you telephoned ... you mentioned the stories. About the marsh, the Winston Cemetery where he's buried. Things people claim to have seen?"

I smiled uncomfortably. "Well, you know ... I guess the story's been going around for a long time ... ."

"What story?"

I cleared my throat. "Well, you know, like the red signal light shining out in the marsh...?"

She bowed her head. "Ghost stories," she breathed.

"Yeah, like that." I swallowed hard.

She tossed her head, recovering her gentle manner, but touched her hair self-consciously while her eyes settled on me. "Oh, I know. I know what kinds of tales they tell ... what they claim to have seen...." She turned to study me, and I felt my face redden. She leaned back, and inhaled sharply. "You. You've seen something, too, haven't you?"

My skin went clammy in an instant. I nodded. "I'm sorry, Mrs. Runyon, and I don't mean any disrespect to you or your father. For a long time, I wasn't sure if I was crazy or not, or if my imagination had gone wild ... but now I know – I know what I saw, and what I felt...." I went on in a rush to describe the light, the phantom train and all its sensations, the storm of emotions that filled me in the marsh.

Mrs. Runyon nodded with understanding. "You believe he is out there?"

"I do. I've sort of ... met him."

The old woman paled. "Have you *seen* him?"

"Only in my mind's eye, I guess you'd say – not with my eyes. My eyes have seen his signal light, and vague things I can't describe.... At first, I was scared, but now it's more sad than scary."

She looked up, a little indignant. "Certainly there should be no need to be afraid."

I laughed nervously, "That's easy for *you* to say!"

Mrs. Runyon drew back, then smiled. "Oh, I shouldn't fear my own Papa, you mean. But neither should anyone else!"

I bit my lower lip. "Seeing things like that – that can't ever be good, can it? I mean, all the stories … everybody who's ever seen him believes that the Ghost of Jamie McVay means trouble … some kind of accident, or a disaster of some kind … some kind of … evil."

"James McVay, an evil Spirit?" She stood and paced to the windows and back. "No, no, never!" She paused. "Sometimes I think he's just caught," she said sadly, turning back to me. "Caught among the echoes, as I think of it. Some moments in this life are so powerful, you know … so emotionally intense that they transcend the normal limits and laws of the universe, the usual boundaries and dimensions … including Time. Like the echoes of voices in a cavern, some events must reverberate through the caves of Time. The Marsh Disaster was such an event – and poor James McVay was caught among the echoes. So there are times when his light shines through time, just an echo of that terrible night."

I was thinking, that wasn't too different from Uncle Bob's theory. "Mrs. Runyon, have you seen – *him* – yourself?"

She shook her head. "No, I'm afraid I have not." She looked at me curiously. "You must have a special gift. A special mind, to see through Time and to feel my father's tortured soul. But through the years, whenever someone has seen his light, it's been for a reason. What is that light but what it's *always* meant to be? A warning."

"Warning of what, though?"

"Anything that might help him atone for his sins, I suppose … any sort of impending misfortune."

Any sort of accident, I thought, and then I saw things fall into place: warnings of collapsing scaffolds, runaway trains … auto accidents! I thought of my own state of mind the first time I saw the light on the Prairie Path.

Mrs. Runyon gazed at the photo of Jamie McVay in the open album. "His suffering spirit must recognize despair as well as danger in this world. How he must ache to have forgiveness and put his soul to rest!"

Exactly the maddened yearning I'd felt in waves of guilt and desperation. "Condemned for all these years," I said, "haunting the old railroad and the marsh, looking for forgiveness?"

"Condemned for all eternity, Brian. Or at least as long as this world exists. I pray for him," Mrs. Runyon said. "I pray every day for his poor soul – that one day he'll find peace and forgiveness, and the atonement he seeks."

I looked at the man in the photo, and I wanted to punch that smiling face – not for the death and destruction he'd set loose that night, but for the single teardrop decades later on an old woman's cheek.

CHAPTER TWENTY

That night as I sat in front of the computer, I couldn't get Mrs. Runyon's final words out of my mind: *We should all live our lives, so we have no regrets.* Gramps always said the same thing. I thought about Jamie McVay, and all that regret twisted up in his soul.

I tried Sharon again on her home phone.

"Hiya!" she answered.

"Whoa! It's really you?"

"Um, yeah. *You* called *me,* so...."

"Sharon, I've been trying to get a hold of you all weekend! Didn't you get my messages?"

"Well, excuse me! We just now got home from the hospital. Grandpa had another stroke."

"Aw, Jeeze, Sharon, I'm sorry. How is he?"

"Not so good. Grandma called an ambulance as soon as she figured something was wrong, but...." Her voice cracked. "In the hospital, he was awake and looking around, but he couldn't talk or anything, so ... I don't know."

"I'm so sorry, Sharon," I repeated, and then lamely, "He's a good old guy."

She sniffed into the phone. "Yeah. So...."

"Yeah, I was just calling, and leaving messages."

"Oh, shoot, my cell phone?" Her voice lowered. "I kind of – I don't know if I lost it or what. I think maybe... I might have left it in ... in

Doreen's car or something, but she's staying at her Dad's this weekend and, um, I never talked to her to get it back."

"Uh-oh, that sucks."

"Yeah, and if I lost it, my parents'll totally *kill* me!"

"Yeah, but you can call Doreen tonight, right? She'll be back in school tomorrow?"

"Right, right." She definitely sounded nervous. "So, what were you calling about?"

"Oh – that woman, from the Turner Museum."

"Uh-huh, what's her deal?"

I told her about Mrs. Runyon and how I'd been to her house for "tea."

"Well, aren't *you* Mr. Fancy Pants!" she laughed.

"Ha-ha. So listen," I said. "When are we going to sit down and finish the paper?"

She groaned, "Oh, man, we have to get it done by Thursday?"

"Yep."

"Well, I think we're keeping Grandma company tonight, you know?"

"Yeah, sure."

"Okay, look," she said, "let's get together after school tomorrow."

"After cross-country?"

"Okay, after that. In the meantime, write up what you've got so far and bring it with you to class. Then come over here tomorrow. You can have dinner with us. It'll have to be after *tea time!*" she laughed.

Homecoming Week kicked off with a pep rally in the gym, the band cranking out the Winston fight song while the cheerleaders put on a show of shaky acrobatics. Coach Nelson introduced the football teams and blathered the standard "rah-rah" slogans. When the assembly was over, the festivities spilled out through the school. Gaudy posters (Lasso the Stallions!) and inspirational banners (Warriors Rule!) decked the halls from one end of the building to the other. Bands of kids chanted war cries as they ran through the halls between classes. Announcements blared over the PA system reminding us of all the fun we should be having.

In English class, Rick Wagner was missing in action, so I didn't need to worry about him. Mr. Taylor gave us class time for partners to get together and talk about our projects. "You should be revising your rough drafts by now, people," he warned. "Take turns re-reading and revising the text so you can bring in a polished final draft on Thursday."

"Don't let him know we're still writing the first draft," Sharon whispered.

I showed what I'd written the night before, my dramatic conclusion:

For James McVay, his destiny lay upon the railroad tracks, where he died a few days later, fallen under the wheels of a train as it passed through Roosevelt Marsh. Although it seemed another tragic accident, some suspected that the conductor committed suicide rather than live with the burden of guilt for the disaster he had caused.

"Oh, Brian," Sharon crooned with a tilt of her head, "that's so good, the way you wrote it. Sad."

"Thanks," I said, reddening. "I think we've got all the facts. You already wrote the intro. What else?"

"There's some parts I want to add," she said, "so we've got enough research sources. About the safety measures the railroad started after the Marsh Disaster. We can work on the bibliography tonight."

***

It was dark by the time I got to Sharon's after practice. I was nervous, but it wasn't about the research paper. *No regrets,* I thought. Mrs. Rice had put some lasagna in the oven before she and Sharon's dad went to the hospital to see Grandpa. I enjoyed the dinner in spite of Allen's suspicious looks and Christine's nonstop chatter. After we cleaned up the kitchen, Sharon and I sat side by side at the dining table with our school work. She did some writing on her tablet while I proofread pages. The television droned from downstairs, where the boys watched in the family room; Christine had disappeared into her bedroom with a book. The moment had arrived.

"How's the … uh … float coming along?"

Sharon gave me a sidelong look. "Awesome. If you *really* want to know."

"Yeah, well, I *do* really want to know. 'Cause if *you're* working on it,

I'm sure it *will* be awesome."

"Ohh-kay."

I felt my face getting hot. "So, look, uh … with all this Homecoming stuff going on, I was wondering if you – what are you – in case you are – or *aren't* going with anybody else?"

She folded her arms and glared at me. "Spit it out, Brian!"

"DoyouwantagotoHomecoming? With me?"

The silence was way too long, but her pursed mouth relaxed and turned into a grin. She turned and grabbed my hands, shaking them as she squealed, "Yes!"

Sharon bounced up and began to dance around the table.

"Okay, okay, excellent." I said, giving her some space.

"Ohhh, I thought you'd never ask!" she cried. "What've you been waiting for?"

'Uh, well – I don't know – things always kept getting messed up – between us, you know?"

She waved her hands at me. "No, I know, I get it! But – Brian, it's going to be *sooo* much fun!"

I shrugged, still blushing. "I think so, too. I'm sorry it's so – so *last minute*. I don't know how it'll work. How we'll get to the dance? I mean, I don't have to get a tux or anything, do I? I've got a suit I can wear…. I know sometimes girls get a special dress and all, right? But if you don't, that doesn't matter…."

She slid into her chair, looking thoughtful. "Look Brian. Let me tell you something. I already *have* a Homecoming dress." She flushed and looked down. "I've had it for a year."

Kenny was right, I thought. *Who'd've thunk it?*

Sharon must have seen the look on my face because she started explaining with way too much information. "Last year I thought I was going to Homecoming," she said. "I was convinced that … that *somebody* was going to ask me. But they didn't." Her eyes brimmed with tears. "Because…. Because…."

"Because they knew you were saving yourself for me?" I blurted.

Her bottom lip quivered. "Because I was too fat!"

I couldn't just sit there. I reached over and gave her shoulders a firm squeeze. And that started the rainstorm. In a second she had her face on my chest trying to talk through her sobs and soaking my shirt.

"So … fat … I couldn't… get a date!"

"Hey, hey, now. That's ridiculous. Don't do that. You don't have to cry." She looked up, miserable and tear-stained. "My mom'll have to take in the dress," she said. "A lot!"

Then she threw her arms around me in a damp hug and planted her warm lips on mine in a kiss that left me reeling. "This is going to be the best Homecoming," she said. "Ever."

***

Next day, somehow, everybody who knew Sharon or me also knew we were a couple for Homecoming. Girls made appreciative noises, and guys gave congratulatory head bobs. Doreen scorched me with a look that curdled my chocolate milk. As I walked up to their cafeteria table at lunchtime, she quick stepped between me and Sharon, screening me with her bulk.

"Better see she doesn't get hurt, Dude," she warned. All I could do was shrug and step back to look past her.

I called, "Hey, Sharon!"

She flashed a bright smile from her seat. "Hey."

Seeing Doreen made me think to ask: "Did you ever find your phone?"

Sharon shot a look at her friend and back to me, shaking her head, "No."

Doreen paused a half-beat and said, "You know, it might have fallen under the seat or something, in my dad's car. I'm gonna call him and ask him to look when he gets home from work."

"Whatever. Hey, Sharon, you remember I'm running tonight, right?"

She fluttered over. "Yeah, you know, I was thinking – We'll be working on the float at Kristin's across the street, so we could give you a ride home from school after."

"Sure, okay, I guess. I'm not sure when the team bus will get back."

"I'll be watching for you. Heck, you can see the parking lot from

Kristin's house."

"All right, then," I sighed.

"Good luck in the meet," she called. "You're the fast one!"

***

Truth is, I'd never been in a "relationship" before this. I mean, there'd been group dates, and girls I liked, and messing around in the park or in somebody's basement. But this was different – this seemed more serious, feeling *responsibility* to act a certain way. We hadn't even been on a date yet! Was I supposed to act like Sharon's *boyfriend* now? And what was that anyway?

One more good reason for me to run. Amazing how a lot of crap just falls away behind you when you run. This particular afternoon, racing against the North Valley schools, I ran like a pack of wild dogs was chasing me and ended up in the seventh spot with my fastest time yet.

It was dark and chilly by the time our bus pulled into the school parking lot, and I was glad to be wearing sweats. As promised, Sharon was watching for me. She stood with a small group of kids and parents, hooting and clapping as we stepped from the bus. It was more "rah-rah" wannabe cheerleader behavior. A couple of the guys hooted back at her and exchanged high fives.

Sharon stepped forward as I came up. "How'd you do?"

"Pretty good. J-V came in second, but Varsity was third."

"You guys are awesome! You get better all the time." She led the way across the parking lot into a barrage of pounding music where Doreen waited in her car. "Okay if Doreen drops us at the hospital?" Sharon shouted. "Dad's supposed to be there, and we can go home with him."

I didn't have much say in the matter. Off we went with the doors and windows rattling.

Sharon dragged me up to the 5th floor of the hospital, which was getting to feel like my home away from home. When I was there after the accident I'd been concussed and pretty well doped up, my feelings dulled. This time my senses were heightened. My vision seemed sharper, and every sound echoed. I had the funny feeling of being watched and seeing somebody just slip around the corner, out of my view.

I plopped onto a chair in the waiting area while Sharon entered a room down the hall. A few nurses chatted at their desks as if they were the only ones on the floor. In the faint light, I kept seeing shapes in the far corners, but wasn't I just jittery? Weren't they just shadows?

After a bit, Mr. Rice came out of the room. He stood looking down at the floor for a minute, then noticed me and strolled over. I stood up and put out my hand.

"Hi, Mr. Rice. Sorry to hear about your dad."

He nodded and smiled with his eyes. "Thanks, Brian. Uh, I'm going to talk to the nurse for a minute, and then we can go. Okay if we stop for some burgers or something?" He shuffled out of view just as Sharon leaned her head out of the room, waving me over.

"Come on in," she whispered.

I shook my head no, but she just put more into the wave and repeated more loudly, "Come on!"

I hesitated at the door, but she pulled me into the dimly-lit room. Grandpa Rice lay with his head propped up on a pillow, his body just a wrinkle under the sheets.

"Look, Grandpa, my friend Brian is here to see you." She sat in the chair to his left.

He was slumped to that side, his eyes half-closed, with an oxygen mask covering his nose and mouth. Tubes looped from his swollen white hand up to bags hanging from hooks overhead. Other bags and colored tubing draped from the bedding.

The smell of antiseptic mingled with my own uneasiness, and prickles broke out all over my skin. I leaned over the bed and murmured a cautious "Hello."

The old man focused on Sharon beside him, who chattered away, "You remember Brian, Grandpa? He came over to the house one time this summer and we had lemonade? We were talking about trains and the railroad and the Ghost of Jamie McVay."

The clear plastic mask fogged and unfogged with his shallow breathing. Lights blinked on the equipment, and a wall-mounted monitor displayed the jagged lines of the old man's vital signs.

"Come over on this side," Sharon said. "He might not be able to see you over there."

Standing next to Sharon, I leaned in again and muttered, lamely, "I hope you're feeling better soon, Mr. Rice."

At this he stirred and lifted his head, locking his pale blue eyes with mine. He seemed to flinch, and his eyes grew large, staring so I couldn't look away. He took in a sharp breath and exhaled, "Huhhhhhhhhh…" His frail body seemed to rise under the sheets, and he mumbled into the mask.

I took a step back, but his eyes stayed focused on my own, taking me in. Then he grew calm and nodded ever so slightly at me. A wave of a feeling washed over me, a cool, gentle swell that smoothed out my gooseflesh and flowed over the dread.

I glanced over at Sharon, who stood up alarmed and confused. "What did he say?"

I hadn't understood a spoken word, but I knew what he wanted to say. "He said it's okay," I told her.

When I looked back his eyes were closed and his face relaxed, as he sank into the pillows. Sharon reached out and took his hand, while I backed out of the room.

CHAPTER TWENTY-ONE

Later, back at the Rice's, after the burger bags were cleared away, I ended up at their dining room table once again, tapping out our paper's conclusion on Sharon's tablet. In an hour or so we had a final draft. I read the last paragraph to her out loud:

Some would say that the death of Jamie McVay was the final act of the drama, but repercussions of the Roosevelt Marsh Disaster were felt for many years. Light rail trains would run through the suburbs more safely, and improved technology brought upgrades to the system virtually eliminating the potential for human-caused accidents. The survivors, of course, would bear the scars, and the nightmare would always live in their memories. And some say that the Ghost of Jamie McVay still haunts the railway trail through Roosevelt Marsh.

Sharon gave me a cow-eyed look and leaned over to give me a kiss on the cheek. "Oh, Brian, that's terrific! I knew you'd nail it!" She took over the keyboard and clacked about to make a few adjustments and save the draft.

"Finally!" Sharon groaned, pushing the computer aside. "I'm *so* glad we're done!"

"Yeah," I said, "we're done with it. But Jamie McVay *is* still out there in the dark. I wonder if he's done with us."

***

When I got to English class next day, amid the general milling around, I saw Rick Wagner standing off in a corner with Sharon. They kept their voices low, but whatever was going on between the two of them wasn't "happy talk". Her face was pink as she stood with arms crossed, and he looked ready to kill somebody. His eyes darted around the room, and when he spotted me, he stepped back to shoot a look of pure hate in my direction. *Good,* I thought with some satisfaction. *So much for 'sharin' rice'.* He spun and threw himself into his chair just as the bell rang. Mr. Taylor sashayed to the front of his desk clearing his throat, so Sharon found her seat, and the class settled down.

"Well, I'm sure you feel it's been a long time coming," Taylor said, "but at long last – today you get to turn in those research papers."

Somebody called out, "What research papers?" and Taylor smiled.

"I'm looking forward to reading all the local history you've dug up. I know your work will be worthy of the Winston Sesquicentennial!" He spoke over the sarcastic cheers and comments that followed. "You can pass those papers up now, if you'd care to, and we can move on to our literature assignment." People in the back of the room started handing their papers up, neat folders in a variety of styles and colors. Sharon had placed ours in a classy binder with a clear plastic cover.

Mr. Taylor nodded in acknowledgment. "Brian, I trust you've given credit to Jamie McVay for his collaboration on your paper?"

I'm sure I looked confused.

"As a *ghostwriter*?" He chuckled, quite pleased with himself.

I looked over my shoulder at Sharon, but she was clearly distracted.

"Psst! Hey, Sharon!" I called. Wagner, meanwhile stood up and managed to graze me with an elbow as he walked to the front. He ceremoniously handed a dirty manila folder to Mr. Taylor.

"Thank you, Mr. Wagner, nice of you to join us today." Taylor opened the folder and glanced at the several typed pages. "So this is the 'lite' version?"

Wagner turned as he got back to his seat. "Ain't no light virgins in *this* class, Mr. T."

"Ow!" somebody yelled out, and a few laughs rippled through the class.

Taylor's smile faded, and he stepped up the row closer to Rick. "Let's talk for a minute after class."

I thought Wagner was overreacting, but I could imagine the way he'd look at it. After a couple days of goofing off, playing hooky, and smoking dope with Pete the Pyro, he comes back to school and finds out Sharon is going to Homecoming with me. *So now he's giving her a hard time about it? Not like they had anything going on, right?* A lot of possibilities ran through my brain while we plodded through a discussion of a Nathaniel Hawthorne story nobody had read, filling out a worksheet with guesses and b.s. I didn't get a chance to talk to Sharon until right before the bell, when Taylor gave us leave to wrap it up.

"Everything okay?" I asked her.

She looked up at me from her chair and shook her head. "I'll talk to you later," she said and indicated Wagner with a short toss of her hair.

Rick was watching us, though, sitting there fuming. The bell rang, and Sharon got up to go, but Wagner called over, "Hey, wait up!" Fumbling in his pocket, he slid out a phone. "Almost forgot. You left this in the back seat of my car." He tossed it in Sharon's direction, but, hands full of her books and bag, she fumbled the catch, and the phone hit the floor. It bounced on the tile and came apart.

"Shit!" Sharon scrambled to pick up the pieces.

"Nice move, asshole!" I said.

Wagner gave me a sick grin. "Aww, it didn't work anyway – maybe it just needs a charge, I don't know. Hey, Sharon, you got a couple messages there from *me* – and about forty from some Brian guy."

"Mr. Wagner?" Taylor called from his desk, and Rick sauntered up there.

Sharon stuffed the parts of her phone into her bag and headed out the door with me hot on her tail.

"Did you get it all?" I asked. "You can probably put it back together."

"Yeah, I hope so…" she muttered, moving down the hall.

"Hey, I thought you left it in Doreen's –" Ah, and suddenly I'm Stupid, the last one to catch on. "Sharon? The *back seat?*"

She slowed and glanced up at me. "I'm sorry," she said, in a meek voice I barely recognized. "…I didn't…."

"You didn't *what?* You knew all along where the phone was, didn't you?"

"I… wasn't sure…."

I stared. *She was lying then, and she's lying now.*

Sharon stopped and looked me full on, shame in her face changing to indignation. She tried to rise up a couple inches, and her voice took on a frosty tone. "You can think what you want, but I'm telling you nothing happened. And even if it had, there wasn't any – *agreement* between *us* until two days ago, so you ought to *back off!"* With that, tearfully, she turned and stomped away.

***

That night was miserable for me, wondering how Sharon and I were going to get through this little problem. On the one hand, Wagner had made me look like a fool with Sharon. On the other hand, I did a pretty good job all by myself. Sharon was right – that I hadn't had any claim on her even if she *had* made out with Wagner in his car. I finally broke down and called her at home. Her sister Christine told me Sharon and her parents were still at the hospital. I would have to wait until the next day for the drama to play out.

When I got to my locker in the morning, a note inside from Sharon cheered me up:

"Brian – Sorry about the whole thing with Wagner. I'll make it up to you."

I liked the sound of that. Even so, it seemed Sharon was avoiding me throughout the day, until at lunch time I went over to her chatty female table. I stood there about ten feet away until she acknowledged me with an exaggerated and fake double take.

"Brian! How we doing?"

"You tell me." She followed me over to the end of a half-empty table. I allowed myself a little smile. "Just wondering: How do you propose to 'make it up' to me?"

She ducked and looked to both sides as if she was about to reveal a secret. "I'll show you tonight – when you get back from your meet."

"Hmm. Is this something I'll be able to share with my parents?"

"Well ... sure, why not?"

I hung my head. "I can't tell you how much of a disappointment that is."

She colored a little. "Ha! You'll see, won't you?" She leaned in closer. "When you get back to school, come straight over to Kristin's house across from the ball field. Come to the back door of the garage."

"What's going on there?"

"You'll see."

"Come on!"

She shook her head solemnly. "Nope. It'll be a surprise."

So I had to worry about *that* all day – wondering what Sharon's idea of a surprise peace offering might be. She never gave up so much as a hint, not even when I pestered her in English class. I was glad to see Wagner gone again, so we would avoid any more scenes with him.

That afternoon the team buses took us all the way out to Forest Hills in the south part of the county. Near as I could tell, there weren't any hills to be seen, and the forest had fallen to the ax a long, long time ago. The flat landscape made for good running, though, and once more I managed to score in the top twenty. Overall, the team didn't do that well, though, and the bus ride home in the dark was pretty quiet. I was half asleep when we pulled up outside the field house in Winston.

I stumbled off the bus into the cold, where ten or so parents waited under garish parking lot lights, clapping and cheering mechanically before whisking their kids off for dinner. Shouldering my backpack, I walked from the blacktop and across the street toward a small brick split-level house of cream-colored brick, its driveway lined with cars. I wound my way through to the back door. I could hear their voices – a bunch of kids yelling at each other, laughing and making noise. I knocked and waited, but wasn't surprised when that didn't get anybody's attention. After a minute I pressed the lighted doorbell. Somebody inside yelled "Kristin!" and a commotion of chatter and footsteps erupted before the door opened a crack. The tall cheerleader peeked out at me blankly through the storm door.

"I'm Brian Krueger. Sharon Rice told me to come here."

I recognized the top of Sharon's head as she tried to see over Kristin's shoulder. "Hey, Brian! Come on in. Everything's just about ready." She whispered something to Kristin, who turned and disappeared while Sharon opened the door.

"What's going on?"

"I told you," Sharon said with a laugh. "It's a surprise. Now, close your eyes." She grabbed both my hands and tugged me into the house. "Now keep 'em closed." Shuffling backward she led me around a corner, through a doorway, and down a step into the garage, where a murmur of low voices droned. I felt like I was about to be sacrificed on an altar or something, until Sharon positioned me and yelled, "Okay, you can look!"

I opened my eyes to the secret project that had occupied – no, *obsessed* these people for the last couple of weeks – a garish construction of sticks, plywood and cardboard, decorated in crepe bunting, streamers, and paper flowers – the Junior Class Homecoming Float!

It was a Viking ship. A longship that might have struck fear into the hearts of townsfolk, brought curses to the lips of monks and priests, and haunted the nightmares of women and small children in coastal regions for hundreds of years. The Vikings themselves would have marveled at this pink and red spectacle all aflutter with red and white pennants, lined with posterboard runestones. Red spray-painted garbage can lids served as shields, and real oars stuck out at all angles from the deck of the trailer that served as a platform. Lording over all of it, a paper mâché dragon head leered on the prow, its long pink tongue lolling like a Labrador retriever's.

I must have been grinning stupidly at the thing – the dozen or so kids lining the garage walls now cheered and applauded their dramatic showing. Sharon did a little happy dance and squeezed my hands. "Whattya think? Isn't it great?"

I just shook my head. Honestly, it looked as if a bunch of third-graders had been turned loose with glue and scissors at the Party Depot store. The Homecoming parade route was supposed to go from school and all through the downtown up Front Street and back the other side of the railroad tracks. This thing didn't look like it would make the length of the football field in one piece.

Sharon hopped up and down laughing, "Wait, wait, that's not all! Close your eyes again." I obeyed with a sigh, the smile frozen on my face. Some sort of hat was placed on my head – I couldn't help but flinch, and I blinked to see Kristin Schuh looming over me – in a furry, long-horned Viking helmet, long blonde braids hanging out from under it.

In sudden realization, I pulled my hands out of Sharon's grasp and reached up to take the thing off my head. Sure enough, it was a cheesy plastic replica of the Warrior's headgear, with the braids attached, and stubby plastic horns.

A cheer went up from the kids in the garage. Sharon stepped close to me and gushed,

"Whattaya think? Isn't it cool? This is the best part! Guess what else?"

I couldn't imagine. How could it get any better? By this time my smile was starting to hurt.

"You get to ride on the float!" She chattered on, confidentially, "It wasn't easy, but I talked them into letting you in on it. Andrew Bishop got mono, so you're taking his place. You'll be right up there with me! Yesss! I'm on it too!" she squealed. "Isn't that cool?"

My smile cracked, and I worked my jaw to get feeling back into my face. I drew her aside while the others went back to their business. "Jeeze, Sharon, this is great and all, but… I don't know, I wonder if I can do it." My mind raced to find a way out. "I think Coach wants the cross-country team to be all together, marching in the parade, and all, and then they introduce members of the team at the bonfire…."

"Oh, no, that's nothing! You can go down to the field Thursday night when they introduce the team. And as far as the parade goes, what does he care? You'll still be in the parade, but on the float!"

Kristin bounced up with a smile. "Hey, Brian, congratulations! Have a Coke?"

Handing me a can, she nodded at me solemnly. "We get the crew together here at five o'clock. Do you have anything else for your costume?"

"What? Like a fur coat or something? I don't think so."

"Well … I guess you can use Bishop's outfit. I'll pick it up and bring it here tomorrow."

"Here tomorrow?"

"Yeah, if you're here early enough, you can change and then help get the float over to school. We line them all up behind the bleachers before the bonfire and pep rally."

Sharon was plenty lathered up over all of this, and she was watching my reaction. "Oh, Brian," she broke in, "I'm going to stay at Doreen's after school, and we'll be here around five. Can you get a ride from somebody?"

"Ah… I guess so. Kenny offered me a ride."

"Ohhh-kay!" Sharon exclaimed, and tiptoed up to kiss my cheek.

I glanced back at the float and for a second imagined Jamie McVay hanging onto the stern waving his red signal lantern. But it was just the cracked lens of a tail light on the trailer.

CHAPTER TWENTY-TWO

"Whattya think?" Dad posed in the kitchen, stuffed like a sausage into his only suit. He had managed a huge knot in the necktie in the hope of hiding the loose top button of his white shirt.

"Not bad," I told him. "You don't seem *too* dangerous a felon."

He forced a nervous grin. But it wasn't funny. Dad's day in court hung over us like a buzzard on a branch.

Still in her robe, Mom padded barefoot into the kitchen and slotted a piece of bread into the toaster. She dropped the butter knife, spilled her coffee and fumbled the plastic jar of powdered dairy creamer. We were all nervous. Dad and Mom would be meeting the lawyer at the courthouse. "So you're okay after school, Brian?"

"Don't worry about me. Kenny's giving me a ride to the bonfire – well, his big brother's driving. I'll meet up with Sharon at the float."

Mom patted me on the head and smiled. "Well, I'm glad you're getting to go to Homecoming. It should be a special night." She gave Dad the once-over, sighed and fiddled with his threadbare shirt collar, shaking her head.

"What?" he said. "We don't want the judge to think we're too well-off, do we? This is gonna cost us a bundle anyway."

Mom stared at him. "You'll be lucky if that's all there is to it."

"I'm lucky Bob paid the lawyer's retainer," Dad admitted. "Who knows when we'll be able to pay him back!" His eyes darted over to me. "Listen, if this thing goes late, your Mom'll go on to work, and your

Uncle Bob will bring me home. So...."

"Yeah, well, good luck," I said. We stood there for a couple seconds, three feet apart in the kitchen, looking at each other's feet. "I better get to school."

***

"South Stallions Suck! South Stallions Suck!" The chant had started with football players in one of the gym classes and rolled down the hall, echoed between classes by kids with a sense that the normal rules of behavior had been temporarily suspended. All day long we'd been distracted with Homecoming nonsense – cheerleaders cavorting in the hallways, gaudy posters falling off the walls, and Winston Warriors in horned helmets marching from room to room stirring up school spirit with plastic broadswords.

Even Sharon applauded late in the day when a bunch of the football players charged past us to the locker room, yelling, "Kill the Stallions!"

"Go Warriors!" yelled their escort of pom-pom girls.

"Go Northmen!" Sharon shouted.

I groaned inwardly. The more hyped up she got, the less likely I would be able to get off the Viking Boat Rowing Team. She looked back at me with a grin. I waved a fist in the air for her benefit, but the thought of sitting on that float, with a stupid helmet on my head, in front of the whole school just filled me with dread.

She pulled me off into a doorway. "So, Brian – I'm going over to Kristin's with Doreen. I guess I'll catch up with you tonight."

"Right. When it's time for the floats to come out?"

She chuckled to herself, nodding, and gave my hand a quick squeeze. "I'll look for you on board ship!"

"Aye-aye," I sighed. "I'll be the one wearing the Viking helmet."

***

Back at home, there was no sign of Dad, or any clue of what might have happened in court. That could be a bad thing – or maybe he was out celebrating with Uncle Bob. I puttered around a little to kill time, had a bowl of cereal, and got cleaned up and changed. What do you wear that goes with fake fur and a horned helmet?

I ended up wearing black jeans and tee with a hoodie sweatshirt. Sitting at the kitchen table listening to some tunes, I dozed and dreamed I was running down the Prairie Path through Roosevelt Marsh, led by a flickering flame that stayed always just out of sight. But I saw the fire's glow in the sky ahead of me, and the golden light flashed through the trees. I could feel the ghost of Jamie McVay behind me, and just as I turned to look over my shoulder, I woke with a start. Heart pounding, I sat there in the dark kitchen until the lights of a car swung into the driveway. I met Kenny at the front door.

"Hey. Thanks for coming to pick me up."

"No problem. My brother owes me – I saw him smoking dope out back of the field house last week. Now, his fate is in my hands! Bwahahahaha!" Kenny made a neck-wringing gesture to complete the image. I understood completely why he didn't have a date for Homecoming.

Crawling into the back seat, I exchanged curt greetings with his brother Logan, and we were off.

"Hey, Kenny," I said. "I saw the Junior float last night. And guess what?"

"What?"

"It's a Viking ship."

"Yep."

Logan didn't turn his head. "It's *always* a frikkin' Viking ship, Dude."

"Some tradition," I said.

"But it wasn't always," Kenny said. "Right?"

"Well that's true," Logan admitted. "Back in the day, the Winston Warriors were Indians." He turned to look back. "You know, Red Indians, with feather headdresses and all."

"So how come – ?"

"They'd make floats with tepees on them, and if somebody could ride, they'd put them in the parade on horseback, dressed in an Indian outfit."

"But it wasn't politically correct," Kenny explained. "They didn't want to offend any Native Americans, so they changed it."

"They figured the Scandinavians were a lot less likely to raise a stink about it," Logan said. "So the Vikings came to town."

"And it's been Viking ships ever since," Kenny said.

"Now what?" Logan pulled the car over to let a fire engine roar by with lights blazing and siren blaring. Swinging back out to follow, we were surprised to see the strobe-lit truck slow and turn left onto the high school's street. "Holy shit!"

Kenny looked at me with raised eyebrows. "Do you smell smoke?"

We followed the fire engine into the parking lot, which was a crazy mob scene, kids running every which way, cars parked in disorder with some pulling out while others pulled in behind us. Logan found a spot near the gym, and before the car stopped, I hopped out, racing to the football field.

Behind the south end zone, the freshman bonfire smoldered, a mound of glowing coals the size of Buckingham Fountain.

A ring of people circled the red-hot pile about fifteen feet out. "What happened?" Kenny asked.

"Somebody set it off a half hour early, is what," a skinny freshman said.

"Man, it must have went up fast." Other voices chimed in.

"Almost like they used gasoline or something."

"I could smell the gas as soon as I got here."

"Who did it?"

The fire truck had pulled up in front of the bleachers, but the firemen in boots and full gear just stood and looked. One of them was talking to Coach Nelson.

"Well it *is* kind of confusing," Kenny said. "I mean, it's a *bonfire*! It's *supposed* to be burning. Are they supposed to put it out now or what?"

It appeared the firemen were just going to sit back and watch it burn with the rest of us. Coach Nelson stomped up, broke through the ring of spectators and approached the flaming coals, but was repelled by the heat. In the firelight, his face looked demented and shaken, not at all the tough guy he usually acted. He turned and looked away from the fire, past us into the dark beyond the visitors' bleachers across the field. His eyes, blinking from the heat and smoke, grew large. He pointed and croaked, "Fire!"

The group of kids nearest to him – the ones who could hear what he'd said – laughed and clapped. "Yeah!"

"Fire!"

"Yeah, that's what it is!"

Coach looked about wildly, the whites of his eyes flashing. "The floats!" he rasped and waved his arm toward the bleachers. Behind the stands, another fire blazed.

"Oh no!" I gasped.

Kenny saw it, too. "The floats are on fire!" he yelled, and others took up the shout as we raced across the field.

Behind the bleachers the parade floats – the four decorated trailers hitched to their tow vehicles – had been lined up for the pep rally. Now from across the field, they caricatured the disaster scene in Lincoln Marsh, Jamie McVay's train all aflame as he saw it, with echoes of the shock and fear he felt at the sight.

The end of the Senior Class float flickered with blue fire. Someone had unhooked the shiny pick-up truck and driven it off to safety. A couple guys from the football team were struggling to unhitch Mark Thomsen's '57 Chevy. Colorful flames danced atop the Junior Class Viking ship, licking about the grinning dragon's head, and from the creature's mouth streamed plumes of fire and smoke. The little boat blazed away like a Viking's funeral.

An icy chill flushed through me as I searched for a glimpse of Sharon in the dark. I imagined her doing something desperate to save her precious float. People dashed wildly about shouting, while some stood helplessly singly or huddled in groups, watching the floats burn. Coach Nelson turned this way and that in confusion as the fire engine rumbled past him to the stands.

In a matter of minutes, firefighters had doused the flames. Two trailers sat smoking, their bedraggled paper decorations a soggy pulp of ashes and singed streamers.

I found Kristin Schuh sobbing with the other cheerleaders on a bottom bench of the bleachers. “Kristin, where’s Sharon?”

She looked at me blankly. “I don’t know.”

“I saw her at Kristin’s house,” one of the other girls said.

“Haven’t seen her,” said another.

“How about Doreen?” Someone said, “She was riding with Doreen.”

“Haven’t seen them.”

My stomach churned. “Kenny,” I called, spotting him with some guys by the cars. “Help me look for Sharon. Ask people if they’ve seen her.”

He nodded and trotted off in one direction while I went the other. But no one remembered seeing Sharon since they’d left Kristin’s house with the floats.

Principal Wesley said a few words to Coach Nelson, and a couple other teachers led the dazed coach away like a whipped puppy on a leash. A few minutes later Kenny approached with Coach Konechny.

“Any luck?”

Kenny just shrugged and shook his head.

“Brian,” Coach said, “you can help spread the word. Principal Wesley has canceled the Pep Rally. They want everybody to just go home, and we’ll start over tomorrow night before the game.”

He moved off to another group of students. The crowds milling about started to disperse. A few die-hards still circled the cooling embers of the bonfire, but clearly, the excitement was over for the time being. I scanned the figures there one more time, hoping to see Sharon’s stubby silhouette. Instead, Kenny’s brother broke out of the formation and called us over.

“Whattya say, K-Dog,” he said. “Looks like this barbecue’s over and done. Let’s get outa here. You comin’, Krueger?”

I stumbled along with them to the parking lot, where some cars were still arriving, only to be turned away with news of the disaster. In the midst of the confusion, Doreen’s shadow loomed in front of us.

“Doreen!” I called. “Where’s Sharon?”

She stopped and stood, considering. “Oh, Krueger.” She waved a meaty paw at the people walking to their cars. “What the heck’s going on here?”

Kenny laughed delightedly and told her.

Doreen staggered back. "Oh, no! Not our beautiful boat?" She shouldered past us toward the field.

"Wait a minute! Wasn't Sharon with you?"

Doreen paused, looking me up and down. "Oh. Yeah. I was supposed to tell you. I took her home."

"What? Why? Is she okay?"

Doreen shrugged. "Well… not really. Her mom called while we were at Kristin's. Her grandpa died."

***

Back in the car, Kenny just couldn't shut up. "Oh man did you see the coach, he was freakin' out, man, he's like 'Duh, what's goin' on?'"

Logan cackled, hunching over the steering wheel and gripping it up high. "Tonight he's like 'Hey get that fire truck off the field, man!"

"Who did it, do you think?"

"Some of the football team saw somebody by the floats and chased 'em, but they never caught anybody."

I felt sick, my head was pounding, and the jabbering from the two of them wasn't helping. As we turned down Jewel Road, I leaned toward Logan's ear, "Hey, why don't you let me off here?"

"What? What's here?"

"The Prairie Path. I'll walk home. It's a shortcut."

"Whatever." He swerved over to the shoulder.

Kenny gaped at me from the front seat. "You're walking?"

"Yeah, I'll be fine. Just gotta clear my head."

I watched them drive away and crossed back over to where the path started its slow descent through that cutting to the marsh. I paused in the shadows, out of the light from the street lamp. On this moonless night, the trail was black, graveyard black, and that chilly damp seeped into my bones. I pictured old Grandpa Rice in the hospital bed, just looking at me. Grandpa Rice, the railroad man, who saw the light of Jamie McVay. And where was he now? Did he follow McVay's signal light – to someplace else?

When my own Gramps died, I was pretty broken up, feeling sorry for myself because I'd miss him so much, but feeling sorry for Dad, too. Just the way my heart was breaking for Sharon right now. I remember the reverend at Gramps's funeral, and all the people saying, "He's in a better place," and "his soul's at rest." But I never pictured Gramps in Heaven or anywhere else. To me, he was just gone.

Of course, that was before I'd seen the ghost of Jamie McVay – before I knew there was something – some place *more* – after you died. Now my mind reeled to wonder *where.* All these months I'd been seeing that spirit and feeling the horrible pain of a soul caught *between* this world and the next. And never until now had I ever wondered what that next world might be – where it is, how we come to it.

Searching out in the shapeless dark of the marsh, I vaguely felt his presence – a dull ache of need forever seeking redemption. Then, just off the trail, I saw what I expected – a faint point of reddish light, bobbing and gliding below the embankment. Who was McVay signaling tonight?

Turning my back to the mystery, I walked briskly toward the cold light at Pleasant Hill Road, keeping to the shoulder away from the traffic. Back home at last and Uncle Bob's car was parked in the driveway.

"Dad?" I stepped through the door and saw him lying back in the Lay-Z-Boy with a beer in his hand. "What happened in court?"

His red face beamed. "All good, Brian!" he said. "A year's suspension is all. And the fine – two grand! It's a bite – plus the lawyer and all. But it could have been worse."

"Damn straight, it could've!" Uncle Bob came down the hall from the bathroom. "That prosecutor was pushing for jail time – but the judge was more reasonable."

"Reasonable," Dad echoed and took a swig from the can. "And I can apply for a restricted permit after 30 days, to get to work – if I had job to go to."

"But don't forget about the breathalyzer thing. You got to pay for that, too."

"What's that?" I asked.

"The thing where you blow into a tube, and if you've had alcohol the car won't start."

"The tube!" Dad yelled, raising his beer can. "Here's to the frikking tube!"

Uncle Bob chuckled and staggered against the wall. "The tube!"

I glared at him and stood over Dad in disbelief. "You really think this is the best way to celebrate not going to jail on a DUI?"

He shrugged and looked sheepish, the silly grin on his face fading. "No. You're right. It could've been worse. I could've done serious time." He tried to look serious. "I was lucky."

I nodded. "Yeah you were."

He belched, and Uncle Bob started giggling, and Dad busted out laughing harder. I just threw my hands up and went back to the kitchen, burning my uncle with a look on the way. He followed me in.

"Brian. Kid," he said. "Don't look at me like that. You know I can't make him do anything. You and your mom can't either. It's gonna take something – I don't know – a lot more than us to make him change."

A great concussion shook the house and an orange glow bathed the walls. Outside in the vacant lot, Pete's bonfire went up with a "whoosh" and great tongues of crackling flame. We watched wide-eyed through the patio door.

"Vincenzi," I muttered and eased the door open to slip out.

"Be careful," Dad called. To Uncle Bob, he explained, "That kid's dangerous."

CHAPTER TWENTY-THREE

Long snakes of shadow reached out from the trees behind the house. I walked to the lot line and peered through at the scene. Snapping like a wild beast, the bonfire leaped and writhed, with Pete dancing around it, poking and prodding with a long pole. A shape emerged from the shadows and approached me.

"Some fire, huh, Krueger?" Rick Wagner's beady eyes glinted in the firelight.

'Yeah," I said. "Hot stuff."

"I hear the Freshman Bonfire was kind of a disappointment."

"Is that so?"

"Yeah, that's what I heard. I heard it was a case of premature conflagration!" He made a stroking motion with one hand and chuckled. "Hey, Pete!" he called. "Krueger wants to know when's the Homecoming Parade tomorrow!"

The Pyro pranced over, brandishing his smoking poker and grinning like a demon. "Hooo, Klooger! You goin' to the Big Game tomorrow?"

"Sure he is," Rick said. "He's got a real hot date!"

"Hot date, Haaaha!"

Melkovec and Carla came down from the Vincenzis' deck. "Haaha," Bill echoed, and looked blankly at Wagner. "What's funny?"

"Tell him, Krueger," Rick said to me. "Tell him how you and Rice are ridin' on the float tomorrow! You are, aren't you?"

Vincenzi and Carla grinned, waiting to hear me answer.

I just shook my head. "Y'know, the bonfire – who gives a damn, right? Freshies need to learn how to make a fire!"

"Learn from the master!" Pete laughed.

"But the floats, Pete? That crossed a line. That's another kind of thing altogether."

He stepped back with a phony look of indignation. "What? What about the floats? Do I know something about some floats?"

Carla shoved him playfully, giggling, and Melkovec shrugged, "We don't know nothing about no floats."

"Right," I said. "Well, *whoever* knows something – whoever burned those things – must have been a real asshole!"

Pete lunged at me, his face inches from my own. "Well, maybe there's lots of assholes! Maybe that whole school is a stinkin' hole!" His hands were curled into fists, and his eyes blazed. I tensed, but he stepped back, breathing fast.

I took a step toward him, jabbing my finger. "You could have hurt somebody, Pete! People were trying to put out the fires, and they might have really gotten hurt. Coach Nelson – "

"*Screw* Nelson!" Pete leaped forward again, seething. "I wish that prick burned the hair off his head! He wrote me up, that *shit*!"

"You are *insane*!" I yelled back. "You set the whole parade on fire because Coach gave you a *detention*?"

"Nobody messes with me!" Pete screeched. "I don't forget!"

Carla grabbed him by the shoulders and Wagner stepped between us. He looked me in the eyes. "If you're smart, you'll just go back in your house."

"If you're smart, you'll go back to yours. Don't you think the whole school's thinking that Pyro – and all of you – are the ones who did it?"

Wagner scoffed. "They've got nothing on us. We've been here all night. Right, Carla?"

"All night," she cackled.

"And my mom'll tell 'em the same thing," Pete said. "We're in the clear!"

There was no sense talking to any of them. I backed away, but instead of going home I crossed to the other side of the street, leaving the blaze behind. I could still feel the heat on my back when I turned into the cool dark of Richard Street.

A block down, the little Granny cottage at the dead end glowed with its own warm light behind curtained windows. The looming cottonwoods seemed gathered to protect the place from the black night pushing in.

I started up the walk, but paused to listen at the bottom of the wooden stairs. At first, only a hum of voices could be heard, but then I began to make out individuals – Mr. Rice's even tones, the musical voice of Sharon's mom. A squeal followed by laughter must have been Christine and one of the boys. At first, as much as I strained, I couldn't hear Sharon. Peeking through a window, then, I saw where she sat on the couch – saw the back of her blonde head between the thin white-poof of Grandma's hair and the tousled rusty mop of her brother Sammy. By the motions, it was easy see that Sharon was talking – telling some story, I imagined, her head bobbing slightly, a little wiggle to her shoulders – an easy and natural response to the family's sadness. Typical. The whole family gathered to mourn together and to help Grandma through her pain and loss. That's just the way they operated.

It was late. I turned and plodded home.

Back at the house, Uncle Bob's pickup had been replaced in the driveway by the Jeep. The TV flickered over Mom asleep on the couch and Dad snoring in the La-Z-Boy. The red light blinked on the answering machine.

"Brian, it's me," went Sharon's message. "You ought to have heard about Grandpa. That he – he's gone. He died. I … I was really looking forward to the bonfire with you. But call me in the morning. You can tell me all about it."

At the sound, Mom sat up and looked around, squinting. "Brian? Is everything all right?"

"Yeah – no," I said, and told her all about Sharon and her grandpa, and the Bonfire Disaster.

She shook her head and came over to give me a hug. "Aw, that's too bad. But you've got to let her get over it in her own time. I don't have to tell *you."*

"Yeah, I know. Just – wow – the whole Homecoming thing meant a lot to her, that's all. She doesn't even know yet about the float. You think she'll still want to go to Homecoming at all?"

Mom stifled a yawn. "Yeah, it sounds like she will if she can. She could probably use a distraction. Well, just make sure she knows you're there for her, whatever she needs."

***

Early next morning I walked over to Sharon's. She met me out front with a tight hug, and we walked along Richard Street. A reek of smoldering charcoal from the Pyro's bonfire still hung over the whole neighborhood

"So, I'm sorry about your Grandpa," I said. "I definitely know what you're going through."

Sharon took my hand. "I know you do. I know you *think* you do."

"What do you mean, I *think* I do?"

"*You* know," she said. "What you said at the hospital."

"What did I say?"

"*You* remember. Making it sound like you could hear him. That he was talking to you."

"Ah, Sharon...." I didn't want to get into a discussion about it now. "I just had a feeling, okay? It wasn't anything."

"Ohhh-kay. Let's forget it."

We walked to the end of the block without talking and turned in front of the Pyro's house. I hesitated. "Sharon ... you heard about the float?"

Her eyes narrowed, and her fingernails dug into my palm. "Yeah. Oh, that rat bastard!" She turned and glared at the dingy house with its streaked windows and drooping draperies. "Our beautiful ship," she muttered, choking back tears.

"He won't get away with it."

"No," she said. "Sooner or later, he'll get what's coming to him."

"Well," I said, "I suppose I better get going to school. You're not going are you?"

"No, I'm staying home with Grandma."

"And tonight, the game…?"

"No, I suppose not."

"Can you still go to the dance?" I asked. "I mean, do you want to?"

"You know I do," she said, looking up with her head cocked. "I wasn't sure if I *could* – or if I *should*."

"It'd be a shame now if you didn't wear that dress."

She nodded. "I know. Mom worked so hard to get it ready for me."

I pulled her back to look at me. "So, we're doing it?"

She half-smiled. "If you're still on, yeah."

"All right, then!" I was happiest for her, but in the back of my mind there lurked a sense of closure as I thought about the two of us on an actual date.

"I'll call Doreen for our ride," she said. "If that's okay?"

I shrugged. "Do I have any other options?"

"Guess not," she grinned. "You better get to school." She tip-toed up and gave me a quick kiss on the cheek. Then she spun around and, dodging puddles, jogged back home.

***

Winston North Homecoming couldn't have been more dismal. At dusk, with the frosh-soph game underway, rain began to pour. Hundreds of people fled from the stands, leaving a bedraggled few to watch the boys slip and slide all over the field. I got there in time to see the "Little Warriors" stomped into the mud by the Winston South "Ponies" 28-6. Then the official program began, with Dean of Students Streck announcing over the loudspeaker.

"Welcome to Winston North High School, Ladies and Gentlemen, as we start off this year's Homecoming Extravaganzaaaa!" A scattered response of cheers and applause was drowned out by the brassy arrival of the marching band. I didn't recognize the tune they played – I don't think the composer would have, either. When it wheezed to an end, the cheerleaders splashed out onto the field to do a couple of their routines.

Streck's voice blared, "Let's show those Winston South Stallions how the Northmen celebrate Homecoming!" This was lost on the dozen or so visitors huddled under plastic in the bleachers across the field.

Meanwhile, the Homecoming Parade had done its circuit of Downtown Winston and returned to school. I felt guilty for ducking out, but figured correctly that with Sharon gone, I wouldn't be missed. After a few more band numbers, with Poms Squad line dancing, at last the parade crawled from the parking lot like some kind of a battle-scarred refugee train. The freshman and sophomore floats – Viking ships the both of them – had come through Friday night without fire damage. But the fire hoses had given them a good dousing, and now the rains finished the job, matting down the crepe paper and soaking the streamers into sad wads of pulp. Northmen in raincoats pulled at the oars like doomed galley slaves while the class officers cowered under umbrellas, their teeth chattering in the cold. Rain in sheets pelted the covered-up convertibles pulling the floats. Towed behind, the burned and battered Junior float had been stripped to its basic trailer platform. The Viking ship had become a rusty lowboy furnished with plastic furniture, Chosen Ones waving crudely-lettered posterboard signs. Again I felt a pang of remorse to think Sharon and I were both supposed to be up there. But a closer look at the riders' miserable faces cured me of any regret. And I wouldn't mention it to her, but neither Sharon nor I was even remembered in all that mess.

"Students and Faculty, Friends and Family of Winston North…." Streck paused dramatically. "I give you the Homecoming Queen and her Court!" Last in the parade, pulled by a crew cab pickup and escorted by Poms Squad girls in soggy sweat suits, the Senior Float rolled up.

It had been stripped down as well, just a flatbed trailer with a couple tiered plywood platforms on top. The girls in their gowns were covered in plastic rain ponchos, while the guys in tuxes wobbled along trying to keep their umbrellas from turning inside out in the gusty wind. The effect was less comical than you'd expect. On the other hand, the small crowd in the bleachers broke out with a good laugh when the big pickup truck spun its wheels, spattering the baton twirlers with mud.

Our big moment came when Streck introduced the cross-country teams. "Let's – ot forget – Co—Konech – and – s Warrior – the Trail!" The microphone cut in and out, short-circuited by the streaming rain, and finally quit altogether. I joined the guys on the field where we shifted about self-consciously for a while, until Principal Wesley waved us back to the stands.

Dazzling field lights backlit the slashing rain as the band marched back through the mud, and approximately two people joined the cheerleaders in an emotional version of the Winston North fight song. At least I thought I recognized the tune and the words "Northmen" and "Winston."

Of the game itself, the less said the better. Our team came out strong enough in their first series, but eventually had to punt. When Winston South scored on their first possession, all the war washed out of the Warriors. For all their flailing around in the mire, we were down three touchdowns by halftime. I was guilty of that "train-wreck" mentality that makes miles-long gaper's blocks on the tollway – it's hard to turn away from a disaster like that Homecoming game.

Nevertheless, when Kenny nudged me and headed for the parking lot, I followed.

***

Saturday morning I slept in, and even after waking I just lay there, did some reading, feeling pretty relaxed – until I remembered I still had to get a corsage for Sharon. That sent me on a desperate bike ride to a flower shop in Winston. I got back home in time for a check-in and update from Sharon herself, back from the hair salon and the nail salon and … I think that was about it.

Before long I was squeezing into my old funeral suit doing a little primping, myself. Mom had helped me iron a white shirt. Then I spent a half hour trying to tie the tie. Frustrated, I called my dad. "You showed me how to do this once before, but I can't remember."

He stood up and looked at me critically, rubbing his whiskers. "Yeah, come to Papa. Let's see…."

He grabbed the loose ends and made a few flips and flutters with shaking hands. "Try that." The knot somehow slipped away when I tried to tighten it. Dad scowled and tried again, yanking heavily. "Try it now." This time the knot tightened into a tiny nugget that wouldn't move.

"Not quite," I said, and shook my head.

Dad frowned. "Take it off."

"That was a joke," I said. "Knot quite? K-N-O-T?"

"Give it here." Grimly he snatched at the tie and pulled it up over my head. He plucked at the knot, loosened it, draped it around his own neck, then deftly flipped the ends to make a perfect knot. "There. The hands remember." He slipped it off his head and looped it over mine, drawing the knot up under my chin. "Okay."

I looked in the mirror. "Perfect. Thanks."

Mom, just home from work, called from the kitchen, "Your ride is here! Don't forget the corsage." She handed me the box and grabbed me by the shoulders as I squeezed through the door. "You look great, Hon. Oh, take the umbrella, it's raining off and on."

In the driveway, Doreen was waiting, with Margaret Bork in the passenger seat. We all drove over to Sharon's and dashed to the door. Mrs. Rice drew the three of us into the foyer, where the little kids circled like a pack of coyotes. I'm sure we were quite a sight. Me squeezed into the black suit coat, and the girls looking like nothing they'd ever seen before. Doreen looked amazingly feminine in a satiny blue dress with skinny straps straining to hold up her considerable bosom. Margaret Bork was about halfway between Doreen's and Sharon's height and heft. She minced about in high heels, obviously uncomfortable in a clingy black strapless dress that hung on her hips, showing cleavage that could have hidden the whole Winston Warrior playbook.

But everybody else faded out of the scene like a movie special effect when Sharon made her entrance. She floated down the stairs in a peach-colored dress as light and fluffy as whipped cream. She was gorgeous and classy, with the short flouncy dress tied over one shoulder and her hair done up in golden curls. *Bride-like*, I thought, fumbling with the white rose wrist thingy. The other girls oohed and aahed, but I was mute and breathless until Sharon broke the spell.

"Hey, I got you a white rose, too!" she laughed, and ducked into the kitchen to grab the boutonniere.

Mrs. Rice posed us for pictures. Last-minute adjustments were made to the costumes, leaving me self-conscious in the living room with Sharon's dad and the mocking boys. It was a relief to finally slide with Sharon into the back seat. She turned to me, grinned and hunched her shoulders. "Here we go!" she said. Before I could say a word, Margaret said something, and Sharon answered, and the girls chattered all the way to school.

Doreen let us off at the doors, and holding hands we dashed through the rain into the vestibule. Sharon stopped and looked at all the balloons and bows, streamers and glitter.

"Well, you made it!" I said. "Homecoming at last!"

She nodded with a satisfied smile and edged over against me. "At last! Thanks, Brian!"

"My pleasure," I said and ushered her into the gym with an elaborate gesture.

Of course, like a lot of things, the *idea* of a Homecoming Dance is a lot more attractive than the *actual* thing – especially if, like me, you're not much of a dancer. I went into this fully aware that the last time I danced was two years before with my cousin Joanne at her wedding. I was prepared to stand along the wall with a bunch of other guys, and was content to watch the girls do their thing. And that worked for a while, but Sharon wasn't going to let me sit out all night. She was clever, though. She lured me out on the dance floor for a slow dance first, and when that ended, and a faster number started, I was trapped out in the open. Before I knew it, I was stumbling around doing line dances and other calisthenics with everybody else.

Sharon was going like a crazy person. She had the energy, and she was a good dancer, too – graceful in her short-legged way, with subtle rhythm and excellent timing. But she was trying too hard. As the night went on, I saw signs she was wearing out. She looked pale, her shoulders damp, that classy hair-do coming apart with sweat dripping down her temples.

"Hey, let's take a break," I said, and she let me lead her out into the lobby. Her arm was clammy with sweat, and she panted, her chest rising and falling sharply. An effect not lost on me. "Let's just settle down a bit," I said.

She staggered a little and leaned hard against me. The fresh air felt good in the lobby where the doors were propped open. We stood for a while watching people come and go, until Doreen pushed out and the two of them shuffled off to the washroom. I waited with a couple players I knew from class. Drews and Stiller were a little subdued after their drubbing on the field; the public humiliation humanized them to where you could actually talk to them.

"I see Coach is back to his old self," I mentioned. Coach Nelson was still as big a jerk as ever. As a chaperone, he monitored traffic at the door both ways – keeping some people out and others in.

"All right, stand still over there!" he was saying. "Anybody who goes out stays out!"

"Too bad he wasn't such a tough guy during the game," Drews said.

"Did he coach?"

"Not much," Stiller said. "He was sleepwalking. He kept the same line in all four quarters – the only substitutions were called by the Defense."

"What are *you* doing here, Wagner?" Coach swaggered up to block one door. "Show your ticket or hit the road!"

"What *is* he doing here?" Sharon said, coming up alongside of me.

"Maybe he got a last-minute date with Melkovec."

But Rick appeared to be solo, dressed in black jeans and a white shirt with a skinny black tie. He waved his ticket at Coach Nelson and signed in at the registration table. He had already noticed Sharon and me standing there. His eyes narrowed to glance at me, but his voice was normal greeting Sharon.

"Hey, Sharon, Babes, how you doin'?"

"Okay."

"Hey, listen, I'm sorry about your Grand-Dad."

"Thanks." Sharon eyed him.

"Yeah, he was a decent old guy. I remember when we were little, him and your Gram 'd come to the class parties, Grandparents' Days and all. He was okay."

Sharon sniffed. "Thanks, Rick, that's nice to hear you remember him."

"Okay," I said. "I'm ready to go back in! Let's go!"

Wagner strutted down the hall, stopping to exchange greetings with others.

Inside the gym, the music had slowed again. I two-stepped Sharon around, holding her lightly, but her energy was gone, and her thoughts seemed far away. "Let's go sit down," I said and steered us over to a couple of folding chairs. We sat, not talking, holding sweaty hands while the DJ introduced the Homecoming Queen and her court. When the music started again, the beat throbbed through us both.

"You okay, Sharon?"

She kept her gaze leveled at the stage. "Just thinking. I'm sorry."

"Well … that's okay. It's been a rough couple of days for you."

"I shouldn't let it bother me, though. I shouldn't be thinking about Grandpa. But Grandma and Dad are so sad. It doesn't seem right that I'm out having fun."

"I get that. But I bet they all told you it was okay, you should go and enjoy yourself, right?"

She exhaled a little laugh. "Yeah, you're right."

"And as for Grandpa…." I hesitated, and she looked up at me. "Well, I just want you to know, I think he's okay. I mean, not okay, of course – but I mean, not … *ghostly.* If you know what I mean."

"What are you talking about?"

I glanced around – no one was sitting nearby. "*You* know. I just got that feeling. That everything was, *clean* and all. That your Grandpa was gone, like he should be, and he won't be hanging about like – damaged goods – like Ja – "

"That's enough, now, Brian!" Sharon raised both her hands. "Stop it right now!"

"Well, okay, but – I just wanted you to know, I didn't see anything –"

"Cut it out! That's enough of the *ghost* talk, okay?"

"I just thought you'd want to know."

"Brian! No more of that stupid – *foolishness*! I mean it!"

I stared at her. "It's not foolishness."

Sharon closed her eyes and stood, shaking her head. “Please stop! That’s just enough!”

“I’m sorry, but – *you still don’t believe me, do you*?”

“Come on, Brian!” She turned her back on me, facing the dance floor where bodies leaped and twisted in the semi-darkness. The music’s pounding bass vibrated in my chest. Only when she turned back to me did I hear Sharon say, “I want to go home now.”

CHAPTER TWENTY-FOUR

Sunday was a gray day, misty and cold. I stayed in bed late, reliving the stupidity and miserableness of my big Homecoming "Extravaganzaaa." When I did get up, I was glad I had nowhere to go but to the kitchen table. Mom was sitting there reading the newspaper.

"Hey, here's an obituary on Sharon's grandfather." She skimmed the article and read parts out loud. "Today's the wake, from eleven to seven, at Krage's on Front Street. You're going, aren't you?"

"No," I grumbled. "It's best if I don't go."

Mom stared. "Don't you want to show her you care about her? Seeing her friends might distract her and help her get through the wake. You remember your Gramps's wake, don't you? Didn't you feel better when your friends came by?"

"This is different. I don't think it would make Sharon feel better. It'd make things worse."

"Why?"

Dad shuffled into the kitchen. I looked up at him, and he raised his eyebrows.

"It might just be *me* she doesn't want to see."

"Uh-oh. Why? Did something happen last night?"

"No…." I lowered my head, but kept eye contact with Dad. "I don't know…. Maybe because she took me to meet her Grandpa and all … and we talked, him and me…."

"Sure, about the ghost story, I remember."

"Well, that might make her sad, remembering my meeting him and all."

"Well, that's –"

Dad cleared his throat, interrupting, "Yeah, I get it. She won't want to remember that time you were there. That's normal."

Mom crossed her arms. "Still, you ought to make some gesture. You better send a card at least."

"Yeah, definitely." I slipped into the family room.

Dad followed me in. "Hey," he said quietly, "don't let her talk you into it. Believe me, a funeral home is the last place you want to be."

"What do you mean?" I looked past him to make sure Mom was staying in the kitchen.

"*You* know. You don't want to be seeing … *other* people." He rolled his eyes upward. "*Lots* of dead people have been through there. Lots."

"Oh. I get it, yeah. But… at Gramps's wake, I didn't see anything … or anybody."

"Well, count yourself lucky." He brushed his hair back with both hands and shuddered. "For me, it was like … like having fifty televisions in my brain, all on different channels, the volume going up and down."

"Well … I never felt – or saw anything weird."

"I don't know what to tell you. Maybe you weren't ready, maybe you weren't old enough at the time. But the thing is, now you *are*. You're seeing these things now. And they'll get to you, if you let 'em. You can't let 'em hurt you." He sat heavily in the recliner, looking old and tired.

He was making me nervous. "I've only ever been close to the ghost of Jamie McVay. And I've never actually *seen him*. Just the light."

"And he's the only one?"

"Well …" I thought back to that creepy feeling I had in the hospital. "He's the only one I'm *sure* of. And I've never felt – *afraid*, like I was in *danger*, or –"

"I don't know how dangerous they are." Dad waved the idea away. "But that's not what I'm talking about. What I mean is – all that – *misery* – you can't let it affect your – your mind." He looked me square in the eye.

"Okay," I nodded, "that I get. It's pretty powerful stuff – the misery."

"What's misery?" Mom asked, stepping into the room. She set a bowl of pretzels on the coffee table. "Your Uncle Bob is coming over for the Bears Game."

"We were talking about –"

"Pops's wake," my father answered.

Mom flashed a look at him. "As if you remember anything about it."

"I was in bad shape," Dad admitted. "I needed something to help me through it." He looked at me intently.

"You needed somebody to help you stand up, I remember that part," Mom said. "You fell down at your father's grave the next day."

Dad lowered his head. "I was weak," he said. "I was sick. My mind was full of sick thoughts. It was too much to stand."

She looked at him with pity, I think, and shook her head. "You – " She choked off the rest. With an embarrassed glance at me, she turned away and clomped down the basement stairs.

Uncle Bob showed up a little before noon, and we watched the game.

"So I heard it was Homecoming weekend here," he said. "How'd the team do?"

I snorted and told him about the thrashing the Winston team had suffered on Friday.

"Ouch!" he cried. "Well, let's hope this is a better game today."

Mom sat to watch for a while as if nothing had happened between her and Dad. Just before the half she set out a bunch of Sloppy Joes for us and took off in the car to do some shopping.

We stood eating in the kitchen when she'd gone. Uncle Bob popped open another beer and leaned back against the counter. "So, any more run-ins with your ghost?"

"Hmm, I guess I did catch a glimpse when I walked down the Prairie Path the other night."

"That's the only place you've seen him?"

"Yeah," I nodded.

Dad finished a sandwich and wiped a hand across his mouth. "Except now his mother wants him to go to the funeral home. Tell him," he said to me.

"My friend Sharon's grandpa died. I *should* go. Mom's right."

"I told him he's crazy."

Uncle Bob looked thoughtful. "Well, your dad's right. That can be a real freak show sometimes."

"I've never seen any other ghosts, and never any place else."

"Okay, but remember, the ghosts are a rare thing, in the first place – few and far between – and for that be thankful. But some are stronger than others, for whatever reason – because of their own personalities, or because of the – what would you say, Jim, the *violence* of their deaths?"

"The way they died – that's definitely got something to do with it," Dad said.

"Or sometimes I think – it's just that their *need* is so strong. That's what makes it possible for them to punch through – so we can sense them."

"So don't they just haunt the places where they died?" I asked. "Like Jamie McVay and the railroad?"

"No, not always," Uncle Bob said. "The stronger ones – it seems like they can flicker in and out – to other places – any place – when they think they need to. For them, it's like time and space don't matter. Like I said, I've seen 'em at funeral homes and cemeteries."

"Why there, though?"

He shrugged. "Maybe that's the last place they remember seeing their families or something. Someplace where they might have a chance of – *communicating* with somebody?"

"But if they don't have anything to say…?"

"Then they don't show up at all! They're done, they've said their goodbyes, and they move on."

"Where do they go?" I asked, spreading my arms. Uncle Bob sighed and looked over at Dad and then down at his feet. "Where do we *all* go?" I demanded. "Heaven? Hell? Where?"

Dad stepped up and put a hand on my forearm. "There's no way to know," he said. "If you believe in Heaven and Hell, then maybe that's the truth. Maybe that's where we go. But how can you know for sure? You can't."

I needed to go somewhere, do something – but I walked as far as the dining room and watched rain spray against the patio door. The sky had darkened and I pictured the people in raincoats with black umbrellas filing into the funeral parlor on Front Street. The Northwestern line ran right by the place, commuter trains and long freights sounding their horns in salute to the old railroad man. But he was long gone from there – and that was a good thing, wasn't it? That's all I wanted Sharon to know. Where he'd gone to, I couldn't say.

And nobody wants to think about that, anyway. We let the preachers talk about Heaven and Hell, but it's too deep to understand, too much to deal with, so we bow our heads and say "Amen" and just move on with our lives. No wonder Sharon couldn't listen to me, when it was about her own grandfather. How could I expect anything else? How could I expect her to believe that ghosts are real?

Dad clapped a hand onto my shoulder. "You gonna be okay?"

"Yeah, I'm fine," I told him. "But I'm going to have to make it right with Sharon."

"How so?"

"She got upset with me. I told her I thought her grandpa was okay – that I *hadn't* seen his ghost."

Dad slumped and covered his eyes, while behind him Uncle Bob yelled, "You what?"

I hung my head. "And I got upset with her because I realized she didn't believe me anyway. After all summer, she didn't really believe me."

"Rookie!" Uncle Bob shouted. "What's the number one rule?"

"You don't talk about it!" I recited along with Dad. "I get it. I know."

"So now what are you gonna do?"

I shrugged. "Go make-up with her. Apologize. I'll tell her my imagination just got away from me. That I see now. There's a logical explanation for everything?"

Uncle Bob nodded. "That might work."

Dad rubbed his neck and grabbed another beer from the fridge. He plopped down in the family room, where the second half had begun. "Good luck," he muttered. "That's all I can say."

"Okay then. I think I'll go to the funeral tomorrow."

Dad turned to look up at me. "Aww, Brian, no! I told you! That's a bad idea."

Uncle Bob laughed and fell back on the couch. "Well, you've got to figure it out for yourself. Go ahead, then! *Man up* and face your demons! *Literally.* Right, Jim?"

Dad glowered at him.

On the screen, the Bears' big tight end lumbered across the middle and went up for a pass. As the ball hit his fingers, he got hammered by the linebacker and was driven to the turf. Somehow he staggered back up, still holding the ball, and wobbled off the field to cheers.

Uncle Bob shook his fist. "*Wooh!* Holy crap! *That* took guts, my friends. *That's* one brave dude!"

Dad offered a grudging fist-bump. "They've been giving him a bum rap in the paper. Saying he didn't have the *cojones* to go across the middle. Guess that answers *that* question."

"He answered the challenge. Ya gotta love it!"

In fact, that was a Bears first down, and they went on to score and win. Dad had another drink to celebrate, but Uncle Bob decided to leave for home. He was just going out the door when Mom got back from shopping.

"Mom, I decided I want to go to the funeral tomorrow. Can you give me a ride?"

She raised an eyebrow. "I guess you can afford to miss a few hours of school." She rustled through the newspaper to check the details. "Okay. I can take you before my shift. I'm glad you changed your mind."

I nodded. "Yeah, I've got to '*Man up*,' according to Uncle Bob."

She smiled.

Dad stood in the doorway with a dismal look. "I'm going, too," he said.

CHAPTER TWENTY-FIVE

The day of Grandpa Rice's funeral was way beyond blustery. The spindly poplars on Front Street tossed wildly about. In the parking lot, the wind ripped the Jeep's door out of Mom's grip as she tried to hold it open for me. Krage's Funeral Home sprawled over a whole corner, a typical Winston Victorian house, but bastardized with new siding and fake stone veneers.

I squeezed between my parents like a little kid. Dad had doused himself with cologne, but under that scent lay the sour smell of stale beer. Mom pushed the heavy oak door open. Dad nodded solemnly and clutched my shoulder for a second. "Here we go," he breathed.

We stepped onto a stained maroon carpet, and the ancient floor creaked. Knots of people stood in the foyer talking in hushed tones. A sickly-sweet smell hung in the air.

A tingling sensation tickled my brain, and I braced myself. I expected a gust of somebody else's thoughts blowing over and through my mind. But instead of a speeding train slamming into me, impressions soaked into my skull small bits at a time. First one faded image and then another and then all these different streams flowed together like a flood: strange faces and places. Scenes dissolved one into another: a farm, a green hillside, a rolling sea, all spinning in my mind till I staggered, grasping at Dad's arm. Closing my eyes didn't help, either, except to focus some of the images. Voices rose in my mind – a gabble of talk, not all of it in English, gruff tones of men, musical accents of women, shrill cries of children. No single thing stood out. I fished about in my brain to find myself, and pushed through the broken memories to a clear space, gasping as I opened my eyes.

Dad stood in front of me, arms outstretched with both hands against the paneled wall, his face inches from my own, peering into my eyes. His own expression was strained, intense. Mom had walked ahead, and now she turned and, surprised to find herself alone, edged back. Dad stood up straight and left me blinking.

"Are you all right?" Mom asked. I wasn't sure if she was talking to him or to me. "What's going on?"

"Yeah, I'm okay," I replied, and my own voice sounded weird to me.

"I'll be okay," Dad rasped, but his eyes rolled. His fists were clenched, white-knuckled, and he shook his head like a dog coming in from the rain. We followed Mom, joining the crowd as it filed through a wide doorway.

At the threshold Dad paused. "You can push 'em back," he whispered. "Imagine blowing a bubble – a thought bubble – and you stay inside it. You'll want to look through them, but you can push 'em away with your eyes, too." He squared his shoulders and stepped into the parlor.

People stood in small groups or perched on folding chairs in rows facing the coffin, which was positioned in an alcove with heavy purple draperies. And over and through them all, faded ghosts drifted like a shimmering fog of shifting color, unseen by everyone else in the room.

I searched in my mind for a clear space and created a bubble that spread out and before me, pushing aside the clutter of images. Into that path I stepped, following behind my parents. We shuffled in line a few minutes, and the yammering ghosts receded behind the parlor walls. Eventually, we reached Sharon's dad standing before the casket. The rough contractor looked different, well-scrubbed now in his black suit.

"Mr. Rice, I'm real sorry," I said, and sidestepped, allowing Dad to move up. "These are my parents."

Dad gripped the hand offered, "Jim Krueger. Sorry for your loss," and Mom too introduced herself. "I'm Brian's mother. Our condolences to you," she said.

"Thanks," Mr. Rice said. "It's okay, though. My dad lived a full life –

anybody could see that. He worked hard and raised us the best he could, and he was retired a good long time. Seems he passed away peacefully in his sleep."

"It's good that he didn't suffer, then," Mom said.

"Yeah," said Dad. "I lost my Pops just last year, so...."

Mr. Rice nodded. "So you know how it is. We know we can't keep them forever ... but we still miss them, don't we?"

Sharon's mom rose from a plush sofa where she'd been talking quietly to Grandma Rice, who dabbed at her eyes with a tissue. We exchanged greetings, and each muttered some sympathies to the widow before turning to the coffin. The casket of red oak was polished to a satin sheen, covered with flowers. Grandpa Rice lay peaceful and still as a mannequin in a navy blue suit. His frizz of white hair had been managed into a thin fringe around the bald top of his head. The plump little hands that once worked on the railroad were folded over his torso. It was a thoughtful pose, but Grandpa was gone, pure and simple.

We found seats among the rows of folding chairs. I had just sat down when I spotted Sharon emerging from a back room with the rest of the kids in tow, busy with banter to keep them all in line. I stood up, but a chord of organ music signaled the beginning of the service. She saw me though, with some surprise, and acknowledged me with a nod and a quick smile before herding her flock into their seats.

The music sort of drifted from the heavens – or at least from the speakers in the ceiling tile – but it seemed to stifle the ghostly gibbering that pulsed at the edges of my "bubble." On my right, Dad sat tensed, eyes darting about. On my left, Mom crossed her legs and watched the mourners take their places. A drab-looking reverend stepped up to the lectern.

"Dearly beloved," he began. "We are gathered here today...." He was one of those men – you can't decide if they're youthful-looking middle-aged guys or young men just prematurely gray. The effect on him was accentuated by a gray mustache and a gray jacket over his parson's-collared shirt. He was definitely too young to be saying anything personal about Grandpa Rice. His comments were so vague you could tell he'd never met the guy. I suppose there's no harm in reading a few

Bible verses, as long as it's giving some comfort to the family. Then they came to what I guess is a standard at these things – even I was familiar with it, as rarely as I've been to a church – the 23rd Psalm. And I realized some lines had more meaning to me now:

"Yea, though I walk through the valley of the shadow of death, I will fear no evil," the pastor recited, and I thought, *Yeah, that was kind of the situation for Grandpa Rice when I saw him at the hospital. He knew then he was headed somewhere, someplace scary, but he wasn't afraid. That's the way we should all be.*

Thinking about that, I relaxed a bit, and before I knew it, the noisy spirits of the room had advanced again. Their twisted deathly projections crowded closer around me – flame and smoke, screeching metal, cold water, smothering earth and all the desperate longing for life. I stiffened in sudden terror and closed my eyes against the onslaught, barely keeping *things* from touching me. Some choking sound must have escaped because Mom flinched beside me. I felt Dad's hand on my knee.

"Then, good Lord, in Your kindness," prayed the parson, "open wide the door to Your kingdom: grant us a safe haven and peace at last. Amen."

"Amen," I echoed, while over me swirled a battalion of hopeless ghosts who refused to go through that door.

The service ended with the Lord's Prayer, and we were ushered out to the lobby. Sharon cast a look back at me as the family gathered before Grandpa's coffin. As they said their good-byes before the coffin lid was fastened, their minds could be at peace, completely unaware of the horde of restless spirits all around them.

In the lobby, we waited with the rest of the mourners for the coffin to be wheeled out. Dad nudged me and backed out the door. Mom sighed and grumbled, but a minute later I followed. He stood on the wet pavement of the parking lot with his face upturned, mouth open.

"Hey, you okay?" I called.

"Yeah, sure. How about you?"

"Okay," I said, walking up to him. "Dad, I gotta say it. You were right."

He laughed, and I saw the tension exhaled away. "I told you, didn't

I?"

"Lots of dead people."

"Lots! I'm telling you!" He reached out, his hand landing on my head to tousle my hair.

"I know what you and Uncle Bob said, but still there were a lot more than I thought there'd be."

"There was more than I thought, too," Dad grunted. "But you handled it okay?"

I nodded. "Yeah, thanks, that was good advice, pushing 'em back. That worked."

He smiled, but turned serious. "It doesn't always. These were weak. Or old. I don't know." He straightened. "You think you can manage the cemetery?"

"I can if *you* can."

He winced but squared his shoulders. "We can do it then."

We watched the pallbearers lift the coffin to the back of the hearse. A few of the older godchildren had that duty, and I recognized crazy neighbor Mustache Mike, too. The Rices, with Grandma hobbling along, moved off to one limousine, while Sharon ushered her brothers and sisters into another.

***

Mom let me drive to the cemetery. She might have noticed I was a bit rattled, but I'm sure she didn't realize why. I was still trying to process everything I'd experienced in the chapel, but I got behind the wheel of the Jeep and joined the line of funeral cars. After the hearse and the limos, we were at the tail end of a dozen other vehicles gliding through traffic signals and stop signs.

Winston Cemetery borders North Park. I'd seen it from the Prairie Path. We passed between the flagstone gate posts and down one of a few lanes that fanned out from the entrance past the snapping flags of the war memorial. The procession eased to a stop as funeral directors waved the cars to the side. We got out and followed others converging on the grave, some sticking to the paved road and others, like us, taking to the grass, flowing among the tombstones.

The moment I stepped out of the car, I felt a strange buzz and sensed a sort of a low murmur, but didn't *see* any spiritual projections like the ones in the funeral parlor. I turned back to Dad, who was tottering among the plots.

"What *is* this…this *vibe*?" I asked.

He stopped and looked up. "I don't know. It's not…." He shook his head.

The site wasn't quite ready. Two rumpled gravediggers were just setting short brass railings in place and edging the muddy hole with curbs of some green turf-like stuff. They struggled in the wind to set up a canopy, clanking aluminum poles and driving steel stakes into the soft earth. About two dozen of us milled about while the family stayed in the limos with the engines running. Mom sighed impatiently and strolled down a row of gravestones. I followed along.

We stopped where two paths met in a green plaza of close-cropped grass, enclosed by trimmed hedges. In the center, a tall stone monument supported a pair of carved cherubs. Mom looked down. "This is so sad," she said. "These two little ones both died the same day, look."

She pointed to a pair of identical marble markers side by side, with similar inscriptions: Jonathon Brandt, Charles Brandt, birth dates indicating ages of six and eight, with the same date of death, August fourteenth.

"My God," she marveled, "here's another one!"

An arc of the small stones fronted the tall column. Etched in the broad marble base was the outline of a train, and a list of names to match the twelve identical stones: William Garth, Anthony Franz, Amelia Grover, Cynthia Stolz, Adam Tesko, David Kelly…. There were twelve children who died the same day, and without looking up at the inscription on the monument, I knew what had happened that summer night of August fourteenth, when the sunset had faded and the darkness of Roosevelt Marsh exploded into fiery death.

The thrumming of light and color was rising in my consciousness. I looked back to my father, who had stopped at the edge of the garden square. I let my mother walk on. "Dad?"

He raised both his hands as if pushing away the rising tide. "No, Brian, there's nothing here..."

"But –"

"I know what you're getting – but it's not coming from here. I just got a bad feeling...." He backed away until his feet found the pavement.

"Brian," Mom called. "They're starting."

She and I strode across the cemetery to the grave, where the pallbearers were just setting the oak coffin in place above the gaping hole. The family scuffed to their folding chairs under the flapping canopy, and the other mourners huddled under the shelter. Mom and I edged in at the back. The gravediggers ambled over behind the canvas and lit cigarettes. The younger guy, in a metal band tee shirt, hawked and spit, while his older companion plunked with a grunt onto a neighboring tombstone.

The minister took his place at the head of the coffin, his gray hair standing on end in the wind.

"Friends and family of this our departed brother..." he began. His voice couldn't carry, though, and most of his words just blew away. "We appeal, Lord, to Your boundless mercy, grant to the soul of your servant Albert a kindly welcome, cleansing of sin, release from the chains of death...."

Someone sniffled. The rumble of a motorcycle carried from Jewel Road. The gravediggers stared out at nothing as the preacher droned on. "God of all consolation, open our hearts to your word, so that we may comfort one another, finding light in a time of darkness...."

Well, I thought, *Grandpa Rice saw the light – he told me so himself.* Either he must have had a touch of sensitivity, or the ghost of Jamie McVay had such a powerful need that he could reach through to anyone.

"Because God has chosen to call our brother Albert from this life unto himself, we commit his body to the earth, for we are dust and unto dust, we shall return...."

Sharon's mom and dad helped Grandma Rice up, escorting her to the edge of the grave, where they each placed a red rose on the polished oak of the coffin. Then after a silent few seconds, the undertaker stepped up and made some remarks. The pallbearers laid their gloves among the roses on the lid of the coffin, and the mourners turned back to the cars. Sharon had a firm grip on the two younger boys, while Allen and Christine watched her to see what to do next. They followed the grown-ups back to their limo, but Sharon walked back to meet us at the curb.

"Hi, Brian, Mrs. Krueger," she said. "Thanks for coming to the funeral. It means a lot."

"Oh, Sharon," Mom answered, grasping Sharon's offered hand with both of hers. "I'm so sorry for you and your family."

"Will you come to the restaurant for lunch? It's just down the road here."

"No, Sweetie, I'm sorry, but I've got to get to work – and Brian should get to school, you know."

"Oh, sure."

"Yeah," I said, "Mom already called Attendance and told them I'd be there this afternoon."

"In fact," Mom added, "I should get going now. Don't be long, Brian." She turned away and headed back to the car.

A few people lingered at the grave site, while the workers flicked their cigarettes onto the dirt pile and began cranking the coffin down into the pit.

"Ohhhh-kay," Sharon sighed.

"Jeez, you'd think they could wait until the family left."

"Yeah, but –" she shrugged. "I guess they don't want to hang around here any longer than we do."

"Hey, Sharon, I just wanted to say –"

"You don't have to say anything. I was stupid to pick a fight with you."

"Well, that's the thing – I should have been more ... realistic ... and understanding. I know you can't see the things that ... that I see in my own mind."

She smiled. "The things you see in your own mind? That's a good one, Brian. I like it! I'll buy it!" She laughed, and a whole bunch of tension just disappeared from her face.

I smiled and looked around awkwardly. "Well, you better go."

"Yeah, I better." She reached out and clutched my hand. "You, too, school-boy! Where's your dad? I saw him at the funeral home."

I turned toward the car, where Mom stood at the door. But the car was empty; Dad wasn't inside.

A couple of hundred feet away, across the lane from the Marsh Disaster Monument, he was hunched over looking at a tombstone. I saw him straighten, put his hands over his ears and bend backward. At the same instant, a silent explosion burst from the ground at his feet, an expanding circle of cold fire that flash-froze my brain and burned white in my eyes, rolling through me and Sharon, too. Instantly, with a screeching, like steel wheels on a train track, it all contracted – light, sound, heat and cold – everything sucked into a vortex that vanished where my father lay in a heap on the ground. A smell of sulfur lingered in my nostrils. Sharon yanked her hand from my arm and, wide-eyed, staggered away.

"Dad!" I raced over, hurdling headstones. He was curled on his side with his knees drawn up, sobbing and gasping. I slid to the wet grass and clasped his shoulder.

"What's wrong? Dad! What's the matter?"

His eyes rolled, unseeing, and he kicked out as though scrambling from a pit of quicksand. Sucking in a deep breath, he howled like a wounded animal. Mom, running up, stopped short at the sound, then fell to her knees at his side. "Jim!"

Mustache Mike jogged up, with the younger grave digger right behind him.

"What's this?" Mike asked. He locked eyes on me. "What's the situation?"

"He just – fell," I muttered. Mom plucked at Dad's coat, loosening his tie and unbuttoning his shirt. His face looked like every drop of blood had drained out of him, and he whimpered pitifully.

"I'm calling 911," Mike said, pulling his phone from a pocket. "What's his name? Jim?"

I nodded and stood, helpless. Mike leaned down to put his face close in front of Dad's.

"Jim! Just relax a minute, Jim, and we'll see what's the matter."

Dad flailed out, pushing my mother back, and he floundered a moment, ending up on all fours, panting like a dog.

"Take it easy, Jim!" Mike scolded. "We'll have an ambulance here in a minute."

"No!" Dad gasped, looking up. "No, I'll be all right!" With a grunt, he turned and eased over to sit. His breathing was fast, but the color had come back into his face. He inhaled long and deep, and exhaled, leaning back against the tombstone.

"What happened?" Mr. Rice and Sharon had come over. She sidled over to me, mouth open, keeping an eye on Dad.

"I'm okay," my father told him, and blew out another breath of relief with puffed cheeks. "I just ... tripped, is all. May have hurt my knee."

Mike squatted to peer closely at him, then looked up at Mr. Rice. "He *does* look okay, I guess." Standing, he stepped up to Sharon's dad and with his hand close in front of him, pantomimed swigging from a bottle. "You go ahead, man," he told him.

"All right," Mr. Rice said. "Maybe you can help...."

"Yeah, yeah, I got this."

"Okay, Jim, you take it easy, now." Mr. Rice looked over at Sharon and inclined his head toward the waiting cars.

"I'm coming," she said, turning back to pat me on the arm. "Bri, we've *got* to talk. I – I'll see you la–" She froze, glancing up at me and back down again. "Oh, wow."

I followed her gaze to my father, who had bent over, and to the knee-high granite tombstone behind him, and to the name inscribed in the gray stone.

Dad sat trembling on the grave of Jamie McVay.

CHAPTER TWENTY-SIX

Nobody spoke on the way home from the cemetery, but when we pulled up on the driveway, Mom turned to me. "You better stay here and keep an eye on your father. Call me if anything changes."

She backed out, and when we walked into the house, Dad made straight for the fridge. *Well, nothing ever changes*, I thought. But he didn't open the door. He just stood there with his eyes closed, hanging on to the handle. After a couple minutes, his hand slid all the way to the bottom of the bar, and he lurched to the sink. His hands shook as he ran cold water and splashed some onto his face.

"You sure you're all right?"

He sighed, "Yeah, I guess so. Tired. I might just sit a while, maybe take a nap." He draped his suit coat and tie over an arm of the couch and flopped into the La-Z-Boy.

"You going to tell me what happened?" I asked. "At the grave?"

He looked at me and worked his mouth without speaking.

"Well?" I said. "I know something happened. But what happened to *you*?"

He let his chin drop to his chest. "I don't know, Brian. I never – I'll tell you, if that's what your ghost has been showing you, then ... I'm so sorry! That's as bad as I've ever... *felt*." He closed his eyes and sat back deep in the chair.

I backed out and made my own 911 call. I told Uncle Bob everything.

"Jeez, Kid. Okay, I'll come over after supper. Want me to bring something?"

"No," I said. "Mom left us some frozen enchiladas to heat up. There's enough for you, too, if you want."

I was okay with staying home from school. I put together a PB&J and sat in the kitchen, thinking – about everything I 'd seen this day, from the ghosts at the funeral home to the experience in the cemetery. I could definitely see the difference between the "weak" spirits projecting their woes to anyone who might feel them – and Jamie McVay, on the other hand, just *blasting* people like us with his personal horrors. But why? Why show it to anybody? Why show it to Dad, or to me? Is it just because we can see it? Because we're sensitive? But others sometimes claim to have seen the ghosts, like Grandpa Rice, and –

Sharon. What had *she* seen? She'd been holding my arm, and I knew she felt something when the wave came from Jamie McVay. I didn't know *what* – I could hardly understand it myself, so what could *she* make of it? One thing for sure – she couldn't deny it. She would know for sure that I was telling the truth.

After a while, I peeked back in on Dad. He wasn't sleeping – just lying there with his eyes open, staring at the wall. I left him alone and went to my room to read – or try to.

I'd just about given up on that when the doorbell rang. Standing at the door was Mustache Mike with his beady eyes and suspicious look.

"I just came to check on your dad. How's he doing?"

"Uh, okay, I guess. He's lying down."

"Yeah, I'll bet. Lemme see him." He barged in through the half-open door.

I followed him into the family room, where he stood looking at Dad, who did a double-take at the stranger in front of him. "Who –?"

"Mike. Across the street?"

"Oh? Listen, thanks for helping me out this morning, back at the . . . ." Mike and the gravedigger had half-carried him to the car and stuffed him in.

"No problem. How you doin' now?"

"Uh, fine, I guess."

Mike sat on the couch, looking at him, nodding. "Good, good," he said.

"Um, Mike," I asked, "you want a beer or something? "

He didn't look up. "Nah. I been sober for seven years now."

"Really," Dad said, which wasn't so much a question as a *That's nice, now leave me alone.*

Mike just sat there.

"Well, Mike," I said. "You do a lot of work on cars, huh?"

He grinned, showing a lot of teeth behind the bushy mustache. "Yeah, that's my thing. I work on cars, small engines, whatever you got."

"Oh, sure," Dad remembered. "You're the guy with all the cars in the driveway!"

"Maybe you could take a look at our lawn mower," I suggested. "I'm always having trouble with it."

"Yeah, glad to." He stood up and looked out through the smudgy patio doors, then turned back to study the house – the stained carpet, dusty furniture, the beer cans on the kitchen counter. He gave Dad a pitiful look. "Well," he said.

"Well," Dad answered, rising to the challenge.

Mike aimed a serious look down his long nose. "I just wanted to say: I've been where you been. Or maybe, where you are."

Dad stared. "I doubt that," he said. "But thanks for the thought."

"Uh-huh. Now listen: I used to hit the sauce myself, so we can cut the bullshit." He glanced over at me and offered a crooked smile. "I just wanta say, if you ever need to talk about it, you know, I'm a good listener. Like I said, I been sober for seven years and counting. I'm offering to help."

Dad studied him, made some kind of decision and cleared his throat. "Well you know, I'm supposed to go to a program of some kind. AA or something. I got a little problem of a DUI."

Mike nodded. "I can help you there. I'm over at the Congregational Church in Winston. I been a regular there at the meetings."

"How about that," Dad laughed. Both men relaxed.

"How about some water?" I asked.

"Sure," Mike agreed, and took a sip from the glass I handed him.

"Sorry, we don't have any bottled."

"Ahh! Good old well water. Can't beat it!"

"This water stinks," I said. "Literally."

"Yeah, smells like rotten eggs," Mike said. "I know. But I grew up on it, right on this block. The water softener helps take the odor out – and all the taste, too."

"Yeah," I said, "the taste of rusty iron and dirt."

"It's not that bad," Dad muttered. "We've got a softener, but it's broke. I should fix it. My wife complains that everything is getting rust-stained."

"Yeah, that's the main problem. You know what's wrong with it?"

"Not a clue."

"What do you do? For a living?"

"Do? Factory work. I've been looking for something near here, but so far no luck."

I must have made a noise, because Dad shot me an indignant look.

Mike nodded. "Yeah, it's tough going these days. I work in manufacturing myself. I'm kind of a mechanic."

Dad nodded, "Well … I've done a lot of different factory work – assembly, machine operator – but I been out of it for a while now."

"Hey, you should fill out an application where I work. We're looking for a guy."

"Yeah, where do you work?"

"Woodland Plastics," Mike said, "over towards Rte. 56."

I busted out laughing, and Dad smiled. "Yeah, I know that place."

Mike folded his arms across his chest, bristling a bit until we explained how Dad had gone over there and left without even trying. "It didn't seem there was a chance in hell … ."

"I can tell you," Mike said, "*none* of the guys we hired in the last two months have been worth their salt. We're getting people who don't know which end of a screwdriver to use."

Mike had a way of making things happen by sheer force of will, and somebody like Dad, hesitating on a fence all the time, had to jump to one side or another. By the time Mike left, Dad had agreed to go to the next AA meeting.

A while later, after we'd had dinner, Uncle Bob showed up with a half a cake wrapped up in tinfoil. I put some coffee on, and we all sat in the kitchen waiting for it to finish.

Uncle Bob squeezed Dad on the back of his neck. "So, you had a rough one today, huh?"

"Rough enough," Dad said.

"Brian's ghost, the railroad conductor?"

Dad nodded, head hanging over his arms on the table.

I described the scene to Uncle Bob. "All these years – Jamie McVay is buried a stone's throw from the Marsh Disaster Memorial and the graves of those kids. No wonder he's … tormented. And Dad was standing right on his grave."

"That could've been – um, intense!" Uncle Bob agreed.

"Oh, and there's another thing. My friend Sharon got a taste of it."

"What? How?"

"She was – uh, holding my hand or arm when I felt a wave of – feelings, or whatever – from Jamie McVay. And I'm pretty sure she felt – saw – the same thing I did."

"And what was that?"

"Ask Dad. He got the full dose." We both looked at my father expectantly.

He rubbed his hands over his face and sighed. "I felt like I'd been grabbed by the balls and dipped in hellfire." He shuddered.

We sat, absorbing that, until Uncle Bob shook his head. "Well, let's assume your little girlfriend didn't experience it *quite* that way."

"Ha ha. But, even so…."

"Jimmy? What'd you see, in particular?"

"Ah, it all came so fast! Bobby, you know, it's like – like a ball of life and you're inside it."

"I get it," said Uncle Bob. "You see a whole history – as if time isn't in an orderly line, you know, it's all at once."

"Yeah, all at once, and I saw what he did – the train, running through the marsh, the wreck of the trains and the fire – Jesus, the burning kids!"

"And Jamie McVay, his feelings, too, right?" I put in, remembering the desperation and the guilt. "His thoughts and feelings, what I saw…."

"What was in his mind when he died."

"Yeah, the mind of a miserable drunk! And what I saw was so... *hopeless*!"

"And what's hopeless," Uncle Bob suggested, "that's what McVay wants?"

"Yeah. Well. What he *needs*...to get out of his personal hell? To somehow undo it or to make up for it some way. To save them ... or to save *somebody*."

"Anybody he can," I said, thinking about Grandpa Rice on a scaffold, and Mr. Niederman's uncle in the path of a runaway train, and – a bunch of kids on bikes in the dark. And maybe even me, thinking suicidal thoughts on the railroad bridge in Winston.

"So, you think your girlfriend felt everything?" Uncle Bob asked.

"No doubt about it."

"Well, now she'll believe you. That's what you wanted, isn't it?"

"It is. I think. But now what?"

"I'll tell you," Dad said. "Even if she got a 'dose of the ghost', she won't believe it. She'll keep thinking about it and trying to make sense of it, and little by little she'll convince herself that it was all in her imagination – because *you* put the idea in her head."

"The power of suggestion?" Uncle Bob said.

"Yeah."

"But – how can she deny the fact that something ... *supernatural* happened?"

"Believe me, Brian, it's better if she doesn't. If you ever expect to live a normal life. Am I right?"

Uncle Bob reluctantly agreed. "Your dad's probably right. I mean, I don't worry about it, and I try not to get all upset if I *do* run into a spirit. But if your Aunt Margie was in on it, she'd always be making more of it, and reminding me about it all the time, and – it would be a much bigger deal."

"A bigger deal than being roasted in the fires of hell?" I asked.

Uncle Bob laughed. "That reminds me," he said. "Let's have some of that cake. It's Devil's Food!"

We sat in the kitchen and finished the cake, and then the coffee. It made Dad jumpy. After his brother left, Dad stalked around, restless.

Then he sat for a while watching TV. Then he turned the set off and sat there in the dark drumming his fingers on the arms of the chair.

The doorbell rang once more. Dad jumped. "Jeez, what is this tonight? "

I could see through the sidelight that it was Sharon. "Come in."

She saw Dad in the family room. "Oh. Hi, Mr. Krueger. How are you feeling?"

"Fine, fine." He said, standing. He paced back and forth between the family room and dining room.

"How's *your* dad doing?" I asked. "and your grandma?"

"Oh, you know, she's...." Sharon shrugged her shoulders. "She'll manage. You hate to say it, but she might do better now. It's been wearing her out taking care of him since his stroke."

"Yeah, I can see how that might be."

The two of us stood there in the kitchen, shifting about uncomfortably. Now I know what they mean when they say there's an elephant in the room. "Why don't we go for a walk?" I suggested. "We can talk better outside."

"Ohhh-kay," Sharon sighed.

I grabbed my sweatshirt and called to Dad, "I'm just going out with Sharon, to walk her back home, all right?"

"Yeah, yeah, go on. You guys go ahead – and talk."

"You all right?"

"Yeah, I'll be fine."

I opened the patio door to step out into the yard. Sharon followed, but hesitated at the driveway. "Let's go back the other way," she said, "around the block. Vincenzi and Wagner are hanging out there on his deck, and I don't feel like dealing with them right now."

We walked past the front of our house and down the street, our feet crunching gravel along the shoulder. The night had cleared up, and a few stars shone through between the black shapes of the big maples. There was a lot to talk about, and we both knew it, but now that we were alone, it seemed unnecessary somehow – we understood each other without all the words.

Finally, Sharon spoke. "That was something, there, at the cemetery."

"Yep."

"Something weird happened, didn't it?"

"Yep."

"You're a complete weirdo, aren't you?"

"Nope."

She sighed. "You know, my rational-self tells me that it was just some kind of a mind trick. I keep trying to figure out how you did it."

"I'm just the player," I told her. "I don't write the music."

"Hmph. And the music is coming from...?"

"Dead people."

"Dead people broadcast twisted visions of hell? How am I supposed to wrap my mind around that?"

"Just go with it, Sharon. Just accept it, like I do – like I *have* to."

"But, how can you? How do you keep on doing everyday stuff, when you know... *that's* going on? Doesn't it *change* everything?"

I thought for a bit. "No," I decided, "not really. I thought the same way, that it must *have* to, you know? But – life *does* go on, doesn't it? You still want to have the best kind of life that you can, and you can't worry about what comes after that."

We rounded the corner and approached the Rice's house. "I guess you're right," Sharon said. "What can you do, anyway?" She stopped on the front walk. "Let's try to have the best kind of life."

"And not worry," I added.

"Yeah, not worry," she laughed. "Well, at least it's going to be a short week now."

"True – I've got a CC meet tomorrow, and the Invitational is Saturday."

"And then it's Halloween! Got any plans?"

"Like what, you guys go trick-or-treating around here?"

"Why not? And, you can help us with the Spook Trail at Crosby Park. It's for Christine's Girl Scouts."

"Help do what?"

"Hmm, I suppose you don't want to dress up as the Ghost of Jamie McVay?"

"Are you kidding?"

"Hmm, ohh-kay, not the best idea. But you can come anyway."

"Is this like a date?"

She laughed again, and quick as a bird leaned up to kiss me on the cheek. "Sure, why not?" she said and flitted up the stairs.

Starry-eyed, I walked back home the usual way. I regretted it when I heard the commotion from the Pyro's. Pete and his crew danced around his yard popping beer cans and spraying each other with foam. Seeing me, Pete strolled over to the street. "Hey, Krueger," he cackled, "Your old man's freakin' out!"

Wagner pranced over grinning. "He comes out on the patio in his underwear with a couple six-packs. Then he starts heavin' cans out in the yard, yelling and shit."

"Freaking out," Melkovec chuckled. He gulped from a foaming can, yelled, "Here, catch!" and abruptly lined one at my head.

Ducking, I said, "What are you complaining about? Enjoy!"

"Heh-heh." Squinting at the ground, he snatched up a bottle and lofted it in my direction. Not beer but gasoline spewed out. I backed away fast, but still got a few drops splashed on me.

"What the hell! You moron!"

"Oh, yeah?" Melkovec stood up and made to charge at me, until Wagner stepped in between. "I'm a moron? I'll tell you who a moron is!" He pushed with his burly chest against Rick, who laughed but put some effort into holding him back. "A moron is somebody who gets in our way!"

"Yeah, baby!" Pete howled.

"Anybody messes with *us* is a moron!"

"Tell him, man!"

"Coach Nelson found out! He found out at Homecoming!"

Wagner shoved him hard. "Shut up, Bill!" He wasn't laughing now.

Pete pointed his finger at me, and he wasn't laughing either. "Yeah, you just remember, Kroo-gler." He got right in my face with his long nose. "Stay outa our business!"

I kept backing away and through the trees into my own yard.

"Hey, Krueger!" Rick yelled after me. "Tell your old man we'll be back here tomorrow night, too – in case he wants to throw some more brewskies our way!"

CHAPTER TWENTY-SEVEN

The Prairie Path had changed over the weeks. Dry leaves gusted through skeleton trees with just a thin veil of brown and yellow clinging to the shrubbery below. Fallen leaves carpeted the gravel, soft underfoot. Jogging along, I remembered my first time on the trail, that night I had argued with Dad and gone running off blind. That was the night I'd first seen the ghost of Jamie McVay and when I collided in my mind with that phantom train.

Things had sure changed with Dad. We were getting along now. He was staying sober, so far, with Mustache Mike as his sponsor. He was just finishing his first week at Woodland Plastics, and Mike was even driving him to work. Not only that, but we were talking about buying one of the old beaters lined up in Mike's driveway, a mid-sized Buick we could pay off in installments. With a clear head, a job and a paycheck, Dad was a different person. It was hard on him – and sometimes on us – but he was trying.

I was trying to be better, too – not aggravating him, helping out around the house, particulary now that cross-country was over with. I finished the J-V season one of the top runners, which wasn't too shabby. Next year our varsity would be a real force in the conference. I had to laugh at the Me that just a couple months ago dreamed of being a big man on the football team. But now I kind of liked the nerds on CC, like Kenny and Ray. Yeah, I'd made a few friends. And the most important one was Sharon.

Jogging off the path at Jewel Road, I slowed to a saunter on the sidewalk, swinging my arms and feeling good. The windows of houses along the road were taped up with kids' Halloween decorations: witches pasted together out of black triangles with paper plate faces; raggedy shapes with tails and eyes must have been black cats. Here and there ghosts – sheets with soccer ball heads – swung from trees, sailing high and free in the wind. Jack-o-lanterns leered gap-toothed from windows and nestled among gourds below cornstalks tied to lamp posts.

I felt just like one of those grinning pumpkins – monstrously happy with my eyes all lit up. I was on my way to meet Sharon at Crosby Park, and to help Christine's scout group with the Spook Trail. What could be better than Sharon and me in the dark of the woods on Halloween Night?

The old train station and the caboose were dimly lit with jack-o-lanterns, and a string of orange lights shone over a long line of people waiting for their turn to be scared to death. Somebody in a gruesome mask, wearing a lab smock spattered with red paint, popped out of the bushes snarling just as I stepped through the gate. "Get to the end of the line!" he growled.

"Whoa! I'm here to help out. Do you know where Sharon Rice is?"

"She's over by the caboose, I think."

Couples, groups of teenagers, and families with little kids paid their admission at the ticket kiosk and set off into the dark. Murder scenes of blood and gore were staged in and around the station building. Then the trail twisted through the thicket of trees and brush bordering the park. Every so often some ghoulish character would come screaming out of the dark. Zombies moaned eerily and lurched from behind sheds and animal cages. I felt sorry for the poor beasts – they must have wondered who actually ought to be locked up tonight.

I followed the faintly glowing gravel path to the caboose and Sharon. She wore a long, lacy black robe and a peaked black hat right out of the Wizard of Oz as she directed people up and in one side of the caboose platform, where they paused to look in before hopping down the other side.

"Boo!" I yelled and grabbed her around the waist.

She jumped. "Oh! Brian!" she yelped and spun in a circle. "You!" She laughed, collected her wits, and gestured to a family approaching with a kid in a Bat Man costume. "Step right up," she intoned in a movie-gypsy voice "and behold the dark horrors of the vampire's lair."

"The vampire's hair?" I asked.

She struck a pose with upraised chin, giving her head a movie-star toss, and flounced the green wig of hair snarling out from under the witch's hat like moldy spaghetti. "You like?" On closer inspection, she might have been some Euro-trash sci-fi punk rocker, with long nails, a silver face, and blood-red lipstick.

"I like!" The black robe was a gauzy affair, draped over the shoulders of her skin-tight, low-cut top.

"You're late!" she hissed, staying in character. "You will suffer many torments for this!"

"Oh, yuk!" the woman on the platform said, and they hustled their kid away. For the moment, no one waited to step up, so I did and peeked in. Jack-o-lanterns grinned on the window sills, and a black light bathed the interior of the caboose with an ethereal glow. In the middle of the floor an open coffin gaped, and Dracula himself clawed at the sides, struggling with the bloody stake in his heart. I recognized the vampire as a guy from my Spanish class.

"*Muy bien, Humberto*!" I called, and ducked back down to Sharon. "This guy's got potential. A little dramatic, though. I'm not sure he's quite captured the essence of the character."

"You can do better, I suppose?"

I staggered toward her clutching my chest. "You have put a stake through my heart, *Mi Querida!*"

"Yes," she said, "because you are a monster!" Skipping away to intercept an oncoming couple, she called back, "Now go act the part! You can get a mask from Mrs. Harris at the concession stand."

Scout leader Harris dug up a rubbery zombie mask that I fit over my head. It smelled a little pukey. She assured me it was all in my mind.

Maybe so. It looked nasty, putrifying and disgusting enough to get reactions from victims of all ages. My assignment was to first startle visitors to the "vampire's lair" and then encourage them down the steps and along the spook trail to the next attraction. I had fun throwing a scare into people, especially some I knew, confident they wouldn't recognize me. I got to terrorize some brats who thought they were too old to be scared, like Sharon's brother Allen. Creeping up on him and some of his wise-guy buddies as they came up to the caboose, I served up my most blood-curdling shriek, bounding out of the dark, and sent them scattering and peeing their pants.

I also gave special attention to cases such as Vincenzi's girl Carla. When she and her skanky girlfriends stopped on the path to light up smokes, I spooked them off the path and into the raspberry bushes, where I hoped Carla would find some poison ivy to match her personality. But the best thing was sneaking back to grab Sharon so we could laugh and talk like more than just good friends.

The Spook Trail closed at ten o'clock, and then we helped clean up, break down the scenes of horror and pack up the sets and props. Meanwhile, Mrs. Harris, with Christine and the other scouts, set themselves up for the Halloween sleepover in the caboose.

"Bet they don't get much sleep tonight," I said.

Christine squealed, "No! We're gonna tell spooky stories. Hey!" She jumped up and yelled to the rest of the group. "Brian and Sharon can tell us the best ghost story!"

In seconds we were surrounded by a dozen screaming, bouncing ten-year-old girls, all pleading for us to scare the pajamas off them. "Go ahead," Sharon nudged me, "be a sport. Tell 'em the tale of the Ghost of Jamie McVay."

"Yay!"

"Ghost stories!"

"The Ghost of Jamie McVay!"

"Aww, I don't know..." It didn't seem right. Jamie McVay didn't die on the railroad for the merriment of a bunch of overstimulated girl scouts. He wasn't just a story. He was a real person. He and I *knew* each other. In some way I didn't understand, we were ... allies.

Mrs. Harris turned off the lights, leaving only the orange glow of the jack-o-lanterns. Sharon somehow got the girls to shut up and listen. "Let's all settle down and snuggle up together." At this, she put an arm around my waist, while the girls giggled and huddled close on the benches and floor. Sharon pulled me by the belt to sit beside her on a cot near the door. "Hear me now," she said, reverting to the voice of the gypsy witch, "and know the tragic tale of Jamie McVay." Leaning in close, she looked up at me expectantly. What could I do?

It all rushed through my mind, everything I'd learned about the sad ghost of a man, all the pieces of his life at the end – the villain, the hero, the father, the drunk. What could I tell an audience of children? Maybe it was just a tale with a moral.

"Jamie McVay was a railroad man," I began. I portrayed the friendly man with the kind smile, who cracked wise with the passengers and knew all the regulars, how proud he was to wear the uniform, how seriously he took his job, and how he went home every day tired but happy to see his own little girl. "But that one night he was careless," I told them. Christine squirmed, eyes big as jack-o-lanterns, her feet jiggling away. The other girls glanced around at each other nervously.

I described the excursion train broken down above the marsh, the restless kids tired from their picnic at the river. Jamie McVay sets out down the tracks with his lantern, to warn any oncoming trains. Yes, he is careless, and "tired," I tell them, and in my mind, I see my own father slumped in the La-Z-Boy. Jamie McVay "takes a nap" and lets his signal light go out. And when the freight train passes him by at the Pleasant Hill Station (yes, this very building outside) how he races in desperation through the marsh, stumbling and floundering in the muck to warn them, but too late, too late! The crash, the fire, the screams....

The girls in the dark caboose had stopped fidgeting. Eyes wide and mouths open, they hung on every word. I described the scene as if I'd been there, because I had...I had seen it in my mind...the smoke, the flames, Jamie McVay rushing into the burning cars to save trapped children, pulling survivors from the wreckage. And I condensed the tale, omitting the suicide and making up a final scene to match the legend: McVay later that night, crushed with despair, plodding down the tracks in a trance, still clutching his darkened signal lantern, blind to the morning train approaching from the Winston roundhouse. At the last second the engineer sees him, rings his bell and blows the whistle, "but it's no use," I say. "Jamie McVay was crushed under the wheels of the four a.m. milk train."

"And they never found his head," Christine somberly declared at my knee. The entire group exhaled at once, with vague mutterings and a few whimpers of confusion.

"Well..." Mrs. Harris breathed.

But Sharon wasn't done. "That is so," she continued in her spooky voice. "And that is why, on cold, windy nights in October – like this very night – you might sometimes see strange sights and hear strange sounds on the Prairie Path and in the dark, musty marsh." She gripped my forearm and gave it a squeeze, peering up at me, pausing in anticipation.

I thought again of the restless spirit on the trail. What was he looking for? "Yes," I intoned, joining into the weirdness of the moment, "some nights – like this very night – you might see a flickering red light – like the light of a railroad man's antique signal lantern – wavering as it moves along … across the marsh … down the path … seeking – some *thing… searching… coming closer… closer… calling "where?" … "where?" coming closer… closer… calling … "where… is… my… HEAD!"* and that instant I lunged to squeeze Christine in the ribs.

Pandemonium erupted inside the caboose. Christine squealed and tumbled backward; ponytailed heads recoiled against the walls amid screams and other such carrying-on. Poor Mrs. Harris staggered with both hands over her heart, while Sharon fell back on the cot and rolled on her side gasping with laughter.

"All right, now," the scout leader wheezed, "settle down, now."

A loud thump at the back door shook the car, and the place went silent. No one moved as we all stared and strained to hear. A chain rattled and clattered. Something dragged across the railroad ties outside. Footsteps crunched on the gravel and clomped up the stairs to the platform, where someone panted just outside the door. The scowling face of Mr. Freund appeared in the doorway.

"Back door's chained up," he puffed, and scanned the pale faces regarding him. He looked surprised to see me there, narrowing his eyes and giving a nod.

The girls huddled around and stared at him in alarm.

"Don't forget to lock *this* door," he said. "If you need something, I'll be staying in the barn. Have a good night," he muttered over his shoulder as he left.

Mrs. Harris called out from the back, "Don't worry, we're safe and secure here, Mr. Freund!"

"Oh, man!" Sharon exclaimed. "I'm gonna get it if I'm not home pretty soon."

"Don't you kids have a ride coming for you?" asked the scout leader.

"My Mom's coming to pick us up," I lied.

Sharon started to say something, but Christine came up whining, pulling on her sister's witch gown. The two of them put their heads together, whispering. I sidled out of the caboose and stood waiting below at the steps of the old station. Mrs. Harris came out, eyeballing me suspiciously.

"You're going straight home, right?" she asked.

"Of course." I made a show of looking toward the parking lot. "My Mom should be here any minute."

Sharon came out and edged past Mrs. Harris, giving me a skeptical look the woman couldn't see. "I called home," she said, "to let Mom and Dad know we're on our way. But Christine says she's still scared, so I gave her my phone and told her she could call if she got nervous overnight."

"How're you going to answer if she's got your phone, Genius?"

She socked me on the arm. "She'll call the home phone, Genius! We'll be home in a minute, anyway."

A commotion broke out inside the caboose, and Mrs. Harris turned to go in. "You're sure?"

"We'll be fine, Mrs. Harris, honest," Sharon assured her.

"Mom'll be here in a minute – we'll go wait for her up there," I said, and the two of us strolled towards the entrance. Freund had locked the gate, but we easily clambered over into the parking lot. I glanced at the barn, where I imagined the old man pulling up the blankets on his cot. Out at the street, I took Sharon by the hand, and the two of us scampered off down Jewel Road.

Laughing and panting, Sharon grabbed my arm. "What is going on?"

"We're walking home, that's all. My mom's not coming."

"Ohhh-kay." She nodded and grinned. "Walking home."

"That's all right, isn't it? I thought it'd be nice."

"Nice," she agreed, and away we went.

CHAPTER TWENTY-EIGHT

I'd never known it before, but ... there's something about a warm girl that takes the chill out of an October wind. There's a light in her eyes that'll brighten up the darkest Halloween night. We strolled along nice and slow, just me and Sharon in a world of windblown leaves, jack-o-lanterns with flickering candles, and ghostly sheets flapping among the trees.

We left the street lamps and car headlights behind, stepping off onto the gravel path. From here just a few house lights twinkled far off through creaking branches. The Prairie Path was a black tunnel, a tunnel of love just for us, and we both stopped at the same time – for the same reason. It was the perfect place for a kiss. I wrapped my arms around Sharon's body and just lost myself in that kiss, just floated there in that warm pool of love, letting the heat soak in deeper and deeper until the fever burned in my heart.

And with the heat came a trembling from the ground, and a droning that welled up from everywhere at once, with a scuff of metal on hot metal, and it wasn't just the kiss. Sharon looked up at me with wonder in her big blue eyes, just as it hit. The phantom train slammed over us, a blast of icy wind with all the clatter of steel wheels on rails and fire-flash strobing the trees.

The bell clanged and dulled, the rhythmic rattle faded, and the biting electric smoke blew away.

Sharon stared, trembling. "I gotta sit down," she gasped.

We both sat on a rotting railroad tie just off the trail, looking back toward the reality of traffic on Jewel Road.

"This is what you ..." Sharon murmured, and looked at me for reassurance. "The train...."

"It's like I told you."

"Oh, I know you told me," she said with a shake of her head, "but this, this is for real!"

"Real enough in our own minds, I guess."

"Brian," Sharon lowered her voice to a whisper, "it came and went like a real train!"

"I *told* you."

"It went right *through* us!" she hissed. She turned, peering down the path. Her eyes grew larger, and she grasped my hand. "Now, what?"

I followed her gaze.

A red ember glimmered now where the apparition had vanished. As we looked, it brightened and took shape: the glowing red lens of an old-time oil lantern. And faintly, as if sketched by an unseen hand, first materialized the fingers that gripped the bail, and then the arm, and then the outlined form of a man – shifting, fading and reappearing, a small man, a desperate man of mist and dread: Jamie McVay.

Sharon's fingernails dug into the flesh of my palm. As if mocking me for my Girl Scout ghost story, the red circle of light carried him closer... closer. The specter turned his free hand toward us in a pleading gesture. His vacant eyes were a lens, and through them, we saw the splintering railroad coaches burst into flame; and when he opened the horrible crater of his mouth, we heard the roaring fire, the crackling wires, the screaming children.

Sharon gasped, and the ghost leaped away, the red light pulsing at the edge of the darkness, waiting at the street.

"It's Jamie McVay," Sharon breathed. "What's he doing?"

"I don't know," I said, "but – look there." Other lights had appeared, approaching along the street, accompanied by throaty rumbling. One lurched forward with a squeal and turned onto the path away from us, a dirt bike lighting its way to the marsh. It was followed by a second bike, with an ATV bringing up the rear. One loose red tail light swung back and forth on the back of the lead vehicle.

I grunted. "The Pyro, Melkovec and Wagner."

"I hope they get run over by the train," Sharon muttered.

At the edge of the shadowed path, Jamie McVay dissolved further into the circle of blood-red light. It drew me in as well.

I loosened my hand from Sharon's grip and moved out into the middle of the path.

"What are you doing?" she cried. "Get back here!"

"No," I said, "it's all right, I've got to…." I stepped into the pool of light and felt its glow surround me. The fire burned somehow cold, phosphorescent, with a firefly's luminosity. I reeled with the confusion of the other man's mind, the panic of flight down the gleaming tracks toward the marsh. I remembered the crash I'd never seen, the searing heat, the smoke, the screams….

Abruptly I was released, as though I'd been picked up by the brain and dropped. My knees buckled, and I fell to the ground with a gasp. Looking up I saw the light quivering across Jewel Road.

Sharon kneeled beside me, gently touching my face. "Are you okay?"

The red light flashed into the path on the other side, fading into the darkness where Pete the Pyro had disappeared.

"My God." I stood shakily and watched the light disappear. "I've got to get down there!"

"Oh, no!" Sharon tugged me back. "Don't think you're gonna leave me here alone. No way!"

But I staggered away, turning to her as I went. "No, you don't understand. I've got to warn them about the fire!"

Sharon shook her head, tears ready to cut loose. "Brian, I saw what happened – the fire, the train wreck. Jamie McVay. But you can't change it. It happened. Nobody can change the past."

"I'm talking about Vincenzi. He's going to the park! We've got to stop him!"

Sharon stared. "Oh, God!" she moaned. "Christine!"

I shook her by the shoulders. "You've got to call the cops – get the fire department over to Crosby Park!"

She made a helpless gesture with her hands. "I don't have my phone," she groaned.

"Well, go on, then – run! Get to a phone and call from a house or something." I nodded toward the nearest house with lights showing in the windows, half a block away and fenced off from the path by a thicket of evergreens.

"And *you're* going to the park?" She stood for just a moment. "Yeah, you're the fast one," she decided. "Okay." And she took off in a scattering of gravel. "Be careful!" she called over her shoulder.

I dashed across Jewel and flew down the path's gentle grade. Ahead I caught sight of McVay's light once more, wavering among the trees at the broad curve of the marsh. In no time I reached the clearing where the water glistened black and silver.

The sky was a ceiling of crazy draperies, black masses all running together in the murk. I stood, panting, straining to see some human form among the waving reeds and cattails below. I could just hear the faint rumble of engines until a quick flash of red light drew my attention to the cycles emerging from a stand of sumac.

"Pete!" I yelled, but the wind had risen, blowing up a noisy storm of rustling reeds. A freight train rumbled across the marsh on the Northwestern tracks, and besides, the Pyro wouldn't hear anything over the sound of his machine.

Down the embankment I scrambled, striking out among the hillocks and humps of the marsh. I tripped and stumbled, ran and crawled, sloshed unexpectedly into stinking bog water and struggled to pull myself out of the black muck. Frantic, I drew myself up on a grassy mound and looked around.

The Crosby Park buildings loomed, dark rectangles on the verge, but an impossible tangle of briar roses and grasping raspberry bushes blocked the way. Wind slashed across the marsh. Then below me, a red beam spread across a patch of trampled rushes. Clambering to it, I found it dry enough to cross, and there amid the weeds on the other side, a lantern's glow showed me a dry path.

Hurtling through the cattails, I stumbled into the dirt bikes where they'd been left with the ATV outside the fence. "Pete!" I tried shouting, but not much came out of my dry mouth. Adrenalin must have lifted me over the fence and into the trampled mud of an animal pen. Where *were* they?

The tinkle of broken glass and a sudden yellow glare answered my question. One wall of the barn burst into flame, burning the scene onto the night. Bill Melkovec stood back from the fire with an arm over his face. Across the yard, Rick Wagner crouched in front of the station. And farthest away, at the edge of the dark and the firelight, Pete Vincenzi posed triumphantly, legs spread, arms across his chest. He turned and yelled to Wagner.

"Stop!" I shouted and vaulted over the split-rail fence, waving my arms as I rushed toward Wagner. He held one of the gasoline bottles at arm's length and with the other hand flicked a lighter. He didn't see me running out of the dark until I was right on him, smashing him to the ground with my shoulder. He sprawled face first on the gravel, still clutching the bottle. Reaching out, I slapped it from his hand and saw it skitter down the walk.

"Krueger!" Wagner growled, picking himself up.

"Are you crazy?" I shouted in his face, and shoved him against the station wall. "Are you?"

He was looking over my shoulder, though, fear flashing in his eyes. "Look out!" he yelled and dove to the ground.

I turned in time to see the Pyro follow through on an underhand pitch, letting fly with a bottle that sailed and turned over, a fiery tongue blazing in its wake. "No!" I shouted as it struck just a few feet away. A wave of flaming liquid spread across the shingled wall of the old train station, creeping across the platform and licking along the eaves.

From the burning barn came the screams of terrified horses. The big doors flew open, and the Crosby Park cows swarmed out in a bellowing herd. Surely Freund had roused from his little sleeping alcove, hadn't he? Surely he couldn't sleep through this! Knees wobbling I dodged the panicky cattle trying to make my way up the path. A circus of bleating lop-eared goats ran and leaped around me. "Mr. Freund!"

But I couldn't ignore Pete the Pyro. In just a few seconds I'd lost sight of him. Hesitating, I turned away from the barn. The sides of the ramshackle caboose were awash with false yellow daylight cast from the burning station. “Christine!” I shouted. In the shadows I saw movement, and flushed with relief to see the girls emerging from behind the caboose, wide-eyed Christine in the lead. “Get back!” I yelled. “Get away from the caboose!”

But Christine was transfixed. Before the girls, a singular flame danced. The light that had guided me through the marsh, the red signal of Jamie McVay’s lantern glowed, pulsating bloody and brighter as we watched. Nervous, uncertain, it seemed to hover in midair.

Then, ducking out from behind a kiosk, Pete the Pyro stepped back into the flickering light, posing glassy-eyed and drunk with the power of fire.

“Stop, Pete!” I yelled, and for a second I thought he might have looked over. But he turned matter-of-factly to the caboose, raising his firebomb in salute as if it was a champagne glass, and cocked his arm back to hurl it.

In that instant, the ghostly red flame of Jamie McVay leaped through the air to the Pyro’s upraised hand. Glowing brighter, flaring like a red giant star, it expanded – swelling until it completely enveloped Pete, pinioned in its circle of hell. Then – *whoosh!* – a fireball rose with the sound of crashing locomotives.

I dove to the ground and lay flat in the mud, covering my eyes as the sounds descended on me from all everywhere at once. Screams rose above the roar and crackle of the burning buildings. Shouts, terrified voices, a fiendish chorus of animal cries. Melkovec’s booming voice mixed with the squealing pigs and panicked horses, bawling goats and sheep and cows. It may have been the sound of Freund’s voice that brought me back to my senses.

“Here now!” Freund called from inside the barn. “Here girl!”

I rushed past the wild-eyed pony into the building, dark after the blazing fires outside, and roiling with smoke. Freund was doubled over just inside the doors, convulsed with coughing. Grabbing him by his singed and smoking shirt, I half-dragged him outside.

“That-a girl,” he wheezed, “that-a girl!” The pony galloped off through the gate.

I turned to gape at the hellish scene.

Pete the Pyro was a human torch charging wildly across the barnyard screaming, flapping his arms all aflame, with Melkovec and Wagner in pursuit. Girl Scouts darted past Mrs. Harris at the steps of the caboose as the scout leader tried to corral them into the picnic grove. Sirens whooping and lights flashing, a fire truck pulled through the gate and up the lane while men hustled to their tasks with axes and hoses. A cloaked figure appeared before me. "You all right?"

I nodded to the fireman, "Yeah, but –" I looked at Freund. An EMT knelt over him. I pointed down the path where Wagner had finally caught up with Pete, tackled him and somehow wrestled him into the duck pond. The firefighter rushed to them, shouting into his radio.

Like a child calling for its mother, a small black goat cried and trotted over. I hugged it against me, and we sat taking it all in. Hoses spurted, and torrents fell on the barn, drenching us with a cold spray. Sirens screamed, smoke billowed, steam hissed, but I felt it all with a strange detachment, deep relief, and a sense of release, of broken chains and open highways.

Sometime later a policeman found me and the goat huddled against a pig sty. The fires were out, though firefighters still tromped about dousing the smoking embers of the barn. Pete Vincenzi had been hauled off to the hospital – he was obviously in bad shape – and Rick Wagner too had some minor burns. The cows nailed Melkovec – the farm herd had run scared through the fence and were blundering around in the marsh when Chuck, making his getaway on the ATV, found himself in the middle of the stampede and was damn near trampled. The machine flipped over, the cows mooed for help, and the cops got their man.

Freund had taken some oxygen but now was gentling the horses in the corral. I could have cried to think of him facing those flames, but my heart swelled with pride at the old man's bravery handling the animals. Meanwhile, cars pulled in and out of the parking lot as parents came to pick up their daughters.

Sharon ran up just as the cops finished talking to me. One good hug and a kiss from her warmed me up considerably. "Man, I was worried," she said with a shake of her head. "Hey, who's your friend?"

"New kid," I said, rubbing the coarse fur between its ears. It backed away on its dainty hooves and bawled once before scampering off. I smiled at Sharon – still in her witch makeup, fairly glowing in the bright flashing lights.

"What?" she demanded.

"Nice run! Fast work to get the fire department here." She might have blushed – hard to tell with all the make-up. "And also – you look a lot nicer without the green wig."

She narrowed her eyes and smiled. "You like?"

I did.

"Ah," she said, pulling back, "my mom and dad are both here. And we stopped to pick up your dad, too. Not sure where he is now."

I sought through the chaos for my father. "Hey, remind me to call that Ms. Runyon, to tell her what happened."

"Yeah.... Uh, Brian? What *did* happen?"

I told her everything, including the details of Jamie McVay's light show.

"Oh my God!" Sharon cried. "Jamie McVay saved the girls' lives!"

I looked across the marsh to the dark tree line of the Prairie Path, straight as a train track against the backlit black-clouded sky. "I don't know if anybody's keeping score," I said, "but I think, tonight ... I've just got a feeling. It's like the echoes from that time, all his memories – they've stopped. I can't hear them anymore. Jamie McVay's just *gone* ... someplace else."

Sharon smiled and pulled me toward the brightly–lit caboose. "There's Dad with Christine. Come on."

The bright-eyed fireplug sister danced around Mr. Rice, telling her version of the story. "I saw the signal," she said, clambering up on a picnic table to look her father in the eye. "It was the Ghost of Jamie McVay! He gave us the signal to come out!"

"Is that so?" Mr. Rice chuckled. "Well, it *is* Halloween!"

I looked up when I heard my name and here came my father, tripping over fire hoses and practically knocking people down as he looked this way and that. I waved; he caught the motion and stopped.

"Dad!"

He opened his arms as I ran to him. "Son!" he sobbed. We broke from our hug, wiped our faces and laughed, looking about self-consciously.

Nearby, a tall fireman, his face streaked with soot, was showing something to his lieutenant.

The officer looked over at me. “It’s an oil lantern,” he explained, holding up the dented brass object. It was greasy and smudged from smoke. The red lens was broken out. “You were the one who saw the fires break out?” I nodded. “This was lying out here on the platform – anything to do with the fire?”

“No,” I told him, and stepped up to examine the light. “That’s Jamie McVay’s lantern.”

Sharon winced and covered her eyes. Dad cleared his throat and started to say something.

“Who? Who’s that?” the fireman demanded.

I laughed, “No, it’s nobody here – just some local history. It belongs to one of the museum exhibits.”

The lieutenant shrugged and handed the lantern to the taller man. As they walked away, he tossed it back into the charred interior of the old Pleasant Hill Station.

Sharon slid up and took my hand. “So much for the past,” she said.

I nodded and smiled. “Let’s think of the future.”

THE END

ABOUT THE AUTHOR

R. G. Ziemer was born and bred on Chicago's south side where he learned to appreciate a good story. He has taught English from junior high to college, but also worked in construction. These days he might be found canoeing near his home on the DuPage River west of the city. He also teaches writing at the College of DuPage, publishes poetry and short fiction, is a practicing genealogist, and participates in local writing groups.

Thank you so much for reading one of our **Crime Fiction** novels.
If you enjoyed the experience, please check out our recommended title for your next great read!

Caught in a Web by Joseph Lewis

"This important, nail-biting crime thriller about MS-13 sets the bar very high. One of the year's best thrillers." *–BEST THRILLERS*

View other Black Rose Writing titles at www.blackrosewriting.com/books

and use promo code **PRINT** to receive a **20% discount** when purchasing.

CPSIA information can be obtained
at www.ICGtesting.com
Printed in the USA
FSHW021654220219

9 781684 33215